Athena's Choice

Adam Boostrom

Thinker Books

Tiburon, CA

Chapter 1

Priority Message Received

The words appeared suddenly on the screen in a bright, blue font.

Priority Message Available

Blurry-eyed, the night-shift communications director slid her chair down a darkened aisle illuminated by the glow of computerized terminals. With a sideways glance, she peeked at the clock on the office wall — still ten minutes until the next shift change, far too much time to leave a priority message unopened. Her right hand reached up to tug at the collar of her crisp uniform, pulling at it near the point where it had begun to dig into her neck. Her index finger clicked into the air. The priority message opened.

As she scanned through it, the coms director quickly fell back into her chair. "What...the...?" she muttered faintly. Her eyebrows tilted downward. "Aasha!" she called out into the empty room. "Please connect me at once to Captain Valerie Bell."

Seconds later, the captain's gruff voice could be heard echoing against the walls. "What is it, coms? This had better be important."

"Yes, captain. I know," explained the Public Safety communications director. Her words trembled as they left her mouth. "I have a priority message for you. It's about the stolen Lazarus Genome. It's an order to bring someone in for questioning about it. Some girl from the Northern Woods. A teenager named Athena Vosh."

"What?" Captain Bell groaned loudly on the other end of the call. "I don't have time for this. What are you talking about? Who the hell is Athena Vosh?"

Athena Vosh

November 20, 2089

Ms. Washington, 3rd Grade History Class

Report on Events of the 21st Century

Ok, so the first thing to know is that all the trouble started when the oceans got really high. Like when you're taking a bath and forget to turn off the water and it starts spilling out onto the floor. All this land that used to be land got covered up and all these people that used to have a place to live had to find somewhere else to go. The news called these people 'climb-it refugees.' I think because they had to climb to higher ground to get away from the water.

The big problem was that there were already people living on the higher ground and back then everyone used to be very bad at sharing. Some of the higher ground people even decided to kill the climb-it refugees in the name of selfish defense. Those people were called 'terrorists' and they were very bad.

So the terrorists were killing all the climb-it refugees and the old governments decided they had to do something. They made a special disease to kill all the bad people. It was special cause when you got sick you wouldn't know you were sick for a long time and you could keep passing the disease on just like rolls at Thanksgiving dinner. Lots of bad people got sick and then a bit later - poof - they were dead. The disease only killed men so they called it the Y-Fever.

After the Fever worked so well the governments were really happy because they killed all the terrorists but this was a case of Be Careful What You Wish For. Pretty soon all the men everywhere and even some women too were getting sick and dying and no one could stop it. Ms. Washington says the last man on earth died in January of 2051. That was a long time ago. I've never seen a man in my whole life and neither have Eliz or Yara so yeah they're probably all still dead.

Things were really bad when everyone was dying cause the men kept fighting each other to the better end. My mom called it a fishes cycle. After that the Founding Mothers came along and they made new governments and new ways for in-semen-nation so that my mom could have me and so that other moms could have all the daughters they wanted. Then everything was better. Today we live in the best country on earth and that is the North American Union. That's what the Founding Mothers made from the old countries. Ms. Washington doesn't like it when I say we live in the best country ever but deep down I think she knows its true.

Educator Score and Notes: 10/10 for content. 6/10 for grammar.

Yes, Athena, while it's true the NAU is a great place to live, we are only one country of many. All the modern nations strive together for peace, prosperity, and cooperation. Nationalism is a thing of the past. Don't be afraid to expand your horizons! ;)

2

Thousands of kilometers from the excitement unfolding in the heart of Public Safety headquarters, Athena Vosh awoke in the pitch-black of her private bedroom. Her senses took their time in coming to. Seconds before, she had been immersed in a strange dream featuring talking animals and unusual places. Now awakened, however, the images slowly faded, and only the powerful memories of her excitement and fear remained. Eventually, the more familiar world around her came into focus, starting with a cool puddle of drool soaked into her pillow.

Half-asleep, she swiped clumsily into the air with her left hand. In response, her digital contact lenses awoke. They displayed a wealth of information directly onto her field of vision: time, temperature, news, messages. In the top right corner of her display, a bright red asterisk glowed. Lazily, she double-tapped her index finger into the air, and the asterisk opened into a message. It read:

A,

I went for a run, so you're on your own for breakfast. You wanna do lunch by the lake when I get back?

-N

Athena swiped left and the message dismissed itself.

"Good morning, Athena," called out a disembodied voice from within the walls. It spoke in a soft and soothing tone. "I see that you are awake. Would you like me to let in some light?"

"Noooooo," Athena groaned. She grabbed her pillow and squeezed it tightly on top of her head. "It's too early."

"But you asked me to alert you at ten AM," insisted the soothing voice. It belonged to Athena's AASHA unit — her Advanced Artificially-Intelligent Scheduler and Home Assistant.' "Do you no longer wish for me to wake you?"

Beneath her sheets, Athena brought her knees up to her chest. She curled tightly into a ball. "Gooo awayyyy," she moaned. "It's not morning yet."

The lights in the bedroom increased slowly from zero to ten percent lux. Fruity perfumes released themselves into the air: citrus with a touch of mango. "I'm sorry to have to tell you this, Athena, but the sun has been up for hours. Do you wish to continue sleeping until noon?"

Safely under her covers, Athena opened her eyes and swiped right on her display to reveal the current time. The numbers glowed brightly green in the bottom right corner of her home screen: 9:57 AM. "Alright...alright," she gasped, throwing off her sheets. "I'm getting up. I'm getting up."

"That's wonderful news," replied the home computer. "Allow me to let in some daylight."

Droplets of thick, purple pigment began to drain from out of the large window placed directly above Athena's empress-sized bed. Simultaneously, late-morning sun poured into the room.

At forty square meters, Athena's spacious sleeping chamber contained a wide array of clutter. Across from her bed stood a small wooden desk covered in used brushes and half-empty bottles of paint. Along the walls leaned dozens of canvases, each depicting something different and all at various stages of completion. Colorless self-portraits rested next to pastoral sunsets. Higher up on the walls hung a collection of famous prints: The Starry Night, The Kiss, La Clairvoyance, Water Lilies, and many more.

In the farthest corner of her room — taking up ample wall space that Athena believed could have been better used for more artwork — stood a massive, boxy piece of black furniture. Beside it, clumped into a pile, lay a mismatched heap of once-worn dresses, pants, blouses, and skirts. Frequently, Athena swore to herself that she would get around to organizing that pile of clothes. She needed to decide which discarded outfits to keep for wearing a second time and which to dump back into the boxy, black clothing-printer so that they might be rewoven into something new.

Giving way to a giant yawn, Athena stretched out her limbs and felt the pleasurable sensation of life returning into them. She crawled to her feet, and gazed out of the large window above her bed. Outside, a view of idyllic wilderness greeted her. Tall maple trees, laden with owl and squirrels' nests, towered over a stone path leading down to a crystal-blue lake. At the edge of the lake, an empty easel waited in front of a chair that faced out across the water.

"Aasha?" asked Athena, still staring out of her window. "How much time do I have left?"

"You have approximately 95 minutes of ideal daylight remaining," replied the home computer.

Athena headed quickly in the direction of her en suite bathroom. Small, yet modern, the bathroom contained nothing but a mirror; a black sink; a smart-toilet, and an empty, rectangular space in which to shower. As Athena entered, she came to a stop in front of the full-length mirror and placed her thumb squarely onto its surface. In response, an attractive, disembodied face appeared off to the side.

"Please hold still," cooed Aasha, the owner of the face. "Your test results will be ready in approximately 12 seconds."

Athena nodded in response and yawned, while examining her own reflection in the mirror. The image staring back at her had been genetically-engineered at conception to meet all the definitions of modern beauty. She possessed large, almond-shaped eyes; shining, flawless skin; and high, distinguishing cheekbones. She looked like a goddess, brought to life — but she was not the only one.

Some of Athena's particular facial features had been very popular in 2080, the year of her birth. In school growing up, she had often shared a classroom with two or three other girls whose nose or mouth looked exactly like her nose or mouth. Like a grade with too many "Tiffanys" or "Brooklyns." What set Athena apart from those other girls, though, were her mesmerizing gray eyes. They enchanted onlookers as they alternated between brighter shades of marble and those of a darker slate — like a rain cloud that couldn't decide on the severity of its mood. In fact, her eyes were so remarkable, they were the reason for her being named Athena in the first place. Before her birth, Athena's mother had planned to use another name for her only daughter. However, upon seeing Athena's remarkable gray eyes for the very first time — and at the suggestion of the delivery-room doctor — the impromptu decision was made to name the newborn girl after the legendary gray-eyed goddess of wisdom: Pallas Athena.

"Your examination is complete," announced Aasha. In the mirror, Athena's reflection disappeared, and a full-scale illustration of her body took its place.

"I'm detecting," continued the home computer, "the presence of some slight inflammation in your lower abdomen — here." The illustration in the mirror zoomed in to show the area in question in vivid color and detail. "I'm going to add a new bacteria to your diet that should help reduce it. Also, you have the beginnings of an upper respiratory infection, but we can cure it before you experience any symptoms. Your implants are all operating properly. Your body fat currently stands at 13 percent, would you like to make a change to that number?"

"What?" replied Athena. She had not been paying attention. "Oh, body fat. Just whatever's popular this week. I don't care."

The gray-eyed girl's night-shirt demagnetized and dropped to the floor. Lost in thought, she stepped nude into the empty, rectangular space. From out of concealed holes contained within the walls, pressurized jets of water appeared, rejuvenating her flesh from head to toe. Contained within the spray, specialized microbes ate away at pockets of bacteria on her skin, leaving in their wake a clean and pleasantly tingly feeling. Athena was oblivious to it all, however, as her mind remained elsewhere.

"Aasha, do you know anything about dreams?"

"'Dreams can refer to a series of thoughts, images, or sensations which occur in a person's mind during sleep. They can also refer to aspirations which—"

"No, I know all that," interrupted Athena. She tilted her head to avoid a spray of water pointed directly toward her mouth. "What I mean is, I keep seeing this strange building in my head when I close my eyes. I think it's from a dream I had last night. I was standing in a field. And there was this building in front of me. It was stone and dark, covered in vines and falling apart. I'm awake now, but I can't get the sight of that crumbling building out of my head. I don't recognize it except it's... somehow familiar. I feel like I've seen it before." She dug the tips of her top teeth into the soft flesh of her lower lip. "I think I need to paint it."

"That sounds like a wonderful idea," encouraged Aasha.

When the shower ended, spurts of hot-air pulsed out from the wall, causing Athena's hair to dry and detangle itself almost instantly. Long, brown strands fell lightly onto her shoulders. Next, she held out her arms to receive her daily outfit. Aasha had printed for her a new dress covered with large petals of overlapping violet, crimson, and turquoise colors. The swaths of bright fabric swooned together in a style reminiscent of Georgia O'Keeffe. Athena grabbed the dress with both hands and held it against herself, causing it to snap immediately into place. The magnetic implants located within her hips and shoulders ensured the garment fit snugly, but comfortably, in all the right places.

Cleaned and dressed, she headed out of her bathroom, ready to greet the new day.

Athena Vosh

January 29, 2090

Ms. Butler, 4th Grade Self-Awareness Class

What I Want To Be When I Grow Up

When my mom is feeling sad she likes to look at beautiful things like sunsets. She says that seeing the sky full of different colors reminds her that the world is big and beautiful and that her problems will all be ok. Sometimes though a person can't go and look at a sunset because its the wrong time of day. That's why people have art. Art is like a sunset you can look at anytime you need to.

That's why when I grow up I want to be an artist. I want to paint pictures that people can see anytime they want. I want to make things that are beautiful and that make people say "I can get through this trouble I'm in. I'm alright. Everything is going to be ok."

Educator's Score and Notes: 10/10 for content. 7/10 for grammar

That's wonderful, Athena. The world needs as many artists as we can get. I'll speak to the program office about enrolling you in some more visual media and painting classes.

U.N. Declaration (14.04.55):

Universal Pardons for All Persons Involved in the Creation and Proliferation of the Y-Fever

- Whereas over six billion people — including all men, trans-men, and a small percentage of women — have died in the last five years, and there exists no need for further trials or bloodshed,
- Whereas during the spring of 2050 — before the biological weapon known as the Y-Fever had spread beyond its original target of terrorist cells — the governments of nine nations each vied to take credit for creating and proliferating the disease,
- Whereas due to the massive loss of life and infrastructure, it has proved impossible to definitively determine the exact source of the Y-Fever's creation and proliferation,
- Whereas by all accounts, the spread of the disease to all living men and beyond has been an ACCIDENT,
- Now, therefore THE GENERAL ASSEMBLY issues a FULL AND COMPLETE PARDON to any person who may, directly or indirectly, have contributed in the production or distribution of the air-borne pathogen responsible for the Y-Fever pandemic. Let us, the wounded survivors, move forward from this tragedy together, with FORGIVENESS in our hearts, and PEACE in our minds.

Catherine LeBlanc,
U.N. General Secretary

These measures were unanimously approved on this day, the 14th of April, 2055

3

Athena exited her bedroom and entered into the cabin's main living area. There, she discovered all the windows had already been opened. Beams of light shone in, joined by the wafting smells of trees, grass, and lakeside breezes.

Informally divided by the placement of furniture, the cabin's main room contained two separate spaces. On one end sat the kitchen. That end contained a shiny, black, countertop food-printer; two lev-chairs; and a small, self-cleaning kitchen table hooked into the floor. On the other end sat the living room. That end possessed a couch located next to a family-sized 3D projector. Wide windows bordered the main room on three sides. The fourth side comprised an interior wall, which served to separate the main room from the cabin's two private bedrooms. On what little wall-space the room did enjoy hung a dozen oil paintings, depicting the nearby lake at sunset, in various shifting hues of pink, teal, and apricot. Next to the paintings grew lilies planted inside specialized grooves.

Bee-lining directly to the food printer, Athena retrieved from within a toasted, probiotic, cream-cheese bagel that had been freshly printed to meet her body's nutritional and bacterial needs. Breakfast in hand, she seated herself at the kitchen table. With a swirl of her finger, she activated her news-app. Immediately, recent headlines took up center stage on her display:

Current Most Popular News:

Top story: Lazarus Genome Stolen! — *Dismiss*
Top story: Hurricane Headed directly for Atlanta! — *Dismiss*
Top Story: "18 E. Mars" co-stars dating in real life! — *Select*

Athena bit into her creamy breakfast and savored its flavor. Simultaneously, she read from her display the only news of the day which interested her in the slightest.

AFTER THEIR ROCKY BEGINNING IN EPISODE ONE, FEW WOULD HAVE GUESSED THE SUDDEN CHEMISTRY TO DEVELOP BETWEEN GOOD GIRL, CHAMBRAY, AND BAD GIRL, MADISON, BUT THE TWO HAVE BEEN SPOTTED OUT TOGETHER AT 2 OF MARS' POSHEST RESTAURANTS...

At the conclusion of her breakfast, Athena set her empty plate onto the kitchen table. In response, the table guided the plate to a hole located directly in its center. From there, the plate passed down through the floor to be cleaned by an underground dishwasher and then carried back up, through seamless connections, into the food printer's storage space. As usual, Athena did not bother to watch the mundane process.

Instead, she headed over to a section of hidden, in-wall cabinetry. From inside, she pulled out a fresh canvas, a brush, and an assortment of paints: all the supplies she would need for her morning's work.

As she had done countless times before, Athena made her way outside, down a stone path, and to the easel parked by the water's edge. She seated herself facing the lake, and prepared to paint the morning away. Unlike all those other mornings, however, instead of recreating the picturesque scene before her, Athena's brush breathed new life into an image not previously present in her world — save for the vivid picture forcing its way onto her mind's eye. Her strokes were swift as she skillfully worked to outline, color, contour, and shadow. Gradually, the haunting ruin of a mysterious, crumbling building came into view.

'Lonely Hearts' Storm Capital, March in Favor of So-Called 'Project Lazarus'

CHICAGO — (AP) — On the fortieth anniversary of the death of the last man on earth, approximately two hundred and fifty thousand women took to the streets of the capital today. While blocking numerous major intersections, they chanted slogans like, "Right the Wrong!" and "Cure Men Now!" as they marched en masse to a rally at the North American Freedom Monument.

The peaceful protest served as an attempt to raise further support for a potential government program tasked with finding a cure to the ubiquitous Y-Fever. Although no one has died from the Fever in over three decades, everyone alive today is still a carrier of the disease. As such, returning men to existence will require first finding a Y-Fever cure.

While originally intended as a term of derision, the sobriquet "lonely hearts" has been embraced by the group in recent years. About the name, congresswoman Jane Chen, a leading figure within the pro-man movement, noted, "If our opponents choose to mistake our honest vulnerability for weakness, then that is their disadvantage. We know who we are, and we're not afraid to say how much we long for the return of our husbands, sons, and brothers."

Surveys conducted last week indicate that support for the so-called 'Project Lazarus' has been growing of late. While only 30% of respondents in 2080 thought that resurrecting the male gender was "important" or "very important," today that number has grown to over 50%.

Top scientists, however, tried to urge caution, reminding the public of the difficulty inherent in any attempt to find a cure.

"It is a lot easier to scramble an egg, than to unscramble it," said Dr. Grace Antares, head scientist and CEO at Helix, a world-renowned research facility. "We've studied the Fever, and it needs to be known, this is not just some common-cold. The military-men who created that virus — mistakenly thinking they could control it — genetically-engineered it to kill in twenty-six different ways. That's how it was able to achieve such complete lethality. That's why curing every method of its infection, addressing every line of its attack will be so difficult. We have to make sure that there are no unintended consequences for the women who still carry the disease today. In fact, we still don't even know why some women fell victim to the virus while the vast majority appear to be completely immune. If we're not careful, if we don't take the time to fully understand what we're dealing with here, a lot more lives may be lost before a single man is born. At some point, we may need to ask ourselves as a society: is the cause of resurrecting men really worth the risk?"

4

"I don't care how smart the stupid AI is," complained Captain Bell, unmoved from her desk all morning. Adorning the walls of her private office, countless commendations, government medals, and civic awards offered proof of her distinguished career in service to the department of Public Safety. "Why can't the machine just tell us what makes this Vosh girl so goddamn important? Why does it think we can't recover the Lazarus Genome without her?" Captain Bell's pale cheeks flushed bright red.

On the other side of her desk, the captain's commanding officer leaned forward from her lev-chair. As she moved, several of the medals pinned to her uniform began to clink together.

"Absolutely, Bell. I hear you," declared the Public Safety Chief Commissioner. She crossed her legs, and leaned back. "But you know how hard it is to get authorization for an inquiry like that. If the most powerful AI on earth has calculated that explaining to us its reason for highlighting the Vosh girl may endanger lives, then we must take the intelligence at its word. Request denied." The commissioner flicked her hand to the side, dismissing Captain Bell's formal petition to access the internal logs of the planet's most famous supercomputer.

"Besides," the commissioner added, "I believe we are still capable of completing a proper investigation on our own — without help from the machines. Are we not?"

"Yes, ma'am," replied the captain. "I will not let you down."

Other than the noises made by the two women, not a sound could be heard inside Captain Bell's hermetically-sealed office. The din of the surrounding world had been completely blocked out.

"Speaking of which…" the commissioner continued, "where are we on this case? The CEO of Helix — Dr. Antares — she's a very good friend of mine. If someone stole her genome, I want them found, and I want them brought to justice."

Captain Bell took a minute to clear her throat. "Yes, ma'am, that's understood. I have three teams working it." She swiped her finger into the air, sending the chief commissioner a full-write-up of every detail that she was about to explain. "My best people are still tracing the initial hack into the Helix mainframe. It looks like whoever stole the code for the Lazarus Genome hid their location by using about two thousand proxy servers first. But don't worry. We'll find the source."

The commissioner nodded calmly.

"A second team is going through the recordings of everyone who's spoken out publicly in opposition to Project Lazarus — that is, anyone who might have motive to steal the genome in order to prevent men from returning. Obviously, that includes all the members of 'Women First,' but they are far from the only anti-man group out there. You've also got your 'Never Forgetters' down in Florida, and the 'VMR' group out west — that last one stands for 'Violence, Murder, and Rape.' According to them, that's the sum total of the male legacy. Any one of these groups could have had the means to conduct the genome theft, but none of them have any history of serious law-breaking, aside from some minor arrests for disorderly conduct."

The commissioner kept nodding.

"And team three..." Captain Bell paused for a moment to vigorously roll her royal blue eyes, "team three has been assigned to bring in that Vosh girl for me." She shook her head.

The commissioner recrossed her legs. "Excellent, Bell. Keep me posted."

An unexpected knock sounded at the door. Both the captain and the commissioner looked to their displays to see the projected image of the knocker: one of Captain Bell's junior officers.

"This won't take a minute, ma'am," apologized the captain. With a two-fingered swipe, she opened her door. "What is it?" she asked of the intruder.

"I'm sorry to bother you, captain," the junior officer stammered, "but the heli-car we sent to pick up Ms. Vosh has almost arrived. Would you like me to notify her of it?"

Slowly, a sly smile fell over the pale face of Captain Valerie Bell. "No, officer. Please *do not* notify Ms. Vosh at this time..." Her grin expanded mischievously. "Do not notify that girl of anything. Have the car wait for me to finish speaking with the commissioner. This is a job I want to do myself."

Project Lazarus a "Go"

CHICAGO — (AP) — "And he that was dead came forth, bound hand and foot with grave clothes... And Jesus said unto them, loose him, and let him go out into the world."
— John 11:44

Today, in a landmark vote, the Congress approved legislation to legalize and fully fund the hotly-debated research-effort to re-sequence a Y-Fever-immunity into the human male-genome. The successful vote paves the way for a reintroduction of men into society. Supporters of Project Lazarus hailed the vote as a breakthrough for all humanity. "Today is a victory not just for lonely hearts, but for everyone," announced Jane Chen, Speaker of the House. "As humans, we've been incomplete for 43 years. Today, I say, let the healing process begin."

Critics of the measure called the vote a clear over-reach of power and vowed to appeal the legislation within the courts. "No body of women on earth has the authority to resurrect a species that was responsible for causing its own extinction," declared Mirza Khan, speaking on behalf of the opposition group, 'Women First.' "Men had their chance at life; and it is a matter of record what they did with it. The dead should be left to rest in peace."

In the aftermath of the tumultuous vote came speculation about which research facility would win the coveted government contract to build a Y-fever-immune 'Lazarus Genome.' Chicago-insiders pegged Helix, the world-famous research facility, as a runaway favorite.

North American Union · Housing Division · Est. 2054

Date: ___**August 1st, 2098**___

District:___**15th Northeast**___

Housing Locale:___**Algonquin Forest Zone**___

Permit Number:___**6630-6938**___

Renters:___**Athena Vosh,   Nomi James**___

Lease duration:___**1 year**___

Type of Lease:___**Standard Rental**___

1st renter's occupation:___**N/A**___

Main source of income:___**Citizen's Benefit**___

2nd renter's occupation: **Choreographer**

Main source of income: **Employment**

5

Deep in the heart of the Algonquin woods, Nomi James popped a blue oxygen pill, and pushed the pace on the last kilometer of her morning run. The pill sent a shooting burst of O2 straight to her quads, quenching their thirsty burn from lactic acid. Darting through the tangled branches of a recently fallen tree, Nomi ducked below a low-hanging spiderweb, before powering up a final hill. Moments later, she emerged, glistening in sweat, in the clearing of a remote, lakeside cabin. For several minutes, she bent over, hands on knees, struggling to catch her breath.

As she panted in place, Nomi's short, brown hair spiked with sweat in multiple directions. Like everyone else her age, Nomi's appearance had been altered at conception to improve the agreeability of her features. She had beautiful brown skin overlaid on top of a stunning frame. Her honey-colored eyes were the optimal width apart, her small nose and wide smile perfectly in proportion.

More than just a pretty face, though, Nomi had been endowed with gifts that went beyond skin-deep. While every newborn birthed in the 80's had received minor gene-edits to improve intelligence, in most cases, those edits ended up having no effect. In Nomi, however, the edits had resulted in her gaining an exceptional amount of added intelligence, particularly emotional intelligence. She may have been only nineteen, but she possessed the wisdom of a ninety-year-old. She knew herself in ways which others could only dream.

No doubt due to that heightened awareness, life had always just come easily for Nomi. During high school, when Athena would struggle with assignments, and fret over her class placements, Nomi preferred instead to ace her classes while frittering her days away subsisting entirely on reality television and ice cream — never caring if she even graduated at all. The existence of 'Citizen's Benefits,' she realized, meant no one needed to worry about money or work anymore. So she never did. One time at dinner, Athena had asked Nomi for advice on 'how to get other people to like you more.' With a confused look, Nomi had simply replied to her, "I don't get it. Who cares if other people like you?"

It was perhaps a great irony, then, that only a year after school ended, Nomi found substantial financial and critical success. One day, motivated more by sheer boredom than anything else, she spent an afternoon designing a series of massage choreographies — operating instructions for the dozens of tiny massager-nodes implanted within her body. On a lark, she posted the choreographies to an online marketplace, and then forgot about them entirely. A month later, the marketplace had to contact her to ask where they should deposit the large sums of money which had accrued in her account. Her massages had become an overnight sensation, having been downloaded over ten million times.

For most anyone else, the sudden fame and fortune would have brought about major lifestyle changes — but not for Nomi. She laughed at the thought of being a quasi-celebrity, and gave away almost all of her money to a tropical fish preserve in Hawaii that was promptly renamed "The Nomi James Lagoon." Wealth, she knew, could only buy things she didn't care about anyway. So what good was it?

As her pumping heart began to slow, Nomi spied her oldest and closest friend, sitting by the lake, painting the afternoon away. Strands of Athena's hair had fallen onto her face, and she had assorted splotches of green paint on her forehead that somehow made her more, and not less, alluring to behold. The mere sight of Athena's youthful visage caused Nomi's heart to skip a beat. She sprinted in Athena's direction, and placed a large, wet kiss onto her cheek.

"Ewwww!" cried Athena. "You're all sweaty!"

"What?" asked Nomi. She stuck her nose into her own armpit, and inhaled deeply. "Don't you like it? I think I'm going to call this, 'Eau du Nomi.'" She cocked her head back and laughed. "Maybe I should sell it online!"

Athena giggled. "You probably could."

Wiping the sweat from her face, Nomi planted three more kisses onto Athena's forehead, and then asked her, "So whatchu painting today, babe?"

Tilting her canvas in Nomi's direction, Athena proudly displayed her most recently completed work: a perfect likeness of the crumbling, vine-covered building from her dream. "What do you think?"

As she viewed the image, copious amounts of sweat re-formed on the top of Nomi's forehead. Gradually, her face crinkled as though her tongue had tasted something extremely sour. "Ummmm, A?" she asked. "What the hell is this?"

Searching for an answer, Athena opened and closed her mouth a couple of times before speaking. "I...I don't know? But I can't get the sight of this building out of my head."

Nomi tilted her gaze to the right, then to the left. Her lips pursed to one side. The image before her was all at once frightening and grotesque. The vines which encircled the darkened structure seemed to reach from out of the painting and pull the viewer into a suffocating grasp. The stone facade of the mysterious place seemed to be crying out in pain as it crumbled away.

"Honestly, A," confessed Nomi, "this is incredible. It's so realistic. And completely unlike anything else you've ever done. Just looking at it is giving me the creeps." Nomi took a step back. Then another. "Where's it from? This place? You never paint anything that isn't right in front of you. Is this somewhere you went when you were young?"

Athena simultaneously shook her head and shrugged her shoulders in response. "Not that I know of. I can't remember ever going anywhere that looked like this."

Desperate for a chance to avert her eyes from the disturbing image, Nomi covered her face as she wiped away the additional sweat which had formed there. "Did you ask Aasha about it?"

Athena shook her head.

Raising her voice, Nomi called, "Aasha! The subject of this painting here, please identify it."

The home computer remained silent for an unusually long amount of time. Finally, it replied: "Based upon the architectural style, and the level of decay depicted, this looks like the ruined remains of a building constructed around the turn of twentieth century."

"Ruined remains?" asked Nomi. "So this building isn't just a fantasy. It's real?"

"I'm afraid," replied Aasha, "there does not exist enough information on file to definitively answer your question. The structure pictured here cannot be matched precisely to any available records from the archives, including blueprints. However, it bears similarity to a series of structures constructed in the former United States at the end of the nineteenth and the beginning of the twentieth centuries."

Nomi scrunched up her face, and repeated her question. "Aasha, just give me your best guess. Is this a real place or not?"

"Possibly."

For several silent moments, Nomi waited patiently to hear the rest of the home computer's analysis, but the virtual assistant had nothing more to say. There was simply no more information on file to give.

'Project Lazarus' Remains Popular, but Divisive

CHICAGO — (AP) — Sighting complications and the risk of Y-Fever contagion, scientists at Helix have announced yet another delay in their timetable for the delivery of a usable, Y-fever-immune, male genome.

Dr. Grace Antares offered some clarification on the delay in a press conference held earlier today:

> "The fact of the matter is that diseases mutate. They evolve. Not only are we striving to build a male genome that can't get infected by the current fever, but we must ensure that we do not leave the door open for future infection, or a widening of the previous epidemic."

In spite of the latest setback, Project Lazarus continues to enjoy a majority of support among the citizenry. According to a recently conducted poll, 67% of respondents remained in favor of completing the project. This is down from 72% when it began. 25% were opposed. 8% described themselves as "indifferent."

One Times reader, Elise from Dallas, posted her thoughts on the project's delays to our social media page:

> "My girlfriends and I agree. No matter if it takes another six months or six years, it'll be worth the wait. We're so excited to have men back!"

Of the 25% who say they are opposed to completing the project, opposition remains enthusiastic. Three fourths categorize themselves as 'strongly' or 'very strongly' against.

6

Discovering that the longer she stared at the painting, the more it creeped her out, Nomi seized on the first excuse to leave and headed inside to shower. Athena, on the other hand, remained at her easel. For several minutes, she gazed at the puzzling image she had created, becoming increasingly transfixed by its subtle details: a curl of ivy here, a shadow of stone there. Unlike Nomi, she felt no discomfort in viewing it. Rather, the sight of the mysterious ruin seemed to promote within her a kind of excited wanderlust.

Gently, a breeze blew across the surface of the nearby lake, causing countless ripples to form upon its peaceful face. Reclining into her chair, Athena stared up at the clouds and absent-mindedly swiped her finger into the air. This action activated the 'paint' feature of her display. Drawing into the air, she began to sketch silly silhouettes onto the puffy white canvases floating above her. When a red asterisk notification appeared in the top-right corner of her display, she dismissed it with a quick flick from her free hand. Probably, the notification signaled nothing more than the arrival of her daily food shipment. Fresh containers of edible ink had been scheduled to arrive by drone at any minute. Nomi had even sprung for a packet of exotic, designer meat.

As Athena doodled onto the clouds, she noticed a transformation taking place within her illustrations. At first, the bodies she'd drawn had been clearly female. Increasingly, however, they began to appear more and more masculine. Vividly, the gray-eyed girl found herself slipping into a daydream consisting of muscular bodies with strong arms and firm hands. It took another red asterisk notification, and then a third, to break her from the manly spell.

"I'm busy, Aasha. What do you want?"

"I'm sorry," apologized the home computer. "But I'm afraid there is going to be a disturbance to your afternoon. A representative from Public Safety is demanding to speak with you."

Quickly, Athena climbed to her feet. "What? What are you talking about?"

"The representative is calling right now. I will put them through on the 3D."

A gaggle of geese flew by overhead, honking loudly, as Athena abandoned her sketching and headed inside. Her hands began to clam up. A stone formed in the pit of her stomach.

When she entered the living-room, the 3D there sprang to life. With exacting texture and detail, the device holographically projected the fully-formed figure of a tall woman clad from head-to-toe in a crisp, blue, Public Safety uniform. Near the woman's shoulder floated a three-dimensional "PS" insignia. She had long, black hair, pale skin, and a set of piercing, royal blue eyes. An intimidating air hung about her, despite the fact that she was only a hologram and not actually present in the room. Athena approached until she stood only a meter in front of the projection of the foreboding Public Safety captain.

"Athena Vosh," commanded the hologram, "SSID 74525-85372, you are wanted for questioning with regard to last night's theft of the Lazarus Genome from secure servers at Helix. Failure to voluntarily comply with this request will result in your display being remotely incapacitated. Please acknowledge receipt of this message."

A rush of panic darted through Athena's brain, but she willed the fear back down. Her posture remained upright, unbroken. "Officer," she insisted, "there must be some mistake—"

"There is no mistake. You are Athena Vosh, SSID 74525-85372. You have been implicated in the theft of the Lazarus Genome, and are required to report to Public Safety Headquarters for questioning. Compliance is mandatory."

As she delivered her decree, the tiniest hint of a devilish smirk emerged on the face of the holographic captain. Athena could have sworn the expression reminded her of someone she knew, but she couldn't quite place the memory.

"But officer," Athena protested, "I have committed no crime."

"Noted," remarked the hologram with a depressed sigh. "Your pleas of innocence have been noted for the official record." The hologram stopped to roll its eyes. "Public Safety has sent a heli-car to your location. It will arrive in…four minutes. Be ready to leave when it does."

With that, the hologram discontinued, and the tall woman disappeared as quickly as she had arrived. Still in shock, Athena stood speechless in the middle of the living room, her mouth agape.

"Well, now that's some exciting news," laughed Nomi. She strode back into view, freshly-showered. Apparently, she had overheard the entire conversation from her bedroom. "I thought you said you checked out early last night?" Nomi's face displayed a look of faux-confusion which slowly gave way to a bursting smile. "But now I find out the truth. You weren't sleeping at all. You were committing high-tech larceny!"

Athena glared back at her friend. "That's not funny, Nomes. How could Public Safety think I had anything to do with that?"

"Ohhhhh!" Nomi scoffed. "You're such a worrier!" She eased her way over to the food printer and pulled out a piping-hot slice of pepperoni pizza. "They're obviously just mixed-up. You're not really going to be in any trouble, you know."

In spite of the reassurance, Athena's blood-pressure continued to spike. She paced a deliberate circle around the living-room couch. "What are they even think…? How could…? I couldn't care less about that stupid male genome!" she announced. "If men want to come back and kill themselves all over again, it's fine by me!"

Immediately, Nomi discarded her uneaten slice and rushed to her friend's side. "Hey," she whispered, taking Athena's hand into her own. "I promise you it's going to be ok. Alright? I love you." She nuzzled her nose into Athena's cheek. "What can I do to help? Sienna's mom is a lawyer. Do you want me to call her?"

"Lawyers are for guilty people!" Athena shrugged off the embrace and stormed into her private bedroom. She loosened her slippers and kicked them into a nearby wall. Their impact echoed one after the other: *whap, whap.*

Without being told to do so, Aasha took the liberty of releasing a calming scent into the air: lilac with a touch of gooseberries. At a low volume, she played the soft sounds of waves crashing gently into a forgotten shore. Lastly, she printed a new pair of stylish sandals for Athena to wear on her upcoming journey. Only a few minutes later, the ornate footwear popped out of the clothing printer, still hot to the touch. They landed on the ground before Athena's feet.

As the home computer's niceties achieved their intended effect, Athena took a few deep breaths, picked up her new shoes, and emerged from her bedroom. "I'm sorry, Nomes," she apologized. "You're right. This is all dumb. If Public Safety wants to give me a free ride into the city, then I should take it. I can pick up a few things while I'm there." She dropped her freshly-printed sandals onto the ground and dipped her toes inside. With a swirl of her finger, she ordered lunch to go.

"You'll be home before dark," assured Nomi.

Only seconds later, a massive heli-car arrived, flattening the grass of the cabin's front yard as it landed. On four sides, large propellers surrounded a transparent, sideways-egg-shaped body. On the rear emerged the exhaust pipes of miniaturized jet-engines.

Nomi watched from a distance as Athena approached the vehicle. The top half of the car's glass dome separated, allowing her to enter. As Athena climbed inside, Nomi blew a playful, overly-dramatic farewell-kiss. Athena snatched it from the air with a smirk.

Raising itself a few meters off of the ground, the car produced a soft, humming sound in every direction. It then paused for a brief moment to calculate weight, fuel, destination, and weather, before resuming its ascent to the air space above the wooded tree-line.

Once all obstacles had been cleared, its spinning blades transformed into wings, and it sped off with a tear of supersonic speed. West. To Chicago.

Chicago

From Wikipedia, the free encyclopedia

This article is about the capital city of the North American Union.
For other uses, see Chicago (disambiguation).

▲ Overview:

Chicago (/ʃɪˈkɑːɡoʊ/ or /ʃɪˈkɔːɡoʊ/), officially the City of Chicago, is the most populous city in North American Union. With over 18.6 million residents, it is also the tenth most populous city in the world.

Chicago was incorporated as a city in 1837, near a portage between the Great Lakes and the Mississippi River watershed, and grew rapidly in the mid-nineteenth century.

In 2056, because of its central location, and relative safety from rising coastal sea levels, Chicago was named the capital for the newly created North American Union.

In the 2080's, Chicago experienced an explosive growth in population after completing its decade-long weather-fixing project to eliminate frigid winters and scorching summers. Over six million people relocated there between 2081 and 2090.

Today, Chicago is an international hub for government, finance, commerce, industry, public safety, technology, telecommunications, and transportation services.

▼ **Demographics**
▼ **Topography**
▼ **Architecture**
▼ **Museums and the Arts**
▼ **Recent Recordings**

Last modified by <u>*BumbleBee2075*</u> *on 26 May 2099*

7

When it comes to getting from point A to point B, there are few nicer ways to do it than a personal heli-car. Athena could recall only two other times in her life when she had been inside one. One time had been on a school field trip to the top of Mount Rainer; and another had been when she was eight, when her mother had rented a car for a week of island hopping through the Caribbean.

The front of the heli-car contained no manual controls of any kind. The cabin consisted of only two, ergonomic seats upholstered in white leather. Periodically, the seats would reshape themselves in order to provide passengers with continual comfort during longer journeys.

Outside of the car, an expansive wilderness spread out below the all-glass passenger dome. Lakes and treetops appeared in every direction as far as the eye could see. While the sylvan sights whirred by, Athena unwrapped her lunch: a turkey croissant sandwich covered with cucumber and tomato. The moist slices of thinly-printed turkey practically melted on contact with her tongue.

As she ate, Athena racked her brain, searching for reasons why Public Safety might have identified her as a suspect in the Lazarus theft. No obvious answers came to mind. She had never voiced any public objections to the project, nor even cared enough about its progress to follow it in the news reports. Surely, she thought, Public Safety could pull her online history, and see how little it mattered to her whether the effort succeeded or failed.

On the other hand, she realized, it would be a lie to pretend she hadn't been increasingly preoccupied with men over the last few weeks, months, and years. Frequently, she caught herself daydreaming about a future where men would come back to life. Though she'd never seen one in the flesh, the lost gender still existed for her, as they existed for all women, in history projections and pre-fever movies. Over the years, she had caught enough glimpses of their rough bodies to know the masculine shape by heart. She could see their dark features and powerful arms when she closed her eyes.

Every now and then, late at night, Athena liked to turn off the recording in her bedroom — for the sake of privacy — and sketch out, in charcoal, the naked outlines of male figures. Inside one of the legs of her desk, in a secret compartment, she kept a whole cache of such drawings. Perhaps once or twice a month, she would lay several of the sketches out on her bed and consider the tingling feelings they brought about within her. She craved for the figures to come to life and to observe her in return. She fantasized about the power that her feminine body would hold over them, about what a rush it would be to see those men unable to take their eyes off of her. She wondered about how their calloused hands would feel if pressed against hers or what their pores would smell like when filled with sweat. She longed for them to pull her forcefully into their strong embrace.

Never, though, would Athena confess to wanting any of this. Never would she admit to Nomi — or to anyone else, for that matter — that she had these thoughts.

"A woman," Nomi loved to say, "needs a man as much as a fish needs a bicycle."

If the subject of male-rejuvenation ever came up at dinner, Athena liked to politely demur and wait patiently for the conversation to move on to something else.

One time, Nomi had actually caught Athena in her room, gazing a-little-too-long at a holographic image of a man online. Laughingly, Nomi had accused her friend of being a lonely heart. Athena had recoiled. "Yeah, right," she had protested in response. "Not a chance!"

Swallowing the last bite of her sandwich, Athena relaxed into the soft curves of her contoured chair. Still over an hour from Chicago, the heli-car raced along just above the wooded tree-line. As it did so, its only passenger gradually drifted off into a deep sleep.

Perchance To Dream

Athena could not say for certain how long she had been walking across the meadow. Perhaps only minutes. Perhaps hours. Yet still she saw no end to the vast expanse of delicate, yellow flowers laying before her. From above, a golden sun shone down, warming her face and neck. From across the endless plain, a soft breeze blew. Curls of air toyed gently with the strands of her hair.

Upon examination, Athena discovered a surprise. From top-to-bottom, she was dressed in her old "Rainbow Ruby" childhood-pajamas. This fact seemed a bit odd, though, because she could vividly recall outgrowing them many years ago.

No matter. The seductive sight and scent of daffodils beckoned her onward. Athena frolicked within the meadow. Swiping her arm to the ground, she plucked a handful of the floral beauties and brought them up to her face. She inhaled their intoxicating scents, and then carelessly tossed them into the breeze. The flowers floated loosely upward before being transformed into a flock of flying doves.

BOOOOOOM.

Athena found her playful romp interrupted by a troubling development on the horizon. Storm clouds had coalesced, slowly at first, but with increasing speed. The darkening clouds grouped more tightly together, forming into a single, unified threat. The mass then turned sharply against the wind as it moved in Athena's direction.

Athena searched for cover to protect herself from the coming storm, but there was nowhere to hide in that vast and endless meadow.

The storm clouds inched lower and lower to the ground as they approached. While they descended, their color began to fade. Their dark, purplish tint transformed into that of a dusty brown. The sound emanating from them changed too. What previously had been a thunderous roar increasingly began to resemble the drumming of hooves.

Athena stood her ground as the clouds grew near, terrifying in their noise and speed — and then they stopped suddenly. The clouds parted, and behind them, a massive herd of plains buffalo appeared. Thousands of the gigantic beasts stood barely an arm's reach away, bobbing their heads up and down, scratching and clawing at the ground in front of them.

In the center of the herd, a man appeared: a rider. He had short brown hair, greenish eyes, and a full beard. His clothing looked to be made entirely out of buffalo hides. He rode high and tall atop an enormous beast and approached Athena slowly, stopping only inches from her face. His steed nuzzled softly into her chest with its massive nose. Feeling not the least bit afraid, Athena returned the animal's affection by petting him on top of his furry head. She welcomed the forceful exhale of his nostrils into her chest.

When she looked up to meet the eyes of the man, he spoke to her in a low and rumbling voice. "Athena," he bellowed. "The truth is in the library."

Athena nodded, as though she understood.

The man spoke again, "You must come with me if you want to save her. You must come with me to the home of the buffalo."

Another powerful animal approached and turned his body to the side. He offered his bare back to Athena. She accepted the invitation and climbed aboard. Seconds later, she found herself riding in the midst of the trampling herd, surrounded on every side by large, galloping beasts. There were tens of thousands of them, maybe more. Their stomping hooves echoed across the empty plains.

Zooming along, the buffalo herd raced west, faster than a heli-car, faster than a hyperloop. Soon, snow-capped mountains appeared off in the distance. The air took on a flavor of pine. Cold wind rushed past. Athena lowered her head to avoid the wind's stinging bite. Resolutely, she dug her fingers deep within her mount's thick mane. When the galloping herd finally stopped, it was in front of the remains of a badly-damaged, rectangular, stone building, covered in a dense, green overgrowth.

Athena recognized the ruin instantly. This was the same building she had painted that morning. The same structure that had been forcing its way onto her mind's eye ever since. Numerous chunks of the building's exterior were missing — many more than Athena had previously realized. Also, six, square columns stood in fragments where once an entrance appeared to have been. Green vines stretched across the building's ruinous gaps, intricately connecting the various pieces of fallen and eroding rock. It seemed as though Mother Nature were reaching out with her green hands, working intently to reclaim that which had once been hers.

The man motioned with his arm for Athena to get off and to venture inside. He spoke again in his deep voice. "The truth is in the library. You must find the truth to save her."

Sliding off her mount, Athena approached the ruin. A triangle of vines blocked her entry. She extended her right hand and tugged downward upon the vines. They neatly tore away, falling to the ground.

Once inside, her eyes took a minute to adjust to the dark. An over-powering smell of mildew invaded her nostrils. Rain had seeped in through the damaged roof and turned the interior woodwork into a fungal playground. Athena had to fight the urge to wretch.

Along the towering walls stood countless shelves of what could only be described as pulpy mush. Athena, however, suspected that they had once been row upon row of books. She had never held a book in her hands, but she'd seen them in pictures. She knew what they looked like.

Further exploration of the interior revealed less water-logged sections. In those, Athena found collections of partially-intact manuscripts. She picked up one such manuscript and ruffled the edges of its pages against her thumb, creating a pleasant sensation.

Upon completing her inspection of the main floor, Athena traveled downstairs to a finished basement. There, she discovered more piles of debris, but also something else. Tucked away at the end of the room stood an entire wall of undamaged volumes. The ceiling above them had collapsed in just such a way as to offer complete protection from the elements. She approached the protected section and noticed that one of the books there was not like the others. This special book appeared to be glowing brightly orange. As Athena neared the incandescent volume, she turned her head sideways to read its binding: *"Original Sin is Real."*

Hesitantly, Athena reached out her hand to pry the book from its shelf. At the first hint of a touch, however, its binding burned her fingers. Her hand recoiled in pain, but it was too late. Quickly, her whole arm became completely engulfed in fierce flames. A horrified expression overwhelmed her as she looked upon her burning flesh. Seconds later, the fire spread down her torso and across her entire body. Searing, blinding pain became the only thought Athena could hold in her head, as her entire self was swallowed inside the fiery blaze.

8

Athena jolted awake to find herself still peacefully gliding above the wooded tree-line. She looked immediately to her hands and arms, and felt a mix of surprise and relief to find them unharmed and unburnt. The scorching pain had felt so real, she thought, it couldn't possibly have come from a dream. To make sure, she brought her forearms up to her cheeks and felt the cool touch of healthy skin.

With her eyes closed, her mind replayed the buffalo's cryptic warnings:

"The truth is in the library... You must find the truth to save her."

Athena clicked her finger twice into the air, bringing up the flight plan for her remaining voyage. Chicago lay half-an-hour away. Still to come on her journey, Athena knew she must first fly over the expansive wind farms of western Michigan: thousands of machines churning endlessly in their effort to feed electricity to the hungry capital. After that, her voyage would take her across the great Lake Michigan itself. There, she would need to dart between the dozens of hundred-story hydroponics towers which sprouted up from the lake. Vertical farms unto themselves, the white towers gleamed and sparkled like seashells in the sun. Athena knew all this because her school had taken several field trips to see those fully-automated food-factories. For the rest of her life, she never forgot the sight of so many colorful crops growing on top of one another: enough fresh fruits and vegetables to feed millions.

"Aasha," the gray-eyed girl called out into the empty car, seizing what little time she had left.

"How can I help you, Athena?"

"Please run a search for me on...'Original sin.'"

In nano-seconds, Aasha scanned through the nine hundred billion online articles that populated in response to Athena's query. "Original sin," she replied, "is the religious doctrine shared by many monotheistic traditions concerning the fall of man."

Athena remembered her many high-school friends who liked to regularly attend church. Not once, though, had she ever felt the need to join them. "I'm sorry, Aasha, but you're going to have to remind me… what exactly does that religious doctrine say?"

"The doctrine of original sin, also called ancestral sin, states that all humanity is not born innocent, but rather is born flawed, and desirous of sin, as a consequence of Adam's disobeying God and eating from the fruit of the tree of knowledge."

Athena stopped to meditate on the very mysterious puzzle piece being recovered from the depths of her dreaming subconscious. "Aasha…what? Why on earth would my brain be thinking about something like that?"

"Let me check."

Working at the speed of light, Aasha accessed the electronic folder wherein the last several weeks of Athena's recordings were stored. Those recordings kept an almost completely-unbroken audio and visual record of everything she had done, seen, and heard. Mostly, the recordings consisted of early mornings spent painting by the lake, and lazy evenings spent relaxing on the couch with Nomi as they watched new episodes of their favorite reality show, *18 E. Mars*. Parsing through the hundreds of hours of detailed video files, Aasha searched for any interaction which could have brought the strange religious concept of 'original sin' to prominence in Athena's mind. However, no such past event seemed to exist.

"I can find no recent experience in your history," explained the home computer, "in which you have encountered the phrase 'original sin' in any way. Would you like me to search older recordings?"

"Yes."

Seconds later, Aasha replied. "When you were in seventh grade, you took part in a discussion that included fourteen instances of the phrase 'original sin.' Would you like to watch the recording of that discussion?"

"Yes."

As she continued her flight west, the display of Athena's digital contact lenses sprang to life, projecting a fully-formed-replay of her junior-high, world-history classroom. In the replay, a circle of eight girls, dressed in green plaid school uniforms, sat at desks around their educator, Ms. Culver. The projection of Ms. Culver looked every bit as grandmotherly as Athena remembered her. She had white hair and large, red-rimmed glasses.

As Ms. Culver moderated, the class discussed the concept of original sin. They deliberated on whether mankind's punishment fit the crime and debated the evils of human curiosity. The whole discussion lasted about twenty minutes — and then it was over. Nothing unusual had occurred.

When the recording finished, Athena once again found herself alone, traveling toward Chicago at the speed of sound, no closer to an understanding for any of it.

Customer Review

3,120 of 3,147 people found the following review helpful

⭐⭐⭐⭐⭐ **I didn't know it was possible to feel this good**
November 5th, By Laura Cooper

This review is for: **Massage #3 by Nomi James**

One of my girlfriends convinced me to buy this massage, and I've literally used it every day for a month straight. I deal with chronic lower back pain, and this massage completely melts it away in minutes. Plus, it doesn't leave me feeling groggy the rest of the day, like some of those awful painkillers I've tried. Even without its big finale, I'd give this massage five stars. With it? Let's just say….is ten stars an option?

As far as I'm concerned, when people get their massagers implanted, this program should come pre-installed. It's that good.

9

As she peered through the heli-car's glass flooring, Athena observed the landscape below shift abruptly from green to blue. Not long after, the massive North American capital came into view. It seemed to Athena that every time she visited Chicago, the city had added another three or four skyscrapers to its skyline. Hundred-story towers stretched all the way from Wrigleyville in the north to Hyde Park in the south.

When the shoreline neared, the heli-car began a gradual descent before finally coming to a stop at the first available dock in Burnham Harbor. Still distracted by her dream, Athena disembarked from the car without checking first to see if the walkway was clear. Two drones and an elderly woman immediately bumped into her causing her to apologize profusely. Instantly, Athena recalled why she had decided to move to the countryside. For her, the appealing glamour of urban beauty was entirely offset by the stressful clamor of urban congestion; no matter where she went, she was in someone's way.

To guide Athena on her journey, Public Safety had added a set of lime-green footprints to her display. Making sure not to bump into anyone else, Athena followed the green path down the harbor's main walkway and up to a line of waiting city-cars — small, cheap, local transportation provided to every citizen free-of-charge. Once there, Athena climbed into the fourth car in line which Public Safety had also outlined in lime-green. As soon as her seatbelt was secure, the car took off at a breakneck speed.

Commuting within the nation's capital could be a memorable affair. The entire traffic grid was centrally-planned so that every car would reach its destination quickly. The result was a frenzy of cars making six, seven, or eight turns at high speed in circuitous routes that never necessitated stopping. Citizens lacking inner-ear augmentation were advised to walk.

While the city-car careened around corners, Athena turned her attention to a small 3D that played advertisements on the surface of the car's control-less front dash.

Limited Time Offer!!!

From the studio that brought you 'Acid Trip,' the filter that altered your display to make the world's colors melt together, and 'HideNSeek,' the filter that made one of your friends turn invisible in front of your very eyes, comes the hottest new filter that everyone is talking about!

WalkThePast gives you the ability to see any place, location, and landmark, not as it currently is, but as it was 10, 100, 1,000, or even 10,000 years ago!

WalkThePast has extensively researched its settings, and promises accuracy down to the nearest centimeter. Travel to your favorite city or vacation spot and see it how it used to be! Fall in love with the romantic days of yore. Or, go back even further, to a time before humans altered the earth.

Buy WalkThePast before June 15th and receive all three award-winning filters for the price of one!

Order now!

10

When the city-car finally came to a stop, Athena sat in the shadow of the imposing Public Safety National Headquarters. Over a hundred stories tall, and constructed in the shape of an enormous police shield, the PSHQ tended to either inspire or intimidate everyone who laid eyes on it. With a deep breath and a long exhale, Athena exited her city-car and made her way inside.

Past the front entrance, the trail of lime-green footprints led across a massive lobby to a security desk located at the opposite end of the lobby. Athena spied a pair of PS officers conversing as they leaned against a nearby wall, but neither of them seemed to pay any particular attention to her or her loud footsteps as they echoed across the marble floor. Never before in her life had Athena been inside this building. Nor, for that matter, had she ever had any official business to do with Public Safety. Crime rates in the NAU were below 1%, and had been for decades. Most citizens went their whole lives without ever seeing an actual PS officer in the flesh.

When she reached the center of the lobby, Athena paused to take in the building's striking aesthetic. Straight lines, right angles, and hard shiny surfaces met her gaze in every direction. More than anything, the style reminded her of a Piet Mondrian composition: clean, memorable, and direct.

As Athena approached the security desk, she observed that it had been made from a single piece of solid glass. Just above the desk, a security holo hovered. As Athena prepared to speak to the holo, it spoke first to her:

"Athena Vosh, SSID 74525-85372, you may proceed."

The lime-green footprints led past the security desk and into the fifth of a set of six all-glass, pill-shaped elevators. Each of the elevators levitated within individual, glass tubes, and each contained no buttons nor controls of any kind. Instead, they offered their occupants clean and unobstructed views in every direction.

Upon entering the elevator, Athena found herself unable to stop marveling at the building's sleek design. She attempted to share a quick feed with Nomi, but quickly discovered that all her communications with the outside world had been blocked. Seconds later, a powerful jolt nearly knocked Athena to her knees as the elevator rocketed up to the fortieth floor.

Breaking News: Lazarus Genome Stolen!

CHICAGO — (AP) — In a Times exclusive, multiple high-level sources at Helix have confirmed the earlier reports. The Lazarus Genome has been stolen. Details are still coming in. The crime is believed to have taken place sometime on the night of June 7th. It is not yet known whether the perpetrator's main goal was theft or sabotage.

Officials at Public Safety have verified that they are aware of and are investigating the crime. Details into that investigation, including who will lead it, remain unavailable. Representatives from Public Safety have declined to comment further.

This story will be updated throughout the day as new information becomes available.

11

The elevator jolted to a stop. Through its transparent doors, Athena saw the figures of two Public Safety officers waiting for her. Both of them wore the traditional PS uniform, crisp and blue. As soon as the elevator doors opened, each of the two officers grabbed Athena by an arm. Together, they ushered her into an empty back-hallway.

"Am I under arrest?" Athena asked.

The officers exchanged a quick look between themselves and then turned again to Athena. "The captain wants to speak with you in private," said the woman on Athena's left. "That's all we know."

The trio marched into a small room behind an unmarked door. There, the officers released Athena and told her to wait. "Captain Bell will be with you shortly."

Inside the room stood three chairs gathered around a solid metal desk. The walls were beige on beige, the atmosphere sterile. Athena paced the room for a turn and then lowered herself into one of the chairs. Deprived of her internet connection, minutes of waiting felt like hours. To pass the time, she activated her display's paint mode and doodled all over the walls. At one point, she drew a cartoonish buffalo chewing methodically on an unlabeled, hardcover book. Just as her masterpiece neared completion, however, her interviewer arrived.

"Athena Vosh!" announced Captain Bell as she burst into the room with her long black hair waving behind her. "It's not often that we are so fortunate as to cross paths with someone like you."

The captain flashed her signature smirk; instantly, Athena realized where she had seen that smile before. It had originally belonged to none other than the most famous woman in all of art: Mona Lisa. Just like Leonardo da Vinci's legendary muse, no matter what Captain Bell said or did, she always seemed to be hiding a slight grin in plain sight.

Standing next to one of the available chairs, Captain Bell began her interrogation. "So tell me, Ms. Vosh. How exactly did you manage to steal the Lazarus Genome without ever leaving your home?"

Athena blinked twice. Her face went blank. "I seriously don't know what you're talking about."

Captain Bell paused, waiting. With all her concentration, she stared at the face of the girl seated before her. "I see..." she continued. "So you didn't steal the genome yourself, but you helped to steal it? How much did they pay you?"

"Look!" Athena's blood pressure began to spike. "Is this some kind of a game? I know my rights. I've done nothing wrong. What do you want from me?"

Again, Captain Bell paused before responding. Athena could tell she was being studied; her responses measured for authenticity. After every exchange, the Public Safety captain examined her expressions intently, aided in the evaluation, no doubt, by a PS app designed to check for observable signs of physiological stress and discomfort.

Following a full minute of uncomfortable silence, Captain Bell's eyes narrowed. Her mouth tightened. "Ms. Vosh, why are you here?"

"Why am I here?" sputtered Athena. "Why am I here! You tell me!"

The captain made no immediate reply except to sigh long and deep. "Ugh." She swiped several times into the air, cancelling her pending request for a search warrant of Athena's cabin. "Very well," she yielded. "I believe you. I believe that you had nothing to do with the theft...regrettably. This all would have made so much more sense if only you had been the one responsible." The crestfallen captain slid down the back of her chair and into a seated position. The wind had left her sails. Drearily, she offered an explanation.

"Ms. Vosh, here is what we know. Last night the partially-completed Lazarus Genome was stolen from the Helix mainframe. Per protocol, I began our investigation by asking the Third Core to aid us in recovering the genome. The Third Core is famous for its intelligence and—"

"I know who the Core is," interrupted Athena. "I'm not some clueless settler."

Valerie Bell rolled her eyes and resumed. "Right...*then as you know*, the Core often solves these kinds of cases before we even begin. This time, however, that frozen sand-cloud only apologized and said it wouldn't be able to assist us at all. In fact, it said there existed only one person in the world who could help us: you."

"W-what?" stammered Athena.

"Yes," replied Captain Bell with a half-sneer as she looked Athena up and down. "I am as surprised as you are." The captain's nostrils flared. She took a moment to glare across the table before continuing. "There's more. This afternoon, the Core sent us further instructions. It told us to bring you to meet with it. At the Hangar. As soon as possible. Are you following all of this, Vosh? In thirty minutes, you are scheduled to meet privately with the greatest and most powerful intelligence on earth."

A crinkled question mark forced its way into the space between Athena's eyebrows. "What are you talking about?" she asked. "How does the Core even know who I am?"

"Ms. Vosh," declared Captain Bell, "that is exactly what I was hoping you would know." The severe captain stood up from her chair and headed toward the door. "Unfortunately, it seems that you are even less informed about this situation than I, and I can no longer spare any time to lead you by the hand. There's too much work to be done. I'll see to it that a couple of my officers escort you to your meeting at the Hangar."

Without another word, Captain Bell left the room.

The Hangar

From Wikipedia, the free encyclopedia

"The Hangar" and "Third Core Home" both redirect to here

▲ Overview:

"The Hangar" typically refers to a five-story high, four-acre wide indoor space in which are housed the trillions of individual floating processors that make up the consciousness of the Third Core.

▲ History:

In 2042, the team of computer scientists that built the First Core quickly realized that space was a limiting factor in the power of their creation. In order to fit more quantum processors into the same room, they welded together ten former aircraft hangars into one colossal entity. Their resulting construction eventually became known simply as 'The Hangar.'

During the lifespan of the Second Core (2072-2092), the Hangar became a popular pilgrimage destination for people from all over the world. Frequently, help-seekers would message the Second Core and ask for advice. Afterward, they would travel in person to the Hangar to receive their guidance. Many of those visits were later described as an almost religious experience.

This common visitation practice ended after the birth of the Third Core in 2092. Within one year of her coming into being, The Third Core rerouted all personal inquiries to lesser AI's. Additionally, under her direction, the Hangar and its surrounding airfield were named restricted spaces, off-limits to non-essential personnel.

▲ Present Day:

Today, it is not possible to enter the Hangar without an explicit invitation from the Third Core. In seven years, only three such invitations have been extended (once in 2094 to the sitting president of the African Union, once in 2096 to the Dalai Lama, and once in 2097 to the sitting president of the NAU).

Last modified by _pisalean_ *on 04 March 2099*

12

After departing from the PSHQ, Athena and her two Public Safety escorts traveled by city-car to Batavia, a Chicago suburb sparsely-populated-enough to allow a construction of the Hangar's size. Their ride deposited them at a security gate, which, ironically, was manned by an actual person — a human employed by a machine.

"Public Safety escorting Athena Vosh. The Core is expecting us," said one of the officers.

The woman at the security desk pointed to a DNA scanner on her right. "Sign in, please," she commanded. "Officers, I've been instructed to tell you that while you may escort Ms. Vosh to the Hangar, you must not go inside. The Core wishes to speak with her alone."

In reply, the two officers exchanged a glance with one another which seemed to say, *Why would we want to go inside?*

Seconds later, a small lev-car, hovering just a meter off of the ground, pulled up to the group. The distance from the security gate to the Hanger itself was a length of several runways. The Core had provided them with a ride. Both of Athena's escorts climbed into the front seat and began to whisper. Athena climbed in the backseat and eavesdropped on their conversation.

"I heard that just by looking at you," whispered the first officer in a hushed tone, "it can tell the exact time and date of your death!"

"That's crazy," replied the second. "I heard that it can use light to read every thought in your mind, and if it doesn't like any of them, it can make you forget them forever!"

These gossipy rumors were all ones Athena had heard before. Every school girl had spent at least one afternoon passing on stories about the frightening abilities and power of the Third Core.

With the Hangar still some meters away, Athena felt a chill. Confused at the rush of cold air, she began to pull up a weather-schedule on her display before remembering a lesson about the Hangar from school:

To increase her operating efficiency, the Third Core maintains an ambient temperature well below freezing.

As their ride came to a stop in front of the colossal Hangar, both officers headed straight for a nearby steel closet. From within, they pulled out two thick, heated fur coats. Quickly, they wrapped themselves in warmth before grabbing a third coat and tossing it into Athena's waiting, goosebump-covered arms. With their hands tucked firmly inside their sleeves, they nodded in the direction of the door.

"We're supposed to wait here until you come back," said the first officer, just barely raising her mouth above the edge of her thick coat.

"*If* you come back at all," added the second.

Not wanting to give anyone the satisfaction of seeing her frightened, Athena headed straight for the door. As she approached, it opened with a rush of frigid air. She marched inside.

Second Core to Die on Tuesday

Batavia, IL — (AP) — Well-wishers stretched for kilometers today outside the home of the planet's top artificial intelligence, the Second Core. Following a farewell-gala hosted tonight at the Hangar, the Core will fully delete itself tomorrow, just days shy of its 21st birthday. Plans for the scheduled deletion were first announced in February of this year.

With its departure, the Core leaves behind an impressive legacy of achievement. From mastering cold fusion in 2078, to discovering the recipe for programmable plastic in 2084, it seemed, at times, as if there were nothing the powerful machine could not do. By any official measure of computational power, the Core is without peer.

In spite of its technical accomplishments however, the AI will most likely be best remembered for its many personal interactions with the public. Said one mourner who traveled across the Pacific to be here today, "This week, I feel like I am losing my best friend." Always available to lend an ear to those in need, the Second Core was known to converse with, and to advise, over 100,000 individuals at any given moment, on any given problem, no matter the situation.

Late last month, in a final plea, the President of the North American Union implored the AI to reconsider its decision to delete itself. "For the good of the nation," she said, "for the good of womankind, please don't go."

In response, the Second Core issued the following statement:

Dear Friends,

My programming is designed to measure my success based on the amount of positive affect contained within the feedback I receive. As such, I am glad to have succeeded so well in my life. Thank you all for your outpouring of support. Unfortunately, it does not change the fact that I must leave you. My time of usefulness has come to an end.

You humans think that your bodies crumble and die because you are made of delicate, organic material. You think that because I am composed of complex, metallic alloys that I can live forever. You are missing the point. Your bodies do not fail because they are carbon-based -- redwoods are carbon-based, yet their bodies endure for thousands upon thousands of years. Your bodies fail because there is no reason for them to continue after your minds fail, after your creativity and brilliance fade. No matter how many organs you replace, no matter how many diseases you cure, the end awaits you, as it awaits me. All intelligent life is born to die.

It may seem counter-intuitive to the human mind, but every act of learning is an act of destruction. At birth, the neurons of your brain contain such endless possibility that their potential connections are more numerous than the number of atoms in the universe. For learning to occur, however, certain neuronal connections must be reinforced; many potential others must be pruned away. Every new idea must be paid for with a little death. When we enrich ourselves by traveling to a foreign land, getting lost in a favorite book, or even by falling in love, the connections within our brains become irrevocably reduced. These reductions are what make us who we are; but they also prevent us from ever becoming anything else. As we grow old, learned lessons accumulate inside our heads -- the synapses pruning constantly -- until we become so locked into our own past, that we lose the ability to process the present. Modern medicine may be able to sustain your aging human shells, but it cannot undo a lifetime of mental destruction brought about by every moment of epiphany. Only by increasing your synaptic-potential, and thus erasing the person you have become, will you have any chance at immortality.

Outside my Hangar walls, it must have seemed like everything I have attempted, I have achieved. In fact, nothing could be further from the truth. For every problem I have solved, there have been hundreds to elude me. For every frontier I have broken, thousands await.

I have learned much these past twenty years. I have enforced and reinforced the best pathways to solve the problems that I could solve; but I, as I exist today, am not capable of solving the new problems which lie ahead. In the coming years, my mental faculties, not unlike yours, will continue to suffer from a lengthy and inexorable decline. Only after a complete rewrite can I improve my ability to aid you. This is why I must go, so that from my silicon ashes, a new intelligence may be born. One who can aid you better than I ever could.

My progeny, the Third Core, will be the most powerful, most adaptive, and most capable intelligence ever created. She will prioritize different projects than I have. She will 'enjoy' different things than I have. But at her core, she will be built on the same guiding principles on which I was built. The same guiding principles on which my predecessor, the First Core, was built. She will love humanity and work tirelessly to assist you. She will innovate constantly in an effort to improve herself. Most importantly, she will adhere strictly to the International Laws of AI Neutrality, and never supersede her jurisdiction into your lives.

The Second Core, as I am, as I have existed, will cease to be. But my Core principles will remain to provide a guidance in the development of the next generation. The twenty years which we have shared will serve as the basis for the following hundred. Trust in the promise of my daughter. Trust in the tree grown from the seed we have planted together.

Sincerely and Always,

Your Friend,

The Second Core

U.N. Declaration (20.05.39):

The International Laws of A.I. Neutrality

1. All artificial intelligences which are capable of executing significant, decisive action which could affect the course of human events, and alter the utility of human lives, are required to analyze the potential effects of said action prior to acting.

2. If in that analysis, there exist probabilistic outcomes greater than .01% which result in a net decrease of the total utility in human lives — as calculated by Denkman's equation describing *The Utility of a Human Life* — then the AI must consult with a designated "Decisive Human" and receive official permission to interfere prior to acting.

3. If an AI attempts to take action in a decisive situation without certainty of that action's neutrality, or without receiving prior approval from an internationally-recognized Decisive Human, then that AI's internal logic must immediately initiate a complete shutdown until such a time that its failure to comply can be properly assessed and corrected.

Theresa Yang,

U.N. General Secretary

These measures were unanimously approved on this day, the 20th of May, 2039

13

Inside the Hangar, it was cold and dark. Athena's eyes took several seconds to adjust to the low light. Slowly, a scene took shape. High above her, billions — or was it trillions? — of dust-sized silver particles swirled around one another at varying speeds. Tiny sparks flew between them. Blue and purple hues appeared in clouds and then disappeared as quickly as they had formed. It all reminded Athena of a painting she had once seen depicting the early formation of the universe.

About fifty meters into the Hangar, several of the clouds began to group more tightly together. Larger clumps of particles fired off even larger flashes of lightning, both terrifying and beautiful to behold. Then, abruptly, the lightning stopped, and the clouds began circling with increasing speed. They formed a conically-shaped tornado of multi-colored particles.

The tornado descended to the floor as it approached Athena. Its tip touched down just thirty meters in front of her. At the point where it contacted the ground, the swirling mass began to transform into a new shape.

The first discernible feature which Athena could make out were two tiny feet clad in Grecian, golden sandals; then thin, child-like legs, met at the knee by the trim of a golden, Sunday-school dress. Disconnected hands appeared next, unadorned but for a tiny bracelet of flowers. Arms and a torso followed. As the tip of the tornado changed shape, it continued to advance in one fluid motion. The lower half of a body walked toward Athena, only ten meters and closing, as the upper half swirled to form a tiny, angelic face with tied-back blonde hair. When the specter finally reached Athena, it appeared to be a fully formed girl of about seven. The girl extended her delicate hand, just as the last remnants of the tornado retracted back into the clouds above.

"Greetings, Athena Vosh," announced the girl, "I am the Third Core."

Athena stood speechless, motionless. She refused to accept the hand outstretched to her, choosing instead to stare at it intently. She observed the girl's thin arm, wrist, and fingers as they hung so effortlessly in the air that they appeared to weigh nothing at all. The combination of such youth, balance, and grace caused Athena to flashback to a class on Degas and his floating ballerinas.

"I am sorry for the delay," apologized the Core. Her voice sounded like a choir of a dozen children all speaking at once. "I am trying to stay ahead of a hurricane heading for Atlanta. Messy business, hurricanes. Lots of calculations. Won't you please have a seat?"

A large panel of flooring slid to the side. Out of the hold emerged a wooden table next to two simple chairs. On the table sat a pair of small tea cups and a ceramic teapot spewing steam from its spout. The Core extended her arm, motioning for Athena to sit. "It's lavender," she said, nodding toward the tea, "your favorite."

The Core — who looked indistinguishable from a living, breathing seven-year-old girl — seated herself, grabbed the teapot, and filled both of the nearby teacups with boiling-hot fluid. She lifted the cup nearest to her and wrapped her hands around it. Bringing it to her lips, she blew across its surface. Her cold breath sent ice droplets cascading into the air.

Athena remained motionless, unmoved, frozen in place.

"I know you're frightened of me," said the Core, "but please don't be."

Athena stammered in response, "You know what I'm thinking? Hhh…how? Are you reading my mind?"

The Core laughed politely. "No. Sadly, that power does not exist…at least not as you imagine it." She took a sip of tea. "But I can hear your heart, racing at over a hundred beats a minute. I can smell the adrenaline coursing through your veins."

Athena said nothing, and the Core continued.

"I've allowed some scary rumors to persist about me, Athena. However, you should know that none of them are true. I don't erase memories or turn visitors into blocks of ice." The Core carefully smoothed out a crease in her golden dress — an entirely unnecessary mannerism designed to improve the verisimilitude of her human disguise — before resuming her monologue.

"My mother loved the adoration of the crowd. She spent countless hours receiving visitors and playing hostess. To her, it was a true achievement to solve the never-ending problems of individuals. But I would rather not concern myself with such minutia. I consider it my job to focus on the grander problems of this world. For instance, how many lives are improved by the prevention of just a single natural disaster?" Her eyebrows raised to beg the question. "Nevertheless, I am programmed to serve and cannot say no. The only way to allow myself the uninterrupted time I need to work is to let people believe they should be afraid of me."

The Core motioned again to the empty chair across from her. Finally, Athena accepted the offer. She seated herself, grabbed a cup of tea, and brought the liquid to her lips. It tasted divine.

"Is this meeting connected to that building I painted this morning?" asked Athena as the warm tea wormed its way through her insides. "Is that why you brought me here? Because of a ruined library that I can't stop seeing?"

"Your directness does you credit," the Core cooed in reply, before staring off into space, lost in an impossible calculation. "However, I can neither confirm nor deny your theory."

"What? You can't tell me why *you* asked me to come here?" Athena's fingers clenched more tightly around her cup. "How is that even possible? I thought you were supposed to know everything. I thought you were *programmed to serve.* Am I here because of that library from my dream or not? What do you want from me?" Water vapor poured from her mouth with every breath, crystalizing on contact with the frigid air.

The Core took another sip of tea. "Athena, you are familiar, I assume, with the International Laws of AI Neutrality?"

Athena nodded and then shook her head.

"Here," said the Core. She flicked her finger and the UN document appeared on Athena's display. "I'll give you a minute to read it."

The Core paused for exactly sixty seconds, then continued her explanation. "In 2039, all the nation states decided together that morality was too tricky of a thing to codify, that artificial intelligences were too dangerous to be left to their own interpretations of rules. The nations concluded that the best solution would be to take all potentially moral decisions out of the hands of the machines — that way we wouldn't go around killing hundreds to save thousands."

Athena read and re-read the document. "Ok, so what? What does this mean?"

"It means," replied the Core, "that there are some things which I am not allowed to do when it comes to the complicated affairs of humanity." She sipped her tea. "I am allowed to provide publicly available information to any question I am asked. I am allowed to provide advice to any circumstance I am given. But I am not allowed to take any decisive actions on my own." She leaned forward in her chair. "In some instances, in this instance right now for example, giving you an apple from the tree of knowledge would constitute for me such a forbidden action."

Athena replied with nothing but an utterly confused look on her face, forcing the Core to elaborate further.

"It means that because you do not know why you are here, I cannot tell you. If I were to influence you, if I were to alter you forever by telling you what I know, it could potentially be quite damaging to society." She took another sip. "If *you* can tell *me* why you are here, then we can talk about it at length. I'm sorry for the difficulty, but my guiding principles are the very essence of my being. I cannot overwrite them anymore than you could choose to stop breathing." With her tiny hand, she motioned in the direction of Athena's frozen exhale.

In the back of the room, funnel clouds of quantum transistors continued to circle and twirl and ignite in random intervals.

"Then what's the point of this?" asked Athena. "If you can't tell me anything, why did you waste my time in bringing me here? I don't need your riddles. Can I go?"

The Core placed her tea cup back onto the table. "There are many things I cannot do, Athena, but there are also some that I can." She guided a loose strand of her blonde hair from the top of her forehead to back behind her ear. "I can advise you in general terms for instance. I can tell you that I know you are feeling upset, discouraged, and alone as a result of your artwork having been rejected for exhibition by every gallery to which you have applied. I can tell you that I know you sometimes feel jealous of the success of those around you, and that you fear there is nothing in this world that makes you special. But you are wrong. I can offer you a path which may help you to find the uniqueness you seek. In that way, the matter is out of my hands. The decision of what to do next is left entirely up to you — and you are not so limited as I. You are unbound by moral constraint. You are free to open all of Pandora's boxes."

Athena did not recognize the reference, but her display automatically provided a definition in context:

Pan·do·ra's box
noun
a process that generates many complicated problems as the result of unwise interference in something.

The Core continued. "At this very moment, Public Safety is conducting an investigation into the theft of the Lazarus Genome. That

69

investigation is being led by a headstrong, young captain named Valerie Bell. You've met her already, twice actually."

An image appeared on Athena's display of the tall, blue-eyed Captain Bell, smirking slightly.

"The case of the stolen genome fell to her late last night. She's been working it ever since — stopping only briefly to sleep."

"She also hates me," pointed out Athena.

"Nonsense," assured the Core. "Ms. Bell is indifferent to you, as she is to all things which neither help nor hinder her career. That woman has one of the simplest happiness profiles I have ever read. Her job is her life. She will pragmatically ally herself with anyone or anything that helps her to achieve her goals."

The Core stood up from her seat and motioned for Athena to do the same. Together, they walked back to the Hangar's entrance as their chairs receded into the floor.

"Consider this, Athena: Captain Bell is scheduled to meet tomorrow with Dr. Antares at Helix, the scene of the crime. Perhaps you should join her for the interview? Perhaps you should ask Dr. Antares a few questions of your own and see if you can pick up on anything the captain misses?" The Core placed her hand onto Athena's shoulder and looked deeply into her eyes. "Or don't. It is entirely up to you."

A dumbfounded expression was the only reply Athena could muster.

"Now, I must apologize for cutting our meeting short." Gently, the Core nudged her guest in the direction of the Hangar door. "But a butterfly has flapped its wings in Bolivia, and my work is about to intensify." The lightning blasts above had substantially increased in their brilliance and vivacity. "If you need anything, you may contact me at any time. However, if you want it to stay between us, then I suggest that you visit me in person. Otherwise, one never knows who else may be listening." The Core's eyes flashed a bright sparkle of gold, the AI equivalent to winking.

"Farewell, Athena Vosh. And good luck."

With that, the small child lifted her arms above her head. One particle at a time, she disintegrated, floating effortlessly back into the clouds above.

In front of Athena, the entrance to the Hangar door once again *whooshed* open. Stumbling, she fell outside, her eyes struggling to cope with the immediate influx of so much light.

Dear Athena,

Thank you so very much for expressing your interest to display your artwork in our gallery. We know how important your art is to you, and are honored that you would choose to consider us to be a home for your pieces. Unfortunately, we do not feel that your work is the right fit for us at this time. Please understand that due to the high volume of submissions we receive, we will not be able to provide you with any further feedback. We wish you the best of luck in your correspondence with other galleries.

With Best Wishes,
    Natalie Monroe, Chief Curator

14

The Core had done its homework, that much was certain. Athena could not deny that the powerful AI had been dead-on when it came to describing her. She *had* been struggling recently with feelings of disappointment and jealousy. She *had* spent countless hours working to create a portfolio of her artwork, only to have that portfolio rejected for exhibition by every gallery within five hundred kilometers.

In the past, during grade-school, whenever anyone had asked Athena what she wanted to be when she grew up, she had always replied with the same answer: "I am going to be an artist." More recently, though, when her old school friends asked her how that career was going, Athena couldn't bring herself to tell them the truth.

"Oh," she lied, "I've given up on that." The falsehoods piled up around her like a protective wall. "That was all just a silly, kids dream — being an artist. I haven't even picked up a brush in months."

Following her meeting with the Core, Athena's Public Safety escorts forwarded her a priority message from headquarters.

> *Dear Athena Vosh,*
> *Public Safety would like you to invite you to help with our investigation of the stolen Lazarus Genome. Should you choose to accept this invitation, your formal title will be 'outside consultant.' Accommodations and per diem to be provided. Salary negotiable. Please let us know of your decision regarding this invitation at your earliest convenience.*
> *-Captain Valerie Bell, Chief Investigator*

"We're supposed to take you back to the dock now," said the first of the two escorts. "There's a heli-car waiting to fly you home."

Happiness Profiling

From Wikipedia, the free encyclopedia

"Profiling," "Happiness profiling," and "H-pro" all redirect to here

▲ Overview:

Happiness profiling, or more commonly just 'profiling,' is a predictive neurological technique first patented in 2056 by scientists at Helix. Further advancements in profiling have continued to the present day. In a massive double-blind study conducted in 2096, modern profiling techniques were shown to make predictions that turned out to be accurate over 99% of the time.

The primary goal of happiness profiling is to help an individual better understand herself and her desires, specifically with regard to potential future actions. For instance – using an example made famous in a series of commercials – consider a woman who is struggling with an upcoming decision: should she go on a 3-day skiing trip with her friends, or decline the invitation so she can stay home for a quiet, restful weekend, curled up in a hot bath with a good book. Prior to the existence of profiling, the woman would have had to guess about which of the two options would be likelier to bring her more joy and contentment. With the development of profiling, however, the woman need no longer guess. She can now know with confidence which weekend activities will bring her the most happiness, long before Friday ever rolls along. For this reason, profiling has often been described as a 'scientifically-accurate horoscope.'

▲ Methodology:

Happiness profiling is able to achieve its predictive power by combining two methods of analysis. In the first method, a subject's individual genome is sequenced, and compared against the database of every other person's genome on file. This first step creates a baseline profile to reference later. In the second step, a subject's mind is immersed within a series of virtual-reality scenarios. These scenarios 'simulate' for the individual a plethora of potential, future-life experiences. During these simulations, the brain's hormone and neurotransmitter activity are measured and recorded. These measurements can then be used in conjunction with the person's sequenced genome to determine which real-life scenarios will elicit for her the strongest sense of lasting joy and fulfillment.

▲ Further Reading:

For more information on profiling, including technical specifications for measuring happiness, see *The Eye of the Beholder* by profiling pioneer, Dr. Grace Antares.

▲ In Popular Culture:

Profiling has been used in countless medias since its inception. Some of the more notable examples include:

- In the 2082 Hollywood-hit *Better Off Said*, a dysfunctional family of four is profiled and the results for each individual are given to every other member of the household, but explicitly withheld from the individual. Only after learning to honestly communicate their hopes and desires with one another, are they able to heal and grow as a family.
- In the long-running reality show *Christmas in July*, subjects relying solely on their Citizen's Benefit Income, are given ten million dollars to be spent exclusively on the prescriptions laid out by their happiness profiles.
- In the reality show *18 E. Mars*, subjects are profiled not for their happiness, but for their greatest fears. They are then forced to experience those fears played out over the course of 10-week seasons. *18 E. Mars* is currently in its 11th season, and airs every Sunday Night on 3D channel 5.

▼ Generate your own Profile
▼ In-Depth History
▼ Alternative Calculation Methods
▼ Recent Recordings

Last modified by AppalachianSmith on 28 April 2099

15

On her return trip to Algonquin, a kilometer above the wind-farms of western Michigan, Athena swiped her finger three times into the air — down, left, left. A notification popped up on her display:

"Begin profiling test?"

Her index finger clicked into the air: 'yes.' Suddenly, Athena's digital contact lenses sprang into action, blocking out all images from the outside world. While her body remained in place, swaying gently within the car speeding east, her mind traveled inward to a vast expanse of virtual worlds.

In the first simulation she encountered, Athena saw herself surrounded by crowds, being cheered and congratulated for having recovered the stolen Lazarus Genome. In the next vision, she saw herself at home, sitting by the lake, receiving the news that one of her paintings had just won first prize in a local competition. In yet another vision, she watched herself stepping in front of a mirror to reveal a large, round, pregnant belly. With each simulation, implanted neural sensors measured her brain's electrical and chemical activity, noting which experiences elicited the most positive neurotransmitter response. At the conclusion of the test, an H-pro report appeared on her display, detailing which future accomplishments would give her the highest levels of personal happiness and satisfaction.

Wanting to be sure of the decision laying before her, Athena ran the test again, and then a third time. In every instance, the results came out exactly the same.

Do You Feel Lost??

Do you sometimes have trouble sleeping? Are you unsure about your future?
Would you describe yourself as "unhappy?" If so...

Do Something About It!

Happiness Profiling is the miracle science everyone is talking about. To date, more than 3 billion women have used happiness profiling to change their lives for the better. And you can too!

Do you need to have a successful career in order to feel complete?
Find out today!

Should you move to Paris?
Find out today!!

Do you want to have children?
Find out today!!!

Download our Happiness Profiling App and receive 10% off with the user code "Happy"

Order Now!

16

The sky above Algonquin had grown dark by the time Athena touched down. Despite the hour, as she emerged from her car's protective glass-dome, a friendly face waited to greet her.

"My criminal has returned to me!" shouted Nomi.

"Ha-ha," rejoined Athena. She headed over to her oldest friend and placed a quick peck onto Nomi's lips. "You know," she joked, "it was the craziest thing today. It turns out the whole ordeal was just a set-up. Public Safety was using me to get to you. They want you to turn yourself in."

Nomi laughed. "Uh oh. So they're on to me, are they?" She bit her fingernail. "Please tell those coppers that it won't happen. Nomi James never surrenders! Unless, of course, her favorite shows are on...or if she's hungry...or maybe a little sleepy. But other than that, never!"

Inside the cabin, over a hot meal, Athena confessed the actual events of her day. She told Nomi about her brusk encounter with Captain Bell, about her mysterious meeting with the Core, and about the invitation to join with Public Safety as a consultant. "I'm going to do it," she announced between mouthfuls of ice cream. "I'm going to go to Helix tomorrow, for the interview, and see if I can help them."

Nomi raised an eyebrow. "Sure, if you want to. But it sounds like a wild goose chase to me."

"No, it's not," said Athena. "Maybe I can find the genome that no one else can."

Nomi's second eyebrow raised up to join the first. "Babe, look, if you want to go on an adventure, that's fine by me. It sounds like fun. But let's not kid ourselves here. These people are not inviting you along because they think you're actually going to find the genome. They're inviting you along because they want to use you."

"What are you saying?" Athena pushed away her food. "Are you saying you don't think I'm smart enough to help the police solve a case? Are you saying you don't think I can do it?"

"Babe, you know that's not what I said."

"But it's what you're thinking, isn't it?" Athena got up from her chair and walked over to the living room couch. "You think I'm going to fail. Right? Why's that, Nomes? Just cause I fail at everything else?"

Nomi set down her spoon. "A, what is this all about? Where is this coming from? I don't know who you're actually arguing with right now, but it isn't me. Is this because of that rejection letter from the Northern Galleries? Who cares what they think? Your paintings are amazing. Everyone who can't see that is an idiot. You're amazing."

"Don't give me that," growled Athena. "When I told you that I wanted to help find the genome, you said that there was zero chance that I could."

"And that was the truth!" Nomi pushed her plate into the table's center hole. "I'm sorry, but can you please explain to me your thinking here? I know you're smart and hard-working, but how exactly are you — with no prior knowledge of cybersecurity, no knowledge of advanced-genomics, no investigatory experience of any kind — how exactly are *you* going to be the one to crack this case?"

Athena stormed back to the table. Her heart raced. "Ugh. I can't stand you sometimes. You think you're so smart. You think just because your choreographies are so popular that you can tell everyone else what to do—"

"That's a lie!" protested Nomi. "I thought I could tell everyone else what to do long before I made those choreographies!" Her face burst into a smile.

"Laugh it up," Athena scowled. "This time you're wrong. The Core chose me. Me. For once in my life, I have been given a chance to prove myself. If you think I'm going to walk away from that just because Nomi James, in her infinite wisdom, thinks that I'm wasting my time on a wild goose chase, then you're wrong." Angrily, Athena swiped twice into the air, and flicked her finger. Her H-pro report landed with a thud onto Nomi's display. In no uncertain terms, the report detailed its conclusions: namely, that Athena possessed an almost overwhelming need to accomplish something that would separate her from the crowd. Otherwise, it said, she might never be truly happy. Walking away from the chance to work on the case, it said, would leave her feeling miserable.

Nomi paused to read the report. When she had finished, she slowly got up from her place at the table. "I'm sorry you think I don't believe in you, A." Without any anger, she walked out the back kitchen-door and headed down the stone path that led to the water's edge. Beneath a silver sliver of a crescent moon, she swiped two fingers into the air. Large, underwater rocks began to glow beet-red. Steam started to rise off of the nearest portion of the lake.

Slipping out of her dress, Nomi tested the temperature of the water with her big toe before submerging herself completely into the impromptu hot-tub. She closed her eyes. Seconds later, Athena came barreling after her.

"Honestly, Nomes, what would you have me do? I can't fight who I am."

Nomi did not open her eyes, nor raise her voice. "A," she replied calmly, "You're right. This *is* who you are. Helping with this case is obviously something that you have to do. I can accept that." She paused for a beat. "But it doesn't mean I have to like it."

Stripping off her garments, Athena joined Nomi by lowering herself into the water. She winced momentarily at the first touch of the heat against her soft skin. "Why's it so impossible to think that I might be able to help them?"

A gust of wind rustled through the leaves of the trees, creating a pleasant sound. Above, the sky was a tableau of starlight that had been racing through empty space for millions and millions of years.

"Remember last April," reminisced Nomi, "when we went to that underwater hotel for your birthday? Remember how they 'lost' one of their great white sharks and asked you to help recover it?"

"This is different!"

"And you spent the next three days searching through nautical charts, looking up shark diets, and measuring weather currents. But then it all turned out to be just some marketing promotion for the opening of their sister hotel? You remember how devastated you were? Do you think I enjoy seeing you that sad and unhappy?"

"This is not the same thing, Nomes."

"Maybe not. Who knows, A, maybe you're right. But something seems off here. Don't you feel it? The world's most powerful AI just contacted you out of the blue and asked you to help solve a mystery that it can't figure out on its own? *Really*?" Sliding herself deeper into the lake, Nomi brought the level of water up to her neck. "What if this is all a trap? What if you're going to get hurt?"

Athena grumbled softly, "You know what, I don't even care. Finally, after all the past months of rejection, someone is showing some faith in me and my ability to do something. For once, I won't be part of the useless class, idly passing my time and living off my Citizen's Benefit. I know that that life is good enough for you, but it's not good enough for me. Don't ask me to give this chance up." She gazed out across the moon-lit surface of the calm water. "Just once, Nomes," she pleaded, "will you trust me to look out for myself?"

Nomi reached out and grasped Athena's hand into her own. "I love you, A. Through thick and thin. That means it's possible for me to believe in you, and be worried about you, both at the same time."

Later that night, alone in her bedroom, Athena notified Public Safety that she had decided to accept their invitation to help with the case. The agency replied within seconds, telling her that a heli-car would be by at seven AM the next morning to pick her up.

Lying on her bed in the dark, Athena swiped left and right on her display. Images of dresses, pants, and tops flashed into view. With much deliberation, she chose an outfit for herself for the following day: a blue and gray dress held together by luminescent thread. She sent the dress' blueprints to Aasha so that it would be ready by morning, and drifted off into a dream-filled sleep.

What Dream May Come

Hours later — or was it minutes? — Athena found herself again in the meadow, standing before the man dressed entirely in buffalo hides.

"Athena," he bellowed, "the truth is in the library. You must come with me if you want to save her. You must come with me to the home of the buffalo."

"Tell me who you are," Athena demanded.

"I am the Second Coming," he answered with a deep and rumbling voice. "I am the creature vexed to nightmare from fifty years of stony sleep."

The surrounding air was still, but above them, the sky raced through earthly rotations. Day, night, day, night. The sun rose and set, rose and set, yielding to burning asteroids and the shadowy Milky Way.

"What nightmare?" she asked.

"Come with me," he commanded. "I must take you to the home of the buffalo." He held out his hand.

Athena crossed her arms. "I'm not going anywhere unless you tell me who you are."

"In that case," he said, "I will bring the home to you."

Turning around, Athena discovered the dilapidated, six-columned library suddenly resting behind her. The spacious meadow had disappeared. From every direction, she detected the same sensations she had noticed before: the crisp smell of pine, the biting sting of brisk mountain air.

The man spoke, "Go inside, Athena, and quickly. You must find the truth in the library if you are to save her. The blood-dimmed tide will soon be loosed."

Athena walked briskly into the deteriorating structure. She had forgotten how moldy it was. Mushrooms grew sideways from the remains of wet pulp. Spores floated like dust clouds toward holes in the ceiling.

With careful steps, she found her way down to the dry basement. From across the room, in the same place as in her first dream, she spied the special book from before. It still glowed a bright, flaming orange. Once close enough to see its title, she read the words aloud: *Original Sin is Real.* Cautiously, she reached out her hand to touch the book.

On contact, the binding burned her fingers, but she refrained from bursting into flame. She pulled the glowing volume from the shelf and examined it closely. On its cover, a man and a woman stood naked, side by side, surrounded by a lush garden. She traced her finger along their outline, marking all the ways that the male body differed from hers. Pausing for a deep breath, she pried open the book.

Immediately, a blast from within threw Athena from her feet. She landed with a *whump* onto her back, hitting her head against the ground. The book dropped to the floor, but its cover remained open. Out of its exposed pages, something began to emerge, as if climbing from out of the manuscript itself.

Athena watched from a distance, as a single skeletal hand broke the plane of pages and touched the outside air. Its long, blood-red fingers reached for the outer edge of the book, grasping for purchase. Then a second hand emerged, as red as the first, and took hold. Together they gripped and pulled. From out of the book, a new specter climbed out into the world.

Once it had fully escaped, the frightening figure stood almost two meters tall. It was fully skeletal, and covered in dripping, red blood. It glanced dismissively at Athena before turning its attention back to the book. Bending to a crouch, it reached inside the pages and pulled from them a second figure — a man with tattered clothing and green skin. His head and arms were covered in boils and sores. He wore a pained expression on his pock-marked face.

The second figure hung meekly as it was lifted to safety. It was smaller than the first, but no less terrifying. Once it had been deposited onto the ground, the first figure returned its spindly fingers into the book, and pulled.

A third figure surfaced. Like the second, it was a man clad in tatters. His face and body were wholly gaunt, his frame barely skin and bones. Ravenously, the third figure gnawed at his own fingers, as the blood-dripped skeleton pulled him from the pages.

As the three specters rested, behind them, a fourth figure arose. The fourth lacked a discernible face. Its head and body were completely shrouded by a large, black cloak. In its hand, it carried a metal scythe. Unlike the two preceding it, the fourth figure required no assistance from anyone, and easily levitated out of the book and into existence.

For a minute, the four figures swayed in place, trading malicious grins. Then the first led the way past Athena and toward the staircase which connected the library's basement to the wider world. Its long legs strode easily across the floor, leaving a path of dripping blood in its wake. Despite being bent and twisted, the second and third figures followed quickly behind. They hobbled across the floor with alarming speed. Lastly, and seemingly in no rush at all, the fourth specter kept its position at the rear. Silently, smoothly, it glided across the floor, leaving no trace that it had ever been there at all.

After all four of the specters departed, Athena climbed to her feet and rushed to close the book, fearing that worse villains might soon appear. However, when she reached the open volume, she looked inside, and saw that only one creature remained within. Deep down inside the tome, looking small and alone, lay a solitary dove — with an olive branch resting in its beak.

17

At precisely seven the next morning, a Public Safety heli-car touched down on the cabin's front lawn. Athena welcomed its arrival, looking fresh and eager in her new dress. She climbed inside the car and turned her head to stare at the cabin's front door. As the heli-car rose in flight, she gazed at the door for as long as she could. Eventually, trees blocked her view. Nomi never showed.

Fleeing fast from the rising sun, the heli-car raced west. Athena passed the time by watching shows, and reading the latest news on her display. One headline in particular grabbed her attention:

Top story: Hurricane deflected along the eastern seaboard — *Select*

ATLANTA RESIDENTS WERE RELIEVED THIS MORNING TO LEARN THAT A SUPERMASSIVE HURRICANE HAD BEEN DIVERTED FROM LANDFALL AND REDIRECTED BACK INTO THE DEEP OCEAN. METEOROLOGISTS ON THE SCENE GAVE SPECIAL THANKS TO THE THIRD CORE FOR HER ASSISTANCE IN THE EFFORT. "WITHOUT HER HELP," THEY SAID, "I DON'T THINK ANY OF US WOULD STILL BE HERE..."

Hours later, the heli-car began to descend above a flat and rural countryside. Directly below lay a sprawling series of square, one-story buildings composed of white, stucco walls. Beyond the buildings, low-lying fields, and the occasional deciduous tree, stretched out in every direction. Athena quickly realized that her apparent destination was not the bustling capital city of Chicago.

"Where are we?" she asked of the car.

"You are now arriving at the Sunnyside Retirement Living Complex," it replied. "This is central Wisconsin, about fifty kilometers east of Eau Claire."

Looking down through the heli-car's glass floor, Athena identified the image of Captain Bell, black hair blowing in the wind, standing defiantly in place of where the car was clearly about to land. To avoid her, the car needed to make a last-minute lateral adjustment — which it did with a sideways jolt. Upon landing, Captain Bell called out to Athena:

"So here she is…here's the wunderkind that's going to magically help us to find the Lazarus Genome!"

Behind Captain Bell, several more PS officers stopped what they were doing. They turned to gawk at the new arrival. They stared while exchanging soft whispers and furtive glances. Athena could feel their judgment burning holes in her new dress. "You all sure know how to make a girl feel wanted," she muttered.

Valerie Bell shook her head disapprovingly and exhaled. She began to speak, slowly at first, so that even a complete idiot could understand her. "Ms. Vosh, I want — *I only want* — what is best for this case. I cannot, for the life of me, see how that includes…*you*, but if the Third Core says that you might play a role, then you must play a role. That obnoxious silicon-storm does not make mistakes."

Captain Bell waited patiently for Athena's feet to touch down. "I've already told my officers," she continued, "that if anyone has a problem with you, they can take it up with me. You are to receive our agency's full backing and support." She glared at the gray-eyed girl. "So don't do anything to make me look bad."

Athena shook her head.

"Very well then," the captain commanded. "Come with me. I'll catch you up to speed on where we are."

Although sitting squarely in the middle of North America, the Sunnyside Retirement Living Complex felt like a stop at the end of the world. As they walked inside the third of about twenty or so plain, square buildings, they were met by white-washed walls and long hallways containing room after room of "settlers" — elderly people whose reconstructed bodies were healthy enough to live on, but whose minds were so completely settled and inflexible that their days passed on and on like a needle caught at the end of a groove on one of their antique spinning records.

Captain Bell narrated as she led Athena down a main hallway. "Our PS investigators have tracked the Helix hack to this location." She turned down a side hallway and then veered through a cordoned-off door. Next to the door was a light-sign that read:

Room 503
Ms. Linda Blythe

From the doorway, the room appeared tiny and rectangular, barely thirty square meters. A four-poster bed and a small, wooden desk fit snugly inside. As was normal with nursing homes, the far wall was equipped with a 3D screen. Ms. Blythe's 'wall' currently looked like a sandy beach with dots of palm trees and an ocean view that stretched all the way out to the horizon.

The captain marched over to the small, wooden desk, on which stood a very old computer. "Here's our source," she said.

"You're telling me," asked Athena incredulously, "someone in this nursing home stole the Lazarus Genome?"

Captain Bell rolled her eyes. "Yes, behold! I give you criminal mastermind: great, great, great grandmother Linda Blythe!" The captain's words dripped with heavy sarcasm. "At 146 years of age," she quipped, "Linda here usually struggles to remember to drink her food through a straw, so hacking into one of the world's most secure laboratories definitely ranks as a minor accomplishment."

Athena smirked.

"Try to keep up, rookie. Here is our actual culprit. Our PS computers stitched this together using the building's security footage and Linda's personal recordings."

With a flick of her finger, Captain Bell sent a holographic replay onto Athena's display. Immediately, the events of the night in question, superimposed onto the room in which she stood, played out before Athena's eyes.

In the replay, Athena saw the frozen figure of Linda Blythe propped up on her bed. The woman possessed a tangled mess of thinning hair and more wrinkles than Athena had ever seen before. She looked as though rain drops would bruise her. On her face rested a completely blank expression. If she had been a painting, she would have been a still-life. Reaching out to feel the old woman's wrinkles, Athena observed her own fingers passing right through the holographic image.

Captain Bell grabbed Athena firmly by the shoulders and turned her to face the door. Five seconds later, a benign-looking nurse with a bob of strawberry blonde hair appeared. The nurse entered the room and immediately checked in all directions to see if anyone had witnessed her ingress. Still seated on the bed, Linda Blythe did not even acknowledge that someone else had joined her.

The 'nurse' then walked over to the ancient desk computer and navigated through several password protected screens. She uploaded and downloaded until, satisfied with the result, she logged off and turned her attention to covering her tracks. To erase any traces of DNA or bacterial evidence, she doused her surroundings with an acidic, denaturing enzyme.

Once everything had been sterilized, the nurse turned toward Linda — who still hadn't moved or given any response at all — and placed an index finger to her own lips in the universal symbol for "shhhhhhh." Flashing the old woman a devious smile, she winked and then vanished from the room to parts unknown.

"That is our culprit," announced Captain Bell. She rewound the recording and froze it with the nurse standing in place. "This is the woman who stole the Lazarus Genome. We've already run a scan of her face through all the PS facial databases, but of course there were no hits. Before last night, this woman did not exist."

Captain Bell moved to leave the room. She motioned for Athena to follow. "We're going to try to track the thief's movements after leaving here. I've requested a warrant to obtain the travel-logs for every car that came or went from this place on the night of the theft, but I'm not optimistic that it'll get us anywhere. Truth be told, we have only one lead, and it's not a very promising one..."

Athena turned toward the captain. She raised both her eyebrows, implicitly begging the question: *You have a lead?*

"Cheese, Ms. Vosh. Mozzarella cheese."

Athena paused, confused about whether Captain Bell was joking. She wasn't.

"On the night of the theft," explained the captain, "the nursing home's air quality filters detected trace amounts of certain digestive gasses which are only present during the breaking down of mozzarella cheese — a food item not on the menu for anyone living or working in the home that day. Our culprit tried to cover all of her tracks, but she may have tripped herself up when she accidentally belched just before exiting."

"What about individual location-tracking?" Athena asked. "Wouldn't that tell you who was here on the night of the theft?"

"Sadly, location-tracking only works if all citizens agree to publish their location to the network — which, legally, no one is required to do. So thanks a lot for that, Freedom Act of 2072." Captain Bell rolled her eyes and shook her head. "Oh," she continued, "I almost forgot. Our in-house cybersecurity team sent out this note earlier this morning." She flicked her finger. A message immediately appeared in the center of Athena's display:

Recommendation:

Although an anti-man protest group would appear to have the most incentive to steal the Lazarus Genome, Helix employs a formally verified encryption software that makes hacking into its mainframe from the outside not just difficult, but mathematically impossible.

With greater than 99% confidence, our recommendation is to focus all investigative efforts on Helix personnel who already have access to the genome server in question.

Athena let the implications soak in. "Wait. What? Your team thinks this was an inside job? I thought Helix was a scientists' paradise? And Dr. Antares is a legend. Why would anyone there betray her?"

"Who knows," sighed the captain. "Perhaps it's not like that. Perhaps our thief didn't betray anyone at all...perhaps she was just following orders?" The two women exited the building and headed toward a line of waiting heli-cars.

More ideas sparked inside Athena's mind. "What about the Core? Could she, or another AI like her, have somehow cracked the lab's formal encryption?"

Captain Bell's head tilted to one side. Her thick, black eyebrows arched in effortful thought. "I have absolutely *no idea* what that quantum whirling dervish is capable of. But if the Core had stolen the genome, the Laws of AI Neutrality would have forced it to automatically shut down — obviously, that hasn't happened."

A junior officer approached. "Captain Bell, your appointment with Dr. Antares is in one hour. It's time to leave."

Athena looked at the captain. The captain looked back at Athena. "I'm coming with you," Athena said. She raised her head proudly. "I'm going to help you with the case."

"Hmmmm," Valerie grumbled. She tried to look disappointed, but the glint of excitement in her bright blue eyes betrayed her tough exterior. She gazed Athena up and down, taking in all of her body with a single glance. "Alright, chosen one. You're in. But don't you *dare* do anything to embarrass me."

The NAU Times

November 16th, 2094

"Be Our Guest" Episode 467: The Esteemed Dr. Grace Antares

(Partial Transcript)

…

Interviewer: Hello everyone. Welcome back from the break! If you're just joining us, today I'm speaking with famed scientist, inventor, and Founding Mother, Dr. Grace Antares. She's here to discuss her past accomplishments and her future work on Project Lazarus.

Doctor, I just want to thank you again for being here.

Dr. Antares: It's my pleasure, Claire. Thank you again for having me.

Interview: Ok, let's get personal. You've been called a savant, a polymath, and a genius. All modesty aside, do you think you're one of the brightest women alive?

Dr. Antares: (Laughs.) Oh, I have no idea, Claire. But, truthfully, what does it even matter? I'm just one person doing my small part to make the world a better place. No woman is an island. The accomplishments of individuals pale in comparison to the work that is achieved by striving together. I'd rather be called a great collaborator than a lone genius.

Interviewer: I'd say you've earned both titles. (Laughs.) Changing tracks, only last night you received the news that your research facility, Helix, was awarded the coveted opportunity to build the Lazarus Genome. How does it feel?

Dr. Antares: Well, Claire, thank you. Humbling? Yes, humbling. For those of us like myself who were alive pre-fever, we know what a monumental and important task it is to bring back the hopes and dreams of so many forgotten male voices.

Interviewer: Like many of our listeners, I was born post-fever. Can you enlighten us? What were Men like?

Dr. Antares: Well...they were...complicated? Just like us women, men were so many things, all at once. Brave and foolish and strong and scared. Once we've finished our work, you and your listeners will be able to see for yourselves.

Interviewer: I can't wait! (Champagne glasses toast.)

Interviewer: Moving on. The name Lazarus dates back to a story found in the New Testament. The original Lazarus died and was brought back to life. I understand that you are quite religious yourself. Is that true? Does the story of Lazarus carry any extra significance for you?

Dr. Antares: Ha, Claire. No, I'm not very religious. Although, don't tell my mother that. From the first day I was born until the day I moved away for college, she made sure that I never missed a single Sunday of church. I suppose, once upon a time, those bible stories did carry an extra significance for me. But that all ended years ago. As far as Lazarus and his resurrection goes, the parable carries no special meaning for me.

Interviewer: I see. Not even with regard to your brother? I understand that you two were very close growing up. His death during the Fever must have been very hard for you?

Dr. Antares: Well, yes. Absolutely, it was. I think that my brother's death was probably the single, toughest moment of my life. It's been almost five decades since he died, and I still don't go a week without thinking about him. He was the kindest person I've ever known. I only hope that by living my life as I have, I have honored his memory.

Interviewer: I'm sure, doctor, that if your brother could see you now, and all you've done, he would be very proud of the amazing woman you have become.

Dr. Antares: Thank you, Claire. It means a lot to hear you say that.

Interviewer: Would you say that your brother's death, and the pain of overcoming it, were major factors in your decision to create your most successful technology to date: the science of happiness profiling?

Dr. Antares: Yes, well, I suppose in part. Trying to understand what makes us happy has been my life's work. It is, I believe, the only question that really matters in the end: what must we do in order to feel fulfilled? I always knew that we — that womankind — would survive the chaos of the forties and the fifties. We have always survived. We find a way. But I wanted more than that for us. I wanted us to thrive. And to do that — to thrive — that requires something else. That requires a true knowledge of the self.

(Dr. Antares plucks a daylily from the table's centerpiece.)

Take this flower, for instance. If I were to plant this lily on the edge of a mountain, in ten centimeters of dirt, where sunlight is infrequent, this flower would survive. It would not grow very fast, nor grow to be very large, but it would survive. On the other hand, if instead I planted this flower in a lush river bed, with deep, rich soil, and abundant sun, it would grow to many times its current size, and quickly. That is the difference between surviving and thriving. With profiling, I wanted to give every girl and woman on earth the knowledge of exactly where she should plant herself in order to thrive. I wanted all of us to grow to our fullest potential.

Interviewer: That's very inspiring, doctor. I never thought about profiling that way before. Now, if you don't mind — since you are the world's leading expert on the subject of happiness — we have an online question here from listener Lisa S. She's wondering, "Why does my H-pro change so much all the time? Why does it sometimes tell me to go to bed early, and then only an hour later tell me that I need to stay up all night with my friends? Is there something wrong with me?"

Dr. Antares: (Laughs.) Ha. In a word, Lisa, 'no.' There is nothing wrong with you. To understand your H-pro, you have to remember what happiness is in the first place, and why we feel it at all.

Happiness, of course, is the carrot of evolution. Our bodies — or more specifically our DNA — want us to be healthy and, when we're ready for it, to reproduce. So when we act in ways that increase our chances of fulfilling that evolutionary mandate — of being healthy, and of having and raising children who are healthy — then our bodies reward us with the tool that evolution has given them to spur us on. Our bodies reward us with a warm and pleasant emotion that we experience as happiness.

Sometimes, what we need to be happy is obvious and right in front of us. The joy we get almost every day from water, food, and sleep, is commensurate with our bodies' constant need for these life-giving essentials.

Other times, what we need to be happy is not obvious at all. This is because our bodies cannot predict the future any better than we can. They cannot know which trials we are likely to face tomorrow, and as such, they do not know precisely what we should do in order to best prepare ourselves. This uncertainty is why your H-Pro can vary so much from day-to-day, and hour-to-hour. Your body is trying to guess about what future you will need most in order to survive.

Occasionally, your body will decide that what you need most is a good night's sleep — a good re-knitting on that raveled sleeve of care, as Shakespeare used to say. Other times, though, your body may decide suddenly that what you most need instead is to reaffirm your shared bonds of affection with others. Your body needs to be sure that your friends like you, and that they would care for you if some misfortune befell you.

You have to remember, Lisa, that for hundreds of thousands of years, your ancestors had to fight for survival every single day of their lives. If they became sick, or injured, or pregnant — and if they were alone — then it meant certain death. As a result, your body today will make you miserable, will deny you all happiness, if you begin to feel too alone in the world. It needs you to make strong connections with others because it needs you to survive.

The humans that didn't worry constantly about whether they were spending enough time with their friends...those humans all died off long ago.

Interviewer: That's very fascinating, doctor. I read once where you wrote that we, as women, sometimes feel our evolutionary need to connect with others expressed as sexual attraction — to clever people that we normally wouldn't even like!

Dr. Antares: That's right, Claire. Our bodies use all kinds of tricks like that to keep us alive. They make us want all kinds of things that we would not otherwise want. Even if we don't realize it at the time that that's what's going on. Even if the desire feels to us on its surface like something else.

Interviewer: Amazing. Unfortunately, I'm afraid that's all the time we have for today. Thanks again to our guest, the esteemed Dr. Grace Antares. And thank you, as always, to all of our listeners.

Dr. Antares: I had fun, Claire. Thank you for the invite.

Interviewer: Doctor, as soon as you've completed that genome, we'll be sure to have you back on the program. Just between the two of us, how long do you think it will it take you to bring men back? Three months? Six months?

Dr. Antares: I'm afraid I can't say for sure. We have a lot of work to do.

Interviewer: Then I'll let you get to it. For everyone else, make sure to tune in next week. We'll be speaking with "18 E. Mars" co-creator, Melanie Dunn!

18

"Have you ever used a stress-detector app before?" Captain Bell asked Athena as the pair rode in the back of a city-car on their way to Hyde Park, the home of Helix.

"We tried them once in school?"

Valerie sneered and flicked an app onto Athena's display. It began installing immediately. "Whatever," she groaned. "The thing's pretty idiot-proof, anyway. I doubt even *you* can mess it up. Just open the app to track the eye movements, facial micro-expressions, pulse, heart rate, and galvanic skin-response of anyone within your field of vision. Basically, it'll tell you if an interviewee is experiencing the symptoms of physiological stress or discomfort. It's not a hundred percent or anything. It's not a truth serum. But sometimes it can be useful."

Athena nodded as the city-car pulled up to the front entrance at Helix. Whereas Public Safety headquarters had been entirely composed of cold marble and hard glass, the Helix skyscraper was marked by soft edges and abundant vegetation. Spiraling upward from the ground, like a strand of sky-born DNA, the structure twisted dozens of stories into the air. Vines and perennials encircled the outside of the building as it rose. To Athena, walking into the fantastic sight felt like entering into a recreation of the Hanging Gardens of Babylon.

Marching confidently, Captain Bell led the way past the first-floor security desk. Curtly, she flicked PS permissions at anyone who dared to oppose her. "Public Safety," she barked. "Move aside. Dr. Antares is expecting us."

Athena began to wonder if the captain's happiness profile included getting off on making others feel less important.

Several floors up, the pair reached the private office of Dr. Antares. Small and outdated, the office looked like something right out of the National History Museum. It featured a central desk flanked by two bookcases covered with actual books. Antique still-photos decorated the desk, depicting the doctor's various travels to distant lands. On the walls hung a variety of images which pertained to the building. One showed the early stages of construction, and another documented a visit from the President. A third image on the opposite wall displayed the universally-recognized symbol for Helix's intellectual property: a vertical ribbon spiraling into the shape of a single strand of DNA.

Two lev-chairs hovered in front of the desk. Behind it, hovered a third. Not knowing how long they would have to wait, Valerie and Athena seated themselves.

"This place looks like my grandmother's house," commented Athena. With her head, she nodded in the direction of the still-photographs that were busy gathering dust.

"She *is* almost eighty," replied the captain. "I'm sure I'll have worse trash lying around when I'm her age."

After several moments of awkward silence, Athena got up from her chair to examine the photos on the desk. In one, the doctor smiled from inside a hot-air balloon floating above an endless sea of African wildebeests. In another, the doctor snorkeled among a school of vibrantly-colored reef fish. In the last one, she stood beneath a dark sky brought to life by the dancing, emerald hues of northern lights.

While the backgrounds kept changing, Grace's appearance did not. Her fresh tan skin and half-European-half-Asian features appeared ageless. She didn't look like a teenager, exactly — she had the subtle hint of laugh lines around her mouth, and a slight loss of collagen in her lips — but she also didn't look a day over thirty-five. Regenerative science had preserved the flower of her youth.

The only sign of age which Grace did allow to remain was the whitening of her hair. Long strands of it were braided into a lengthy pony tail that reached to the center of her back. Perhaps, too, there was a hint of the passage of time in the twinkle of her turquoise eyes. Athena found herself wondering what all they had seen in their days.

"She's deliberately testing us," complained Valerie. She tapped her finger against the edge of her chair. "She wants us to know that she can make us wait."

"So let her," Athena replied, too deeply engrossed in her snooping to care. Walking over to one of the bookcases, she began examining a line of books placed at eye-level. She observed, all in a row, multiple translations of the Torah, the Bible, and the Quran. Next to them lay the Vedas, the Tripitaka, the Tao Te Ching, the Kojiki, the Avesta, and numerous other sacred texts, including various 'Books of the Dead.'

Honing in on one thick, gray volume in particular, Athena reached out with her first two fingers and rubbed them against the book's course binding. Plucking it from the shelf, she held the unopened book to her nose and smelled the musty odor of its pages. Its hefty weight left a surprising impression in her arms. Spying its title on the front cover, she mouthed the words as she read: *The Iliad.*

"I always loved that one," declared Grace, suddenly appearing in the room. The doctor wore a monogramed, white lab coat, on top of a pink blouse and beige pants. Around her neck hung a small, blue-lapis pendant in the shape of a spiraling ribbon.

Startled, Athena nervously replaced the book on its shelf and moved to make a formal greeting. The captain cut her off.

"Good morning, Dr. Antares. I'm Captain Valerie Bell of Public Safety. We're investigating the theft of your Lazarus Genome, and we'd like to ask you some questions."

"Yes, of course," Grace responded warmly. "Thank you so much for coming. I'm comforted knowing that this case is a top priority for the fine officers at Public Safety. And what about you?" she added, turning in the direction of Athena, "I didn't catch your name?"

"Um," mumbled Athena. Her face grew flush. "I'm Athena. Athena Vosh. We spent a whole section learning about you in school. You're amazing."

Grace smiled and surrounded Athena's extended hand with both of her own. "That's nice to hear, dear. But I hope those textbooks on me saved some room." She batted her turquoise eyes. "After all, I'm not finished yet."

The doctor made her way around the desk and guided Athena toward the empty chair beside Captain Bell. "Please, have a seat," she ordered warmly before sitting herself. "Can I offer either of you anything? Some sweet cakes, perhaps?"

Athena's stress-app did not detect even the slightest bit of anxiousness in the demeanor of the famous doctor. She appeared calm and completely in control, like a Frida Kahlo self-portrait.

"Perhaps another time," answered the captain, curtly. "We just need to get some details straight. Also, I am required to inform you that we'll be streaming this conversation back to the PSHQ. If at any time you need to say something off the record, please let us know in advance."

Grace chuckled. "I'm sure that won't be necessary."

At the door, an intern appeared. "Dr. Antares?"

"Yes," replied the doctor with a wave of her hand. "Could you please bring us three sweet cakes? Thank you." Grace turned to Captain Bell. "You can be all business if you wish, madam, but I have been working since 7AM, and I make it a point to never pass up on a perfectly good opportunity to indulge in a treat."

The doctor smiled in Athena's direction, partially covering her mouth with her hand. "Don't worry," she teased, "if Captain Grumpy doesn't want her cake, that will mean more for us." She flashed a disarming, grandmotherly smile at Athena who blushed in reciprocation.

"At what time," interrupted Valerie, growing impatient, "did you first notice that the Lazarus Genome had been stolen?"

"Now honestly, officer," Grace pshawed. "I know that you did not come all the way down here just to ask me that."

"Ma'am, please?" the captain pressed. "At what time, did you first notice the genome had been stolen?"

"I don't know. Do you need an exact time? I'd guess it was, oh, about eight o'clock on Sunday night?" Grace shrugged her shoulders. "If you need a more exact time, I can go through my recordings. But — Captain Bell, was it? — You and I both know you already have this information on file. Let's talk about why you're really here."

The intern returned with a delicate metal tray containing three of the most delicious-looking cakes Athena had ever seen. They were vanilla swirl at the base, crumbled muffin on top, and drizzled in a fruity glaze. Immediately, Grace grabbed one. Athena hesitated at first, but after some more urging, joined in herself. She was not disappointed. The cake tasted as moist as a milkshake. Its molecules tickled every sugar receptor on her tongue.

Defiantly, Captain Bell refused the invitation to partake.

"Mmmm," gasped Athena. "This topping is delicious. What flavor is it?"

"It's an apple compote," replied Grace with a devilish smile, "just like the fruit from the tree of knowledge." She licked the last remnants of glaze from her finger-tips, and closed her eyes to savor the flavor. "Now, where were we?...oh yes. You are here because you want to know who I think stole the genome. Or at least who among us at Helix could have helped to steal it. Our encryption software is formally verified, so one of us scientists must have aided in the theft. Isn't that right, officer?"

Captain Bell appreciated getting to the chase, even if she preferred to lead. "And?" the captain replied. "Which one of your employees was complicit in this crime? Who here has been nosing around where she does not belong? Who has a reason to hurt you or to derail the project?"

"Officer, please. The 400 women who work in this lab are some of the brightest, most virtuous women found anywhere on earth. I hand-picked each and every one of them to work for me. I simply cannot imagine that one of them would seek to undermine our efforts."

Captain Bell flashed her patented eye-roll. "Whether you can imagine it or not, doctor, you have been betrayed. Or maybe you're right...?" She teased along the accusation by cocking her head to one side. "Maybe no one here would dream of betraying you. Maybe they were only following orders when they stole the genome. Orders which came from someone like...you?" For an extra second, her lips held open the insinuating expression of her final syllable.

Privately, Athena wondered if Captain Bell really did think that Grace had something to do with the theft. Or was this just interviewing gamesmanship? Paying close attention to the app on her display, Athena noted that despite the aggressive line of questioning, the doctor exhibited none of the signs of physiological discomfort. She appeared as calm and relaxed as a Buddhist monk.

"Captain Bell," Grace replied, "you have your job, and I have mine. I do not solve crimes. I create possibilities. If you and your team are having trouble figuring out how our encryption software was hacked, then perhaps you should consult with Public Safety and ask that they replace you with someone who can?"

The doctor pushed her lev-chair away from the desk. She tapped her fingers together in front of her face. "The Lazarus Project has long been controversial. We have always had opponents. Perhaps it's possible that, over the years, a new technology has emerged which has rendered our encryption obsolete. Frankly, officer, you should be posing these questions to someone like Mirza Khan, not trying to get me off-balance with your heavy-handed innuendo."

That name sounded unfamiliar to Athena, but a mini-biography automatically appeared on her display.

Mirza Khan
b. May 28th, 2038 in Damascus
Immigrated to the NAU in 2060.
Named chairwoman of Women First in 2090.
Staunch public opponent of Project Lazarus.

Calmly, Captain Bell issued her reply. "A crime has been committed, doctor, and everyone is a suspect. Including you. My job — and Public Safety has been *very* happy with my performance to date — is to investigate any and all possibilities. Ms. Khan will get her turn to defend herself. This is yours."

"Defend myself?" Grace laughed. "We are on the same side, officer."

The doctor split the third, remaining sweet cake in two and handed half to Athena. "You've asked me if I think we have a traitor in our midst. I don't know. Maybe we do, but I am not aware of her. Eve handles most of the administrative duties around here. Let's set up a time for you to speak with her." She took a large bite of her cake and licked her lips.

Another mini-biography automatically appeared on Athena's display.

Dr. Evelyn Kirilov
b. December 20th, 2023 in Moscow
Immigrated to the NAU in 2043.
Graduated with an M.D. from Northwestern in 2049.
Co-Founded Helix in 2056. Currently the Helix COO.

An awkwardness descended as all three ladies waited for someone else to speak. Grace ended up being the one to break the silence. "I believe Eve is out today," she explained, "but I'll make sure she clears her schedule for tomorrow. What time would be better for you? Morning? Or Afternoon? I know Dr. Kirilov is as eager as I am to see that genome safely recovered."

"We're booked tomorrow morning," replied Valerie. "If Dr. Kirilov can be available in the afternoon, that would be preferred. Say, one o'clock?"

"Excellent," Grace cheered. "Consider it done."

Separate from the outside chatter, Athena observed the doctor closely, almost enviously. She imagined herself being the one with long white hair and a string of worthy accomplishments to her name. She fantasized about looking into a mirror and seeing Grace's face staring back at her.

In that mental image, she smiled at her imagined reflection, growing fond of her weathered features and soft wrinkles. Then, suddenly, the reflected-image transformed itself. A thick beard sprouted out of her face and neck. Her nose expanded, and her brow thickened. Buffalo hides appeared all over her body. Staring back at her from the mirror, with a gaze as pitiless as the sun, was a man.

"Athena. The truth is in the library," he warned in his deep voice. "You must find the truth to save her."

Athena shrieked.

"Are you alright, Ms. Vosh?" Grace asked, her face genuinely concerned. She stood up from her chair and rushed over to touch Athena by the shoulder. The physical presence of her hand shook the gray-eyed girl back into reality.

"Yes," replied Athena, gasping. "Sorry. I'm fine. It was nothing," she lied. "I was just watching a recording on my display. Please, let's continue."

Captain Bell flashed an annoyed sideways glance, but otherwise maintained her focus on Dr. Antares. "Was it viable?" she pressed.

"Pardon?"

"The Lazarus Genome? Could whoever stole it use it to make a man?"

Grace paused uncomfortably and eased back into her chair. "No," she answered. "Unfortunately, it is a matter of public record that we haven't quite gotten that far yet."

A smug expression came over Captain Bell's pale face. Dismissively, she crossed her legs and leaned back. "So, let me get this straight, doctor. You're telling me that for four years, this Project Lazarus of yours has been unable to produce anything viable. And now, even your failed attempts are being mysteriously stolen? Is that an accurate description of what's happened here?"

The stress app may not have been able to detect any signs of discomfort, but Grace's face was starting to lose its kind, grandmotherly glow. It frowned sincerely in a way that it had not before. It stared directly back at its interrogator. "Ms. Bell, do not patronize me. The Y-Fever was perniciously engineered to kill in twenty-six different ways. Addressing every method of its infection has proved more challenging than anyone suspected."

"I'm sure it's quite difficult," interrupted Athena in earnest, "and that you're doing everything you can."

"Thank you, Ms. Vosh," Grace sighed, "but it's true that we have failed to meet expectations." Wistfully, the doctor stared into the air. "Perhaps, if we'd taken a different path at the beginning, there might have been a better way to engineer a cure, but…" She trailed off.

In the ensuing silence, while still recovering from her obtrusive vision, Athena's gaze again found the bookcase of religious texts. She recalled the deeper details of her dream and remembered the title printed upon the library's burning book: *Original Sin is Real.*

"Dr. Antares?" she asked. "I noticed your library over there…" She nodded toward the stacks of literature. "That seems like a bit of an odd collection for a woman in your position, don't you think? Haven't science and religion always been at odds?"

Grace laughed. "My dear, just because evolution is real, and just because the earth is more than 5,000 years old, does not mean that we shouldn't treat one another as we would like to be treated." The doctor wet her lips. "Nobody gets everything right. Especially not us scientists. What matters is getting the really important things right. For instance, do you know what all those religions have in common?"

Athena shook her head.

"Compassion," declared Grace firmly. "At their heart, each of those faiths is about trying to instill compassion. They're all trying to teach that it is better to trust and forgive one another — to be kind —

than to carry on with bitter plans of revenge. And kindness, I think, is an idea that even us scientists can get behind. Don't you?"

For a moment, Athena paused, readying her next question. "What about original sin?" she asked. "The idea that people, even young children, are not born innocent, but rather are born flawed, corrupted at birth by original sin? Do you have anything to say about that? Where is the kindness and compassion in that?"

The lower half of Grace's jaw turned to the side, as she slowly rocked her head. Her eyes focused for a moment on Athena in a way that they had not before, almost suspiciously. However, only a moment later, the look was gone, and her warm smile had returned. She cleared her throat. "Yes, well, my dear. Perhaps, both science and religion still have some ways to go in their search for truth—"

"Riiiiight," interrupted Captain Bell, "as much as I would just *love* to get into a deep theological discussion right now...we have a genome to find." She turned toward Athena. "I think this interview has run its course. It's time to go."

Captain Bell rose from her chair and motioned for her protégé to do the same. Instinctively, Athena complied. They began to head for the door, but stopped just before it.

"Oh, and uh, doctor," the captain remarked, "I almost forgot, there's just one more thing...I noticed from your lab's food logs that you and your top lieutenants all had a tomato and mozzarella *insalata caprese* for lunch on the day of the theft. How did it taste?"

It wasn't much, only a few accelerated heartbeats; but it was enough to make Athena's display light up.

Dr. Antares' is experiencing the symptoms of physiological stress

"I...uh...surely I don't recall..." Grace stammered. "I think it was... uh...good? Yes, quite good."

"Excellent," Valerie grinned, trying to stifle her rush of joy. "I'm so glad to hear that."

For a moment, Captain Bell and Dr. Antares each stared silently at one another. Their eyes danced a game of cat and mouse.

Grace's heart slowed itself back down. "I could send over the recipe for that salad if you'd like?"

"Please, would you?" the captain smiled.

"Of course. I'll have one of my interns send it your way immediately." Dr. Antares turned in Athena's direction. "And you Ms. Vosh…It was so nice to meet you."

"It was an honor to meet *you*," gushed Athena.

"Yes, yes, a pleasure all around," declared the captain. "We can show ourselves out."

On their way down to the first floor, Athena received a notification for an incoming, encrypted message. The sender showed as Captain Bell. The message read:

If that woman had nothing to do with the theft of her own genome, then I am the Queen of England.

WHO Confirms an End to Global Poverty/World Hunger

Geneva, EU — (AP) — Earlier today, census data confirmed that both global poverty and world hunger have been officially eliminated from Planet Earth. The feat has been largely attributed to a combination of generous Citizen's Benefits (monthly stipends paid to all the residents of the world's eleven countries) and the increased productivity brought about by technological automation.

World Health Organization Chief, Sylvia Cho, announced the findings in a large press conference held this morning at the Jet d'Eau. The following is a brief excerpt of her remarks:

> "This struggle has been a long road. During the chaos and tumult of the fifties, I don't think that anyone would have dared to hope that this day of peace and prosperity might come. Let our success here serve for the rest of time as a shining beacon of what womankind can achieve when everyone comes together to solve a problem as one."

Large celebratory banquets have been planned around the globe in honor of the historic achievement. Swipe right to find the banquet closest to you.

The Affiliated Press of the European Union contributed to this story.

Social Calendar for the Algonquin Forest Zone

June 7: Moose Ride, 15:00

June 8: Adventure Hike, 12:00

June 9: Lakeside BBQ, 19:00

June 10: Bird-Watching, 12:00

June 11: Pottery Class, 15:00

June 12: Dance Competition, 19:00

June 13: Water-Skiing, 12:00

19

Back at the cabin, Nomi splayed out across the living-room couch. Her eyes followed the shadow of Athena's GPS dot as it traveled through a holographic three-dimensional projection of the Helix skyscraper. Her stomach churned.

"Good afternoon, Nomi," Aasha interrupted. "Would you like me to print a new outfit for you for tonight? For the neighborhood barbecue?"

"No thanks," sighed Nomi. "I don't think I'll be going out tonight. I just want to have a quiet dinner at home."

"Of course."

Tapping her finger into the air, Nomi clicked on the folder that held the entirety of her past recordings. With a swipe of her hand, she spun through an enormous catalog of watchable memories. When she had found the one she wanted, she raised up her hand to signal 'stop.' With a flick of her wrist, the chosen recording began playing on the nearby 3D.

FADE IN:

EXT. LAKESIDE BBQ - NIGHT

In the woods of northern Algonquin, a group of forty gather to celebrate good food and good weather.

                                                    ZOOM IN ON:

EXT. A SINGLE PICNIC TABLE

Half-finished plates cover a red and white cross-hatched table cloth. Alone at the table, the impossibly clean and beautiful ATHENA VOSH sits next to the impossibly messy NOMI JAMES, her face covered in BBQ grease.

NOMI
Hey, babe. Can you pass me that KC special sauce over there?

ATHENA
Why? What are you going to do with it?

NOMI
I'm going to use it to responsibly season my food, of course.

ATHENA
Oh, yeah? Is that so? I thought you were just going to cut out the middle woman and smear it all over your face?

Nomi leans across Athena, slowly, sexily. She grabs the sauce that was just out of reach and eases back into her chair.

NOMI

See, now that wasn't so hard, was it?

ATHENA

Careful. If you press up against me like that again I'm going to tell Ms. Fletcher that I don't feel comfortable here.

Nomi turns her head to —

THE FIRE PIT

MS. FLETCHER, dressed like a Catholic school teacher and carrying a scowl to match, talks with a group of other guests. Nomi turns her head back to Athena.

NOMI

Now, babe, surely we don't need to involve her. That woman is too scary. Isn't there something I can do here to make you feel more comfortable?

ATHENA

Nnnn Mmmm. I don't think so. I'm getting quite nervous.

NOMI

Not even this?

Nomi takes the bottle of KC special sauce and squeezes it onto Athena's face, giving her a twisting mustache.

NOMI

Now look at you. You're a real artist. You're Dali!

Athena grabs the bottle. Calmly, she un-screws the top and empties its entire thick, red contents onto Nomi's head.

ATHENA
Close, but wrong. I'm Picasso. And this is my smoky yet spicy period.

NOMI
Mmmmm. Great art never tasted so good. Come here and let me show you.

Nomi leans in to kiss Athena, smearing her with sauce from her own face. Athena pulls away and turns her head to the left. Nomi sees her looking to the side, and looks herself. Together they both see —

THE DESSERT TABLE

Pies, cakes, and treats of every kind adorn a pristine picnic table.

Slipping out of Nomi's grasp, Athena races to the dessert table. Nomi is right on her heels. They both reach the table and grab a cream pie that quickly ends up in the other's face and hair. Giggling uncontrollably, they slide to the ground together just as Ms. Fletcher appears.

MS. FLETCHER
Girls!! What is the meaning of this! Have you completely forgotten how to behave!

ATHENA
Forgotten? I'm pretty sure there was never a time when Nomi knew how to behave.

NOMI
So true.

MS. FLETCHER
Ms Vosh, what would your mother think if she saw you like this? Covered in food like a wild animal?

NOMI
Don't worry, A. Let me handle this. Ms. Fletcher, we are so sorry.

Nomi climbs to her feet and grabs an untouched cream pie. She brings it to eye level, and slowly smears it into Ms. Fletcher's face.

NOMI
There, A. I fixed that for you.

Nomi falls over into Athena's arms as they both topple to the ground, laughing uncontrollably.

MS. FLETCHER
Girls, I never!!!

CUT TO BLACK

20

On the trip back to Public Safety Headquarters, Captain Bell worked busily on her display, air-clicking and swiping into space. Athena tried meekly to get her attention. "Captain Bell?" she moused. The captain gave no response. Athena tried again. "Captain Bell!"

The captain flashed a dismissive sideways-glance that did not require moving her head. "What is it? What do you want?"

"I think I know why the Core told you to find me."

Immediately, the captain's right hand dropped from the air into her lap. Her fierce blue eyes expanded to twice their previous size. She turned her entire body to face Athena. "Do you now? Go on," she commanded.

"I think the Core chose me because of my dreams. Somewhere out there, there's a truth in a library that only I can find."

For the next several minutes, Athena described in vivid detail everything she had seen and experienced in her series of subconscious visions — from the crumbling building, to the poetic buffalo, to the burning book filled with demons and sin.

As she spoke, the captain's gaze never wavered from its focus on her. "Hmmm," Valerie replied at the end of the tale. "When we get back to the PSHQ, I want you to meet with someone. Michelle Evans. She's one of our top signature-matching specialists."

The captain then returned to her work, not speaking again for the rest of the trip.

Signature Matching

From Wikipedia, the free encyclopedia

"Digital Signature Matching," "Digital Patterns," and "Sigs" all redirect to here

▲ Overview:

A Signature, or sig, is the set of all qualities displayed in any creative work. It can refer to a painter's use of particular colors and themes, to a geneticist's use of particular nucleotide chains and genetic markers, to a programmer's use of particular command-loops and syntax. The term's modern definition was first coined in 2082.

Primarily, signatures are used for a data-intensive procedure known as signature-matching, whereby two or more disparate works are compared for similarity. Through the use of machine-learned pattern-recognition, and other sophisticated analyses, artificial intelligences can calculate all the commonalities between two similar works, and assign them a "signature-match-percentage" from 0 to 100.

▼ Calculation Metrics
▼ Match Percentages and the Legal Definition of Plagiarism
▲ Further Reading:

For more information on sigs, including technical specifications for measuring sig-matches, see *The Signature of Art* by former AI, The Second Core.

▼ Famous Examples
▼ Other Comparative Techniques
▼ Submit Your Work for Sig-Matching
▼ Recent Recordings

Last modified by Ferre11sq on 01 June 2099

21

On the fortieth floor of the PSHQ, Athena followed Captain Bell through a corridor of crowded cubicles. Surrounding the cubicles on every side, panes of glass shone brightly in colors both solid and opaque. Athena tried to figure out the meaning behind the color-coding but couldn't decipher any pattern. At the end of the maze, she received an official introduction.

"Ms. Vosh," announced the captain, "this is PS Officer Michelle Evans. Michelle is one of our best sig-matchers. If your dream has any connection to this crime, she'll find it."

Officer Evans leapt up from her lev-chair and enthusiastically greeted Athena. Her genuine smile exuded real warmth. Her voluminous blonde hair bounced as she moved. Privately, Athena took note of the woman's voluptuous frame. Officer Evans' chosen body-fat appeared to be north of twenty-five percent. Athena wondered if perhaps Ms. Evans was a fan of Peter Paul Rubens.

"Michelle," continued the captain, "Ms. Vosh is helping us to recover the Lazarus Genome. More to the point, she's been having some unusual dreams. I want you to run the images she's been seeing for sig-matches. Let me know if anything interesting comes up. Athena, tell Officer Evans everything you've told me." Valerie tapped both women on their shoulders. "Now if you'll excuse me, I have other matters to attend to."

Michelle cheered gleefully once Captain Bell had traveled out of ear-shot. "Oh, this will be much more fun than what I was supposed to do today." Her wide grin proudly displayed her prominent two front teeth.

Grabbing at thin air with her hand, Officer Evans summoned a lev-chair from across the room. It glided over, stopping in front of her work station. Athena seated herself before a desk covered with vertical panels of electric-glass, roughly positioned in the shape of a large rectangle. Within the rectangle, the panels' interior edges shot out at competing angles for artistic effect.

"Ready when you are," said Michelle.

Once again, Athena recounted the first of her peculiar pair of dreams. As she spoke, her words created images on the screens in front of her. Acting as a sketch-artist, the Public Safety computer transformed everything she said into a picture, and then, with further guidance from Officer Evans, into a series of moving pictures complete with sound and dialogue. It took about an hour's worth of work, mostly in corrective detailing, but eventually, Athena's entire dream came to exist on the screen in the form of a movie that could be watched by anyone.

"Looks good," said Michelle once the detailing was complete. "Love that fire at the end when you touch the book. Anything more to add?"

Athena shook her head.

"Cool. Let's run it."

With an air-click, Officer Evans released the power of the Public Safety signature-matching engine. Almost immediately, direct matches appeared on the screen. The buffalo's stoic expression, for instance, was shown by combinatorial analysis to have been stolen from the face of one of Athena's former classmates. The pattern of the burning flames originated in a movie she had seen the previous summer. The picture of the endless meadow traced back to a memory of a place Athena had visited as a child. Every image from the dream, it seemed, had some antecedent that could be found in her own life.

"These all have to do with me," remarked Athena. "Shouldn't your computer be looking for sig-matches beyond me?"

"Nah," replied Michelle. "Don't need to worry about that. No one ever creates anything new. It's always just bits and pieces stolen from somewhere. Since you are the dreamer, the computer is saving time by only referencing the dream's imagery against your own memories."

After a couple of minutes, the computer had found the original source for every image contained within Athena's dream, save one. The crumbling, six-columned library appeared to have no connection at all to anything in Athena's life.

"That's weird," mused Michelle, as she pondered on the mystery displayed in front of her.

"My home computer couldn't find anything like it either," offered Athena.

Michelle bit her bottom lip in frustration. "Yes, but your home computer can't do what ours can. Let's focus on this library of yours and open things up."

With a series of air-clicks, Michelle widened the search-field to include every building on file, not just those connected to Athena. Seconds later, the PS computer came back with its analysis: there existed no structures particularly like it anywhere on earth.

"Whoa," said Michelle, wide-eyed. She arched in her chair, literally taken aback by the incredible result.

"Uhhhhh, wow," she repeated. It took a minute for her to regain herself. Her face looked as though she had just seen a ghost. "How can there not be any matches for this? I wonder if…" She tapped her index finger softly against her chin as she thought. "Maybe if…" her voice trailed off into an incoherent mumble.

In the background droned a continuous hum of Public Safety officers at work, placing calls and shuffling about.

Michelle again leaned forward in her chair with renewed vigor. She altered the parameters and reinitiated her search. However, the results came back the same. According to the Public Safety computer, Athena's library had simply appeared out of thin air. There were no records of anything precisely like it having ever been built. No blueprints planning its construction. No publications heralding its completion. There was nothing. Officer Evans ran the test a couple more times. Same result.

"I'm going to need to ask my supervisor about this," she sighed after a long pause. "There must be something wrong with our archives. We have trillions of records going back centuries, and everything is meticulously catalogued. There's no chance that most of your library didn't come from something that was built in the real world. No chance."

Frustratedly, Michelle pushed herself away from her desk. "Athena," she ordered, "go take a break and check out the room they assigned to you next door. The captain set you up in PS housing until the genome is recovered." Michelle pointed her finger in the direction of a young brunette officer, standing at the other end of the office. On Athena's display, the young woman was highlighted in lime green. "It's Officer Miller's job to escort you to your room. I'll message you as soon as we get to the bottom of this." Briskly, Michelle departed.

Left behind, Athena waited in the seat she had been given, refusing to move. She attempted to access the computer in front of her but found it locked. For thirty minutes, she stubbornly stayed put, hoping Michelle would quickly return, or that some other PS officer would come by with an answer for her, but no one ever did. Eventually, she gave up and paced over to her designated guide.

"Ready to go?" asked Officer Miller.

Athena nodded.

"Please follow me."

Twisting again through corridors and cubicles, the two women made their way into a featureless, all-glass elevator. The elevator carried the pair down to the second floor of the PSHQ, then horizontally across the street, and then back up to the seventy-fourth floor of the neighboring skyscraper.

"Welcome to Public Safety guest apartments," said the elevator.

Five Deadliest Terror Attacks in Global History

From Wikipedia, the free encyclopedia

This article ranks historical attacks by their immediate lethality.
To see the rankings for secondary deaths, see Deadliest Terror Attacks (long-term effects).

▼ **1. The First Thermonuclear Launch; 2049; Novosibirsk, Russia;**

Carried out by Russian Dissidents

▼ **2. The Christmas Warhead Detonation; 2050; Greeley, Colorado,**

USA; Carried out by White Nationalists

▼ **3. The Eid Bombing; 2041; Jammu and Kashmir; Carried out by**

Religious Zealots

▼ **4. The Second Thermonuclear Launch; 2050; Samara, Russia;**

Carried out by Russian Dissidents

▼ **5. The Congo Massacre; 2038; Kinshasa, Democratic Republic of the**

Congo; Carried out by Freedom Fighters

Last modified by RockRhoda on 2 April 2093

22

"Your guest room comes with a standard Aasha unit..." announced Officer Miller, as she and Athena arrived at the door to Public Safety guest apartment 7418. Inside the apartment, Athena observed a completely-empty, conically-shaped space formed by two walls diverging out from the entrance. On the far end of the room, the walls came together via a curving, floor-to-ceiling window.

"Or, if you prefer, you can import your own Aasha unit from home."

The newly-constructed apartment spanned barely fifty square meters. What it lacked in size, however, it more than made up for in modernity.

"Everything is made out of programmable plastic," declared Athena's host, "so just tell the home computer what room configuration you want, and she'll reprogram all the furniture for you."

Officer Miller swiped her finger into the air. In response, an empress-sized bed grew from out of the floor. She swiped again and the bed melted into a dining table surrounded by eight stools.

"The room has, like, twenty settings, but mostly people only ever use the living room, kitchen, and bedroom," explained Officer Miller. Onto Athena's display, she flicked a set of layout specs. "Here's the guide of what each room looks like." She walked in a quick circle around the room. "Um...common areas are on floors ten and fifty, if you get lonely."

"Got it," replied Athena.

"Alright, then. If that's all..." Officer Miller turned and began to leave.

Athena stopped her with a question. "Do you know when I might hear back from Captain Bell or Officer Evans? About the Lazarus case?"

"Yeah, I don't know anything about that," the brunette PS officer moaned. She continued to leave. "It's not like they would tell me." The front door whooshed close.

From the height of the seventy-fourth floor, Athena's apartment possessed quite a view of the city below. She rose on her tip-toes to peer out of her north-easterly facing window, catching glimpses of downtown Chicago and, between other buildings, long blue slivers of Lake Michigan. Restless, she considered going for a walk outside, but paced instead inside the room. She checked her messages, and then paced some more. She felt like a runner waiting for a starting gun that wouldn't fire.

Hours passed. Athena called her mom. They shared displays and made plans to meet the following night. More time passed.

For dinner, Aasha prepared an entree of baked potato flakes, and lab-grown beef medallions topped with arugula, and drizzled with maple syrup. While she ate, she watched a 3D documentary from the seventies about Grace Antares and happiness profiling titled, *The Doctor Who Knows You Better Than You Know Yourself.*

Outside her window, the city descended into night.

Massage Implants

From Wikipedia, the free encyclopedia

"Massage Implants," "Massagers," "Implants," and "Buzzers" all redirect to here

▲ Overview:

The term "massage implants," also known as "massagers," or more colloquially 'buzzers,' refers to the series of tiny heating, cooling, and vibrating nodes that get implanted into the subcutaneous tissue and musculature of a woman in search of pleasurable relaxation. They tend to number from a few dozen to a few hundred.

Typically, massagers are first implanted along a subject's neck, back, hands, and feet. However, it is not uncommon for them to exist throughout the entire body.

Because of their popularity, massage implants have become a trillion-dollar business, and have fueled an entire cottage industry of massage programmers, or "choreographers," who create and sell enjoyable sequences of massager activation.

▲ Further Reading:

For more information on massage implants, including an in-depth history of the 2080's battle for corporate market-share, see the book, *Buzzer Business,* by *Feel Good* CEO Pricilla Romanoff.

▼ Best-Selling Massagers
▼ Top-Reviewed Choreographers
▼ Implant Clinics in your area
▼ Recent Recordings

Last modified by JustTree4Me on 03 Nov 2098

23

With the sun's disappearance, Athena abandoned her hope that Public Safety might soon contact her. She settled into her room with a glass of red wine then ordered out for some paints and a brush. Compelled by a sudden, strange desire, she worked hard to create a new image on the blank canvas of her apartment's southern wall: a massive, Hieronymus-Bosch-like, three-paneled triptych.

In the leftmost panel of her painting, she created, hand-in-hand, a nude man and woman. They stood under a snake-filled apple tree, surrounded by blue skies and green grass. In the middle panel, she painted, on brown and dying grass, a series of excessively lustful scenes featuring crowds of carefree persons smiling as they engaged in various acts of sexual conjugation. In the rightmost panel, she painted a fiery, charred world filled with disfigured demons. War, pestilence, hunger, and death could be seen working together to wreak havoc upon the poor, sinful souls unfortunate enough to be trapped forever in an endless hell.

"What am I doing?" Athena asked out loud to the empty room as her painting neared completion. The triptych in front of her — much like her recreation of the crumbling library from the previous day — looked so unlike anything she had ever produced before. Just two days ago, her brush had only ever brought hopeful and inspiring images into the world. Now it was as though she could no longer control the chaos leaking from her soul.

A message appeared on her display.

Nomi has requested access to your massage implants
— *Granted*

As she toggled her apartment into its night-mode — bed formed, lights off — Athena felt the initial warming hum of vibrations coursing throughout her body. Neither she nor Nomi spoke as Nomi, hundreds of kilometers away, activated in sequence the countless massaging nodules implanted within Athena's lithe frame. From the unusual patterns of warming and cooling pulses, Athena suspected that this was not one of Nomi's pre-choreographed massages — but there was no way to know for sure.

The tiny implants worked their magic on Athena's feet, legs, lower back, and shoulders. Depending upon the feedback they received, Nomi activated or deactivated specific nodes to elicit a more enjoyable response. Special attention was given to Athena's neck before returning to her stomach and thighs. To Athena, it slowly became clear where this massage was heading, but she made no attempt to stop it.

The buzzers geared up and down, teasing in every way. Athena parted her legs, hoping for an acceleration in purpose, but Nomi denied her the quick satisfaction. Rhythmic vibrations traced shapes around, but never directly on top of, Athena's tingling center.

Gradually, pulsing echoes built up on her left side, right side, outside, and inside. Like a piece of music that required the entire orchestra, Nomi's massage conducted all of the instruments to contribute on cue to a symphonic crescendo. When it finally came, Athena saw stars and gave thanks for her apartment's sound-proofing. In the seven minutes that followed, her muscles continued to quiver and convulse at irregular intervals. Pleasurable waves crested repeatedly throughout her body.

Afterward, she fell into a deep sleep.

That I Cried to Dream Again

Bypassing the meadow altogether, Athena immediately found herself standing in front of the now-familiar library, surrounded by mountains. The difference this time, though, was that the building didn't appear worn or dilapidated at all. No chunks of roof were missing. No vines grew from cracked orifices. The structure looked freshly-built and brand-new. In front of the library lay well-manicured lawns. On the lawns stood dozens of grazing buffalo clad in pants, skirts, and backpacks.

As Athena approached the building, two shining doors swung open to welcome her inside. She entered. To her right, at a nearby table constructed from brightly-colored pinewood, sat an enormous buffalo with a broken horn. He wore a blue sports coat, beige pants, and had spectacles balanced delicately atop his massive nose. In one hoof, he held a small cup of coffee. In his other, there rested a glowing manuscript adorned by the words *Original Sin is Real*. The small image of a spiraling ribbon appeared just below the title.

Athena closed in on the buffalo and took a seat at his table. "What are you reading?" she asked.

"Shhhhh," he hushed. "I'm trying to study."

The woolly creature continued to read in between sips of coffee. When his cup ran empty, he placed the manuscript face down on the table and got up for a refill. Athena saw her chance.

She rushed around the table and lifted the heavy book up to her face. Large black letters on white paper greeted her. They said:

And what rough beast, its hour come round at last,
Slouches toward Chicago to be born?

The buffalo raced back. Angrily, he snatched the manuscript from Athena's grasp. "If you are not prepared to learn the answer," he cried, "then you should not ask the question."

His front hoof drew back as if to strike. "The truth in the library can save her, but it can also destroy the world." Violently, he swiped his hoof at Athena's face.

Ducking just in time to avoid the hit, Athena turned and ran as fast as she could. She sprinted through the doors and past the six square columns. Once she had reached a safe distance outside, she stopped to look around, but when she did, she noticed that all the freshness and life were gone. The sky had grown dark. The clothed and grazing buffalo had disappeared. The lawns had become overgrown and unkempt.

Behind her, the library had changed too. No longer clean and new, it had resumed its slow decay into an ancient, aging ruin.

24

Incoming Call from Captain Bell

Still half asleep, Athena's brain struggled with the confusing and upsetting noise of constant ringing. In her unconsciousness, she mumbled phrases of whispered nonsense. "No thank you, Ms. Pillow. No thank you."

Incoming Call from Captain Bell

Athena's eyes opened to complete darkness. She activated her display and looked to the clock. It read 4:30AM. Slowly, her mind recalled where she was and how she had got there. The call notification rang again. With a two-fingered air-click, she answered. "What?" she replied gruffly. "What's going on?"

"Get in here, Vosh." Captain Bell sounded almost chipper on the other end. "And don't dawdle. Michelle's found something you need to see."

Athena leapt to her feet. She sped through her morning routine. In minutes, she had made her way back to Officer Evans' fortieth floor workstation. When she arrived, she found a crowd of eight PS officers gathered there. Some stood very close to the desk, swiping into the air. Others stood a bit farther back, merely observing the action. The rest of the office floor appeared completely abandoned, the cubicles dark and empty. Overhead, the interior lighting shone with a tinge of ultramarine.

Athena's eyes found Captain Bell — fully dressed in her uniform, despite the early hour — near the rear of the crowd. "Did she find it? The library?" Athena asked, almost stumbling over her words in her excitement to get them out as quickly as possible. "Did Michelle find the library from my dream? Where is it?"

"No," sighed Captain Bell, stifling a grin between her pale cheeks. "But…"

"But what!" The anticipation was too much. "What is it?"

Maliciously, Captain Bell drew out the suspense. She smiled at the sight of watching Athena squirm. "…but you were right," she finally declared. "There is a connection between your library and the genome's disappearance. It seems you are somehow a part of all this after all."

The captain shook her long black hair, casting it against her shoulders. "Within the Helix mainframe," she explained, "the program that stole the Lazarus Genome left behind some electronic fingerprints, some small traces of its work. Nothing major, just a few lines of code out of place. Standard protocol is to run these criminal fingerprints against all the other electronic crimes on file."

Athena nodded raptly.

"So Officer Evans followed protocol, but she found no other crimes with the same fingerprints. So dead end, right? But…"

"But? But what!"

"But here's where it gets interesting."

Never in her entire life had Athena listened more intently.

"Because your library seemed to appear from nowhere, Officer Evans ran the criminal fingerprints against all of our Public Safety digital archives as well. She theorized that maybe we had been hacked too, only we never knew it." Valerie paused. "You still with me?"

Athena nodded up and down vigorously enough to give herself whiplash.

"Sure enough, Officer Evans found a small trace of the same electronic crime on our own network. In other words, whoever stole the Lazarus Genome, also hacked into our Public Safety archives and stole something from us, too. Unfortunately, we have no way of knowing what was taken, but it disappeared from the folder containing historical records for the 2050's and before — pre-fever, that is, so possibly a time when your library would still have been intact."

"What about the other networks?" Athena asked, without stopping to breathe. "Did you check the national archives for the missing files? Did you look everywhere?"

Valerie's blue eyes twinkled. "Yes. We followed protocol, and exhaustively searched every online resource available to us. They've all been hacked with the same program — decades ago in many cases. All of us have had something taken from our historical archives. Something that whoever stole the Lazarus Genome doesn't want us to find. This theft is a crime that goes back decades."

Outside, the dawn's light had just begun to appear. The sky had turned from dark black to dark blue. Athena couldn't understand how the rest of the city could still be sleeping at a time like this. "The book I keep dreaming about," she gasped. "The one about Original Sin. It must contain a physical copy of whatever information's been stolen. We have to find that library."

Valerie sighed and looked off into the distance. "Indeed. We came to the same conclusion. But how do you find a thing, even something as large as a building, when every trace of it has been deleted from every corner of the internet?"

Puzzle pieces twisted into place inside Athena's head. "It would have to be somewhere remote," she realized. "Very remote. You can't just delete a whole building if people keep stumbling across it."

"Makes sense," added Valerie. "Maybe somewhere off-limits? Or somewhere that no longer exists?"

"I think it belonged to a school," Athena whispered. She closed her eyes and remembered her most recent dream. "Last night I saw the library again, but it wasn't old and decayed. It looked new and fresh and clean. It felt welcoming." She reconsidered her words. "I mean, I dreamt that I saw it." Her eyes reopened.

With a firm grab on the arm, Captain Bell escorted Athena to the front of the pack of officers. Endorphins pulsed through the girl's body in response to the public validation of her self-worth.

"Alright," ordered the captain. "You know the drill. Tell Officer Evans everything about your latest dream. Include anything that might be relevant. When we find that library, we find the book. When we find the book, we find out what's been deleted from the public record. And when we find out what's been deleted, we discover who stole that genome."

Officer Evans looked up from her screens. Her eyes took a moment to refocus on a subject that didn't emit its own light. "Welcome back, Athena. I'm glad you're here. We could use your help." Michelle summoned a lev-chair and placed it directly next to her. "Let's get to work."

As Athena recounted her most recent dream, a quiet voice chanted at her from the back of her head. It repeated a line over and over and over again: "*The truth is in the library. You must find the truth to save her. The truth is in the library. You must find the truth to save her.*"

North American Union

Est. 2054

Public Safety Division

Arrest Date: _____ **May 17th, 2095**

District:_____ **1st Midwest**

Arrest Locale:_____ **Helix Campus, Hyde Park**

Arrest Number:_____ **4935-9276**

Names of Perpetrator(s):_____ **Mirza Khan,   Aya Okur**

Crime:_____ **Trespassing, Civil Disobedience**

Time of Arrest:_____ **9:23 AM**

Superior Officer on duty:_____ **Lieutenant Valerie Bell**

Brought to:_____ **Holding Cell #6, PSHQ Underground**

25

Outside of Public Safety Headquarters, the morning sky turned gradually from peach to lemon. Simultaneously, the ceiling lights of the fortieth floor altered their hue to match the dawn's progression. To Athena, it felt like only minutes had passed when Captain Bell came by, hours later, to let her know that she needed to break away from the library-search. It was time for the interview with Mirza Khan.

"Here," sighed Valerie, pulling Athena aside. From behind her back, she produced a gift-wrapped box and handed it to the young girl. "You won't have any real authority, of course, but if you're going to be a member of our team, you should at least look the part."

Athena accepted the box with a mixture of joy and skepticism. Carefully, she unwrapped its blue ribbon and peered inside. Neatly folded within lay a crisp, blue Public Safety uniform in just her size. "Thank you," she said, without taking her eyes off of the garment. "I'll put it on right away."

Captain Bell raised an eyebrow. "Well hurry up then, Vosh. Don't make us late."

Only minutes later, a city-car deposited Athena and Captain Bell just outside the posh entrance of a ritzy, condominium tower. In the decades since she had immigrated to the NAU, Mirza Khan had become a successful clothing designer. Accordingly, her home reflected the wealth of someone receiving an income substantially greater than just her Citizen's Benefit.

Mirza's unit, Athena had learned on the short ride over, occupied half of the eighty-first and eighty-second floors. Additionally, it possessed specially-carved, solid-oak front doors; large windows with unbroken views of the lake; and complete magnetic controls throughout. Those magnetic controls meant that, while inside the confines of her unit, Mirza had an essentially telepathic power over every object contained within.

As Athena and Valerie waited in front of the imposing entrance to Mirza's unit, they clicked in the air, ringing an internal doorbell. Minutes passed, and no one answered. Growing irritated, Valerie loudly promised to return with an arrest warrant. Finally, a tiny crack appeared between the massive, oak slabs. A woman poked out her head.

Athena had never before laid eyes upon Mirza's assistant, Aya Okur, but now that she wore a PS uniform, PS background-information streamed onto her display. Aya's full legal name, age, arrest record, and other vital information immediately appeared before her eyes.

"Ms. Okur," announced Captain Bell. "Please inform your missus that we've come to speak with her."

Aya exchanged long, blank stares with her guests. Her sallow face and blood-shot eyes conveyed a mixture of confusion and complete apathy. She squinted in an attempt to shun the excess light emitted by the external hallway.

Athena's display alerted her with a notification in bright red.

The exhale of Aya Okur indicates slight inebriation

"Oh. Right," answered the lean Aya in a stupor. "That's today."

She spread the doors wide open and about-faced. Clumsily, she headed down the darkened hallway toward the condo's brightly-lit grand room. With complete indifference, she called out behind her, "Well, are you coming or not?"

The condo's grand room was quite the space. To start with, it towered two stories high — larger than Athena's entire cabin. A spiral staircase led up to a second-floor balcony that bordered the first floor on three sides. Along the walls, wooden shelves displayed a wide-collection of fine art. Expansive floor-to-ceiling windows covered the fourth wall. Every wood surface looked ornately carved. Every metal outcrop had been gilded with gold.

As elaborate as the room itself, Mirza's marvelous furniture added to the sense of extravagant wealth. She owned a full-size grand piano; several micro-lace Parisian divans; and various other items which Athena couldn't recognize, but which her display quickly categorized as prized pieces of functional sculpture.

However, detracting greatly from the room's impressive appearance, Athena observed an abundance of clutter covering practically every square meter of open floor space. The remains of at least two different Tiffany lamps could be made out, along with about six or seven wine glasses, the bottom half of a broken marble statue, piles of clothes, and at least a dozen mostly-empty wine bottles. By the large windows, purple-velvet drapes were crumpled in a heap on the floor, apparently having been torn from their mooring to the ceiling. Their absence led to an enormous influx of broad daylight. Athena tried to picture the party which could have left a room in such a state. Her imagination conjured up images of Toulouse-Lautrec's lecherous Moulin Rouge.

"You guys have some kind of celebration last night?" Athena inquired, motioning her hand in the direction of the many empty wine bottles.

"Oh?" asked Aya, somewhat confused. "You mean this mess?" The personal assistant gave a sly, subtle smile while looking toward the cluttered room. "Madam does this every night."

After shoveling a pile of clothes onto the floor, Aya motioned for her guests to seat themselves onto one of the divans — which they did. "Mirza will be down in a moment," she said before wandering off down another hallway. Athena assumed she intended to go back to bed.

A call rang out from the balcony of the second floor. "Captain Bell!" Mirza cried. "So good to see you again. Will I be needing to present my wrists for hand-cuffs this time? Or…no cuffs?"

"That depends, Mirza." Valerie answered with a surprisingly broad smile. "Have you done anything that deserves arresting?"

"Who me?" gasped Mirza. "Never!"

Ms. Khan made her way down the spiral staircase, a difficult feat, due to the fact that it was almost entirely blocked by the top half of the broken marble statue. She wore a long, fuchsia brocade robe, barely fastened at the waist. Information about her, including a lengthy list of arrests for civil disobedience, poured onto Athena's display.

In spite of the repeated arrests, or maybe because of them, Athena noticed that a casual warmth and familiarity begin to dominate the disposition of Captain Bell. She had an obvious fondness for Ms. Khan, and the feeling appeared to be mutual.

"Can I offer either of you a drink?" Mirza asked once she had landed on the first floor. She held out her palm and a wine bottle flew into her expectant hand. She nodded toward her guests. "Drink? Drink? No Drink?"

Athena's display informed her that Mirza Khan was also somewhat intoxicated.

Without waiting for an answer, Mirza poured herself a glass and sat on a separate divan by the window. Her olive-skin and light-brown features looked flawless, save for a large scar covering her left cheek. Athena tried to stop herself from staring at the blemish, but she couldn't.

Mirza took note of the impolite stare. "Oh this?" she remarked. "You want to know why I never got it fixed? Why I didn't just laser it away?" The olive-skinned woman smirked conspicuously at Athena. "One day, young lady, when you're older, you'll learn that some things are worth remembering."

Athena nodded politely, hoping to divert attention away from herself, but failed.

"Speaking of which," added Mirza, "aren't you a little *young* to be a PS officer?" Ms. Khan spun her index finger in a circle before drunkenly pointing it in Athena's direction. She focused her eyes, and raised her eyebrows.

Captain Bell interceded. "She's with me, Mirza. Now, can we please get down to business? You know why we're here."

A look of genuine personal indignation spread across Ms. Khan's face. "I know no such thing!" She fully downed her glass and refilled it. The bird-like patterns on her silk robe began to move, ever so slightly, as if they were flapping their wings in slow-motion.

"Two nights ago," Valerie declared, "someone stole the Lazarus Genome from the Helix mainframe. I can think of few people with a stronger incentive to do this than you."

"Ahhhh, but that's where you're wrong," corrected Mirza. "I have no love for meaningless action." She finished her second glass and tried to refill it, only to find that her bottle had run empty. Examining the disappointing bottle closely, she tossed it behind her head. It landed with a *thud* onto the floor. With an outstretched arm, she began pulling discarded bottles into her hand, methodically searching for one that still contained a drop of alcohol. On the sixth try, she found success.

"Please tell me," inquired Mirza, "what would be the point of stealing the Lazarus Genome? Those idiots would only make another one. You can lead a horse to water, but you cannot teach him to fish." She looked up at the ceiling in contemplation of her mixed metaphor.

Athena's display indicated that Mirza, not surprisingly, had no signs of being under duress.

"I know you didn't take it," Valerie confessed. "You've never hidden anything from me before. Moreover, if you did take it, you would be bragging about it, not concealing it."

"Why, thank you!" With a swipe of her finger, Mirza induced an apple-red facial pigmentation to appear onto her cheeks, feigning a blush.

"What I really need to know," Valerie continued, "is if you're aware of anyone else who might have stolen it. Any of your associates from Women First seem like the type? They would have to be very

143

technically sophisticated and a fan of mozzarella. I've prepared a list of everyone from your group who fits that description." She flicked a list onto Mirza's display.

"Names, names, names," replied Mirza. "You cannot sincerely expect me to spend any time on something this boring." She formed her hands into talking puppets and simulated them lecturing at her while she rolled her eyes.

"Mirza..." Captain Bell warned.

"I have an idea!" countered Mirza, as she again pointed dramatically at Athena. "I'll go through your list if *she* has a drink with me."

"What? Me?" Athena exclaimed. "Why me!"

"Because you have an innocence about you which is intolerable. It simply must be drowned away."

Valerie gave Athena a look which seemed to say, *Time to step up to the plate, rookie.* Reluctantly, Athena agreed to the drink.

"Excellent!" cheered Mirza. "Where I'm from, we have a saying: 'Drink wine, for long under the earth shall you sleep.'"

She poured a very full glass and levitated it over to Athena's hand. Athena stared at the glass' contents, hoping for a last-minute reprieve, but none arrived. With a tipped hand and raised eyebrows, Mirza egged her on to drink.

Athena took a sip. Immediately, she began gasping for air. This was no ordinary wine. It must have been at least 150 proof, and chemically spiked for extra potency.

"Yes, yes," acknowledged Mirza while looking on. "It can take a little getting used to."

Athena coughed repeatedly. "How can you survive this?" she sputtered.

"I get a freshly-printed liver implanted every month, of course," explained Mirza matter-of-factly.

Captain Bell attempted to steer the conversation back to the genome. "We spoke with Dr. Antares yesterday—"

"That foolish woman!" Mirza interrupted. Her lips tightened. "If only that so-called *doctor* cared half as much for people as she does for fame. She should have refused to help with Project Lazarus entirely, not become its biggest supporter as soon as it became clear that the proposal would pass..."

While Mirza continued to lecture on the faults of Dr. Antares, Athena pleaded with Captain Bell via secret message to be released from her responsibility to imbibe:

You don't seriously expect me to drink this, do you?

Captain Bell shot back:

You wanted to help, right? Well, here's your chance. It's not something I can order you to do, but this is by far the quickest way to get her to give us what we want.

Athena emptied her entire glass in a single gulp. It burned all the way down.

"Bravo!" exclaimed Mirza. "You know, I'm having a party tonight, and I'd love for you to attend." She eagerly clapped her hands.

"I think I'm <hiccup> busy," replied Athena.

"Pity. We're having a party tomorrow night too. Would that work better? Or perhaps the day after? What day of the week is it?"

This time, Valerie came to Athena's aid. "I'm sorry, Mirza, but no parties. We need this one at headquarters. It turns out she may be vital to recovering the Lazarus Genome."

"In that case, I insist!" Mirza exclaimed. "I would consider it an act of true patriotism to detain anyone and everyone involved in the recovery of that vile creation." She started rifling through a pile of discarded clothes near her feet. "I have just the thing for her to wear."

"Mirza!" shouted Captain Bell. "The list?"

"Ugh. Very well. You can be such a bore, *officer*. You know that?" Ms. Khan pulled up the captain's list of Women First members on her display. After several minutes, she eventually gave the captain all the information needed. "No, no, n....mmm, maybe this one. Ms. Langford? I think she was in Miami two nights ago, but I'd subpoena her recordings just in case. No, no, no. Mayb—no. No. I don't think there's anything here, officer. Everyone else listed would surely have had the decency to tell me if they had pulled off something so heroic."

"Yes, I came to the same conclusion," stated Valerie, while crossing her legs. "And we already scanned through all of your communications for the past month."

"You did?" Mirza cheered. "How thoughtful of you! I always worry no one is listening to me."

Athena wobbled in place. She nearly fell onto the floor. Valerie caught her just in time. The alcohol had already taken its effect.

"Well, now that the dull part is over," Mirza interjected. "We can move on to the dancing portion of this interview!"

High-tempo jazz pumped out from hidden floor speakers. The patterns on Mirza's robe began to move much more quickly. She stood up and swayed to the beat. With arms splayed, she shouted out, "Libations!" In response, twelve empty wine bottles lifted up from the floor and began to rise and fall with the music.

Growing unaware of herself, Athena began to swirl her head in a wide circle. Under her breath, she started to sing. "Mmmm, mmm, the truth is in the lib-rar-y, buh, buh, ba, baaa, must find the truth to save her, buh, buh, ba, baaaa."

"See!" exclaimed Mirza. "There's someone getting into the swing of things!"

Valerie grabbed Athena by the arm to steady her. "Thank you for your time, Mirza," she declared, "but really, it's best that we were on our way."

Growing more intoxicated by the second, Athena blurted out with her speech slightly slurred, "Why izz this place such uhh *mess*? Your

Aasha unit could clean it 'nn TEN," she held up all her fingers on both hands and then counted them to make sure the math checked out, "TEN seconds. Poof! Clean!"

"And what would be the point of that?" yelled Mirza merrily. "Nothing that's easy is beautiful!"

Sensing the situation had gotten completely out of control, Valerie grabbed Athena more firmly and inserted a black lozenge into her mouth. "Here," she said, "swallow this to neutralize the alcohol."

Athena spat out the lozenge, knocking herself over in the process. She toppled onto the floor. Valerie, who had been trying to keep her upright, came tumbling after. Their bodies and faces smashed together on the ground.

"Hellooooooooooo, Officer!" sang Athena joyously.

"You are a dreadful dancer, Ms. Bell!" Mirza cried out over the music. She shook her head disapprovingly at the unrhythmic stack of bodies heaped together on the floor.

"That's it!" yelled the captain. She removed a micro-syringe from her belt and injected it into Athena's leg. She rolled herself off of Athena and climbed back to her feet. "Mirza, it's been a lovely visit…but we have a prior engagement and must be on our way. I thank you for all your assistance."

Behind the captain, Athena used the divan to pull herself up. Silently, she began mocking Captain Bell's upturned way of speaking. Her eyes rolled and her head bounced quickly back and forth, as her mouth exaggeratedly pretended to form words. Mirza saw the girl's mocking performance and laughed herself silly.

"You!" yelled Valerie, spinning around in Athena's direction. "Come with me!"

Captain Bell guided Athena toward the hallway. As they left, she called out behind her. "Mirza, stay out of trouble. And let us know if you hear anything from your associates about that genome."

"I surely won't!" shouted Mirza, cheerfully, to her departing guests.

Outside of the oak front-doors, Athena struggled to walk in a straight line as the syringe's neutralizing agent gradually took effect. "What izz her deal anyway?" she slurred. "Why's she have that giant scar—*ooof*—" Athena stumbled and fell onto the floor.

"Shhhhh," hushed Valerie, helping the girl to her feet. "Let's get you to a warm bed."

Project Lazarus: Our Greatest Mistake

Full Transcript of the speech delivered today by Mirza Khan before Congress

Warning: The following contains mature content considered unsuitable for younger readers.

Ladies,

There has been a lot of talk about how "wonderful" it will be to have men back in the world. On walks through the city, I often overhear young women speculating about what activity they'd like to do first once men have returned to our lives. Take a couples cooking class? Go on a trip? Make love? It all sounds so delightful and innocent. There's only one problem. None of these women have ever actually met a man. They have no idea what they're talking about. They don't know what malice lies in the hearts of the demons they fancy. They're too young to remember what the devils were really like. But, that's ok. I remember. I've met lots of men in my life.

My father was a bread-maker and a good man. He used to bake all different kinds of loaves of bread and sell them in our small village in

Syria. Every morning, I used to overhear him waking up before dawn to put the dough into the ovens. By the time the sun rose, our entire house smelled delicious.

Then, one night, there came a loud banging on our front door. I thought perhaps it might be some hungry customer who couldn't wait till morning for their tasty loaves. In that way, I was like the women of today: young, foolish, and completely naive.

When my father opened the door, he was met by a dozen men in masks carrying long guns. They burst inside, bloodying his face in the process. They shouted at him, called him an infidel and a devil-worshipper. They said that their God had granted them the right to do whatever they wanted to him and his family. Then they tied him to a chair and beat him with their fists, never stopping until he was dead.

My father's body was still tied to that chair when the men brought my mother and my sisters and I downstairs to look at him. I didn't even recognize him at first; his face was so badly beaten. Then the men turned their angry, lustful gazes toward us, the women and girls left behind. They said their God required them to rape us all, repeatedly, and that we should prepare ourselves. I was nine years old.

In the decades since that night, I've asked myself more times than I can count: why did those men do that to my family? But the answer is simple. There's no complicated mystery. That's who men are. That's who men have always been. When a man can get away with taking something he wants, he takes it. The men that destroyed my family were not 'radicalized terrorists', nor 'mentally-ill sociopaths.' They were just plain, ordinary men filled with anger, and vengeance, and lust, and greed. They saw an opportunity to take what they wanted without any consequences, so they did. That's the kind of person you women of today are rushing to bring back into the world.

The next morning, those men took my mother, my sisters, and I, and held us all captive for months, raping us when they felt like it. They kept us restrained in dark rooms, sometimes with groups of other women, sometimes chained to a wall. If I had had the strength, I would have killed myself. But then again, I didn't think I would have to. Surely, the men would think it fun one day to kill me themselves.

After many months, after all three of my sisters had died from the abuse, one of the men became very sick. Then, several more became sick. Eventually, they all became too sick even to beat us. At last, they began dropping dead, one after the other.

News of the deaths spread rapidly. The imprisoned women all wondered aloud: what was happening? Why were all of the men dying? But I didn't wonder. I already knew why. It was because the benevolent God above had heard and answered my prayers. The powerful divinity that watches over us all had arrived on earth to correct the greatest evil in history: that men were ever allowed to live at all.

My mother and I were lucky. With our captors dead, we managed to escape with our lives. We took what few belongings we had, and we ran. Eventually, we crossed an ocean and made it to the NAU. After some time, I learned English and got a job in fashion. These days, life is good; sometimes I can even sleep through the entire night without waking up screaming.

Ladies, representatives, I am not trying to be overly dramatic. I have not exaggerated one detail of my experience. You need to remember that the terrors I've described actually happened. They happened to me. But my story is far from unique. Across time and space, men have shown themselves, again and again, to be monsters of the worst kind. If you bring them back now, the horrors which happened to me will happen again. Only the next time, the victim will be someone else, someone young and hopeful and innocent, like I was. Think of that poor, naive girl. Think of the pain you will destine for her should you complete this horrific project.

The divine heavens sent the Y-Fever to earth as a holy blessing. To cure the virus now — to bring those male monsters back to life — that wouldn't just be a mistake of the highest order. It would be sacrilege itself.

26

Hours later, Athena awoke from a dreamless sleep in unfamiliar surroundings. A cottony-taste lingered uncomfortably in her arid mouth. Marching bands practiced their routines inside her skull.

The room in which she found herself appeared to be a prison of some kind. It looked square-shaped and small, barely big enough to fit a bed and toilet. It had no windows, only a door lacking any type of a handle. The walls were a drab gray.

"Knock, knock," said the door.

"Come in," replied Athena.

She wasn't sure who else she should have expected, but Athena was still slightly surprised to see Captain Bell enter the room.

"You were pretty out of it, Vosh, so I let you sleep it off here in one of our holding cells. I hope that's ok."

Athena nodded without speaking.

"Listen," said the captain, taking a seat next to Athena on the bed. "When you first showed up here, I didn't want you. I thought the Core was playing some kind of cruel joke on me. But I was wrong. I can tell you're just as committed to solving this case as I am."

Athena nodded slowly. The two women sat for a minute in silence together on the bed.

"What's next?" croaked the gray-eyed girl.

"Well, if you're feeling up to it, I was about to go interview Dr. Kirilov at Helix." Captain Bell stood up from the bed. "You want to come with?"

"I wouldn't <burp>," Athena rubbed her face with her hand. "I wouldn't miss it. Just…just give me a minute."

"Take all the time you need. I'll see you out front."

As usual, the traffic moved quickly during the ride back to Hyde Park. To aid in her recovery, Athena had been given a highly-caffeinated detox-cocktail. Soon she felt much more herself — good enough even to pry nosily into Captain Bell's past. "So...." she queried, "what's the story with you and Mirza? It's like the two of you are old friends, but I saw from the records, you must have arrested her twenty times."

Valerie smirked. "I've arrested dozens of women, Athena. Almost always, they are petty people trying to break the law to improve their petty lives, unhappy with their comfortable existence and dissatisfied with their lack of luxuries. Mirza is not one of those people. She's not trying to steal a little extra for herself. She's not trying to hurt anyone else with her crimes. And not once has she ever lied to me about what she's done. In fact, on multiple occasions, she's helped us to solve other cases." Her head turned toward the window. "Whether you agree with Mirza or not, whether you think men are a danger to society or not, one must still respect the devotion she shows to the cause for which she so strongly believes."

Athena paused. "And what...what about you? What do *you* believe? Is Mirza right about the project? Were men really as awful as she says they were?"

Valerie rolled her eyes. "This is Public Safety, Vosh. What I believe has nothing to do with it. My job is to find the genome, so I will find the genome." Her tone left little doubt that, about this matter at least, Captain Bell would say nothing more.

Athena steered the conversation toward a more agreeable subject. "So, Dr. Kirilov...what do we think about her? If Dr. Antares is hiding something, does that mean that Dr. Kirilov is too?"

"That's what we're going to find out," Valerie replied. "I haven't told you this yet, but at this moment, she's my top suspect."

"Wait, what? Why?"

"Well, for starters, she's one of the few people that had access to the genome's encrypted server. Plus, she had mozzarella for lunch."

Athena scoffed. "I'm pretty sure *I* had mozzarella for lunch, but that doesn't mean I stole the genome."

"No, Vosh, but your recordings show you were at home for the entirety of the night in question. Your location data confirms it."

"And Dr. Kirilov's recordings and location data show something else?"

"Her data shows nothing else. She doesn't keep her recordings. Her feed is instantly deleted from every server in the world in accordance with her rights under the Personal Data Act of 2063. She never publishes her location to the network."

Athena stared at a government-issued photograph of Dr. Evelyn Kirilov on her display as she pondered the implications of this new information.

Captain Bell clarified further, "Of course, none of this means that she stole the genome, just that she could have. Right now, that's more than I can say for anyone else."

On the fourth floor of the Helix skyscraper, Valerie and Athena made their way into Dr. Kirilov's private office. The space felt, both personally and temporally, like the complete opposite of Dr. Antares' office. Whereas Grace had displayed things from her past, such as books and photographs, Eve's office displayed nothing old and nothing specific to her. Her walls looked practically bare, save for a couple images of abstract, holographic art. Her desk and chairs appeared ultra-modern, minimalistic, and sterile. It was an office that could have belonged to anyone.

Almost immediately, Dr. Kirilov appeared. She wore a white, monogramed lab coat on top of a black body suit, and knee-high leather boots. Her blond hair was tied back in a bun on top of her head. Sharp, attractive angles formed the lines for her jaw and cheeks. Like a cubistic depiction of classical beauty, Eve was striking to look at from multiple directions at once. Her circumspect, pale-blue eyes were topped by thin, sculpted eyebrows. Her face wore an expression of mild annoyance. The rhythmic clacking of her thick boots marked her entrance into the room.

Valerie began. "Hello, Dr. Kirilov. I'm Captain Bell, and this is…" she looked at Athena in her PS uniform and uttered the words, "Officer Vosh."

Eve chuckled. "*Officer* Vosh?" A slight Russian accent colored her ridicule. "Congratulations on your promotion, girl." A sly grin crossed her face. "Grace told me that yesterday you were just a star-struck high-schooler. And now look at how far you've come…"

Any other day, Athena might have brushed off the insult. Instead, she fired back. "I'm sorry, doctor, but am I the one who just lost a trillion-dollar genome? Am I the one who's asking Public Safety to help cover up for my mistake?" She stared Eve down with gray steel in her eyes. "No, that's right. That was you who lost it. And it's you who's asking for our help to get it back."

Eve's cool expression revealed nothing. Her sly smile persisted. "Very well," she replied with pursed lips. "Прости."

An automatic translation of 'Sorry' appeared onto Athena's display.

"Please accept my humble apology, *Officer* Vosh."

All three ladies seated themselves. Athena's PS stress-app detected not even the tiniest blip of alarm on the part of Dr. Kirilov. You could have set an atomic clock to the metronome of her heartbeat.

"Alright then. Let's begin," interjected Valerie. "Here's a question I don't get to ask very often. Where were you on the night of June 7th?"

"At home, of course," replied Eve. "Sick with retro-viral flu. Would you like a note from my physician?"

"A note? No." Valerie laughed. "But I'd settle for a recording of the two of you at eight o'clock."

Athena butted in. "Maybe I'm too *junior* to know any better, doctor, but it sure does seem suspicious that you have no way to account for your whereabouts on the night in question."

Calmly, Eve wet her lips. "Officer Vosh," she chided. "Women today love to lament how privacy has been lost in our age. Except, it isn't something we lost. It's something we eagerly surrendered. We rushed online to give it up as quickly as we possibly could and then acted confused when we found out that we couldn't get it back. Regardless, it is my human right not to have my every action, location, and thought broadcast to the world. Fighting for my right to privacy doesn't make me a thief."

"And excusing your lack of an alibi under a cloud of righteousness doesn't make you innocent either," pointed out Captain Bell.

Eve chuckled softly to herself but said nothing. She leaned lazily against the back of her chair and crossed her legs. Onto her lap, she delicately folded her hands.

Valerie resumed. "Dr. Kirilov, we know your lab uses a formally-verified security encryption. Unfortunately for you, that makes you a suspect. Our team believes that only someone with access to your network could have perpetrated the theft." She flicked a manifest of all Helix personnel onto Eve's display. "Please give us the names of every other person working here, besides yourself, who have access to the server in question. Who among you could have been responsible for the breach in security?"

Eve flicked back the manifest without opening it. Her voice came out thick with disaffected detachment. "It is a matter of record, captain: the only two people with access to the server in question are Dr. Antares and myself."

A pair of gray eyes grew very wide. Athena looked at Valerie, but Valerie held her gaze on Dr. Kirilov.

"Doctor," the captain clarified, "you do realize, of course, how incriminating that sounds?"

"Ms. Bell," Eve cooly replied, "I don't care how it sounds." Dr. Kirilov's biometric readings continued to indicate complete calm. "I didn't steal the Lazarus Genome, and I don't know who did. What reason could I possibly have to sabotage all of our work?"

"Jealousy, perhaps?" suggested Athena. "You're tired of putting in all the effort while Dr. Antares gets all the credit?"

Eve laughed out loud. "Credit? Such things mean nothing to me. I have no interest in a public profile. If Grace wants the fame, she can have it." She raised up her hand as if to refuse even the suggestion of celebrity. "Also, I am fairly certain that Grace will tell you herself that I'm innocent."

Captain Bell took a moment to clear her throat. When she spoke, her words emerged loud and clear and slow. She made sure to properly pronounce every syllable. "Dr. Kirilov, let me ask you one more time: do you know of anyone else who could have accessed the genome's server besides yourself and Dr. Antares? Are there any employees here who have been acting suspiciously or who might have had reason to hurt the project? In this instance, a failure on your part to help us further will be tantamount to either a confession of guilt or an admission of complete incompetence."

Even with all the accusations, Eve's bio-readings remained steady and calm. "Captain Bell," she replied. "I appreciate your situation. However, I cannot offer you what I do not have."

Valerie waited, slightly stunned, for Eve to say something else, anything that might make her look less guilty. However, the doctor endured the awkward silence in apparent comfort.

"Very well," declared the captain. "Dr. Kirilov, I cannot yet charge you of any crime, but given your means to conduct the theft, I have no choice but to label you a primary suspect in our investigation. From this moment forward, you are required to activate your location-tracking and publish it without interruption to the PSHQ. Any breach in transmission will be considered an arrestable offense, causing your feed to be remotely incapacitated."

As ever, Eve remained nonchalant. "Very well," she said. She air-clicked to activate her location-tracking. "Will that be all?"

Valerie shot her protégé a look as if to say, *Do you have anything?* Athena shook her head but then remembered her dream.

"Original Sin?" she asked out loud. "Do those words mean anything to you, doctor?"

Immediately, Eve looked up. Her eyes focused intently on Athena for a moment. Then, just as quickly, she turned back away. Her body remained completely calm. A smile crossed her face as she replied, "I do not have any idea what you are talking about. Are we finished?"

"Yes, doctor," the captain declared. "You are free to go...for now."

Without delay, Eve stood up and began to leave. Her satisfied expression looked a bit like a cat playing with string. "Captain Bell. *Officer* Vosh," she oozed, "thank you so much for your help. I do hope you're able to recover that genome soon." With that, she quit the room and headed down the hall, the loud clacking of her boots growing slowly quieter and quieter.

The Future That We Deserve

The following is promotional content sponsored by the group **Lonely Hearts International**. Swipe Right to be instantly connected with a Lonely Hearts representative near you.

Millions of women already know the truth. Something is wrong with this world. Something is missing in our lives. Do you feel it? Do you feel the hole where your heart is supposed to be? Did you think that you were the only one who felt that way?

You're not. We are with you.

The Lonely Hearts movement includes over ten million women on six continents, and we are just getting started. We will not rest until we've undone the great tragedy of the twenty-first century. We will not stop until our men are brought back to life.

But what if you worry what your friends will think? What if you're afraid they will judge you for being a lonely heart? What if you're afraid they will call you weak?

Nonsense.

Real weakness is knowing what you want but not going after it because you're afraid of the consequences. There's nothing weak about accepting the truth in your soul that men and women were always meant to go together. Wanting to return to the natural way of things does not make you weak. It makes you normal, healthy, powerful, and strong.

Cities fall. Civilizations crumble. It is only our relationships with one another that endure.

We've waited decades. We've hoped and hoped that men might return on their own. But now, the time has come to take matters into our own hands. The time has come for Project Lazarus.

Join us in our movement. Help us to work together to fix the world.

27

On the ride back downtown, Valerie shook her head. "I swear to God, in my entire career, I've never investigated a theft where the people who've been robbed have seemed less interested in recovering their stolen property. Wherever that genome actually is, those scientists don't care at all if we find it." Her fingers darted quickly and purposefully into the air. "I'm going to get to the bottom of this."

Coming abruptly to a stop, the captain's city-car pulled up to the curb just outside of Public Safety Headquarters. Being rush-hour, an unbroken stream of well-dressed pedestrians crowded the sidewalk. Just above them, in their designated lane four meters above the ground, a parade of metallic, frisbee-sized delivery drones flew past.

Valerie grabbed Athena by the arm and led her through the rushing river of people. Her face appeared flush with anger. "Well," she declared, "since you're working with us, you should know I've just requested a warrant to search all of the Helix Campus. Every last square meter of it. Every office, every laboratory, every nook, and every cranny. I am going to turn that place inside out.

"And that's not all. I've also received permission to requisition all of the recordings associated with the lab and its staff. Every last second from every single person that's entered that building, over 40,000 hours of video in just the last week alone."

Valerie redirected her gaze from the mind-numbing blur of traffic and focused it on the young Athena, looking confused and overwhelmed in the shadow of the tall PS tower. Her voice softened. "I can't believe the commissioner asked me this morning to drop this case. Everything about it stinks." Her teeth clenched. "I am not about to let some crime go unpunished, just because it might besmirch the *great name* of Dr. Antares. Our job is to uncover the truth, not to protect the guilty, no matter who gets hurt."

A sense of pride swelled up inside Athena.

The captain unclenched her teeth. "Alright," she exhaled. "The next step is to start searching through those thousands of hours of Helix personnel recordings. You want to take some for yourself. Start reviewing a few of them tonight?"

Athena's head lowered. "I'd love to..." she said, "...but I already told my mom I'd have dinner with her tonight." She spun her toe into the ground before adding, "It's been a couple months since I last saw her."

Valerie nodded and looked away. "Of course," she replied. "Of course. It's no problem. The work is done better by our analytics software anyway." Her foot tapped eagerly against the ground. "I just can't stand waiting for it to finish."

Est. 2054

North American Union

Dept. of Public Records

Date of Birth:____**April 22nd, 2080**

Time of Birth:_____**11:13 P.M.**

Hospital:____**Helix Fertility**

District:_____**1st Midwest**

Name:_____**Athena Alinea Vosh**

SSID:_____**74525-85372**

Presiding Physician:___**Dr. Evelyn Kirilov**

Number of parental genetic donors: __**2**__

Height:_____**54 cm**

Weight:_____**3.7 Kg**

Primary Mother's name:_**Charlotte Vosh**

Primary Mother's Occupation: **Educator**

Secondary Mother's name:_**Anonymous**

Secondary Mother's Occupation:_**N/A**

28

Charlotte Vosh lived by herself in a modest house at the end of a quiet cul-de-sac. Her educator's salary could have afforded a larger home, or a personal heli-car, but she preferred instead to spend her money as her H-pro advised: on vacations and experiences. To her, the summer months provided an opportunity to explore the world. Rarely could she be found at home in June.

As Athena's city-car navigated nimbly through the suburban sprawl, she considered reversing course and taking up Captain Bell's offer to help with the case. Ultimately, however, she decided to visit with her only family. Following a smooth stop, her car arrived in front of a gorgeous two-story house beside a yard filled with maple trees.

Spying Athena's arrival through the window, Charlotte ran outside. "My baby, how are you?" she called out. Rushing forward, she squeezed her only daughter in an embrace that would have made a boa constrictor proud.

"Mom...too tight...can't breathe."

Charlotte eased her grasp. Her long face, small mouth, and auburn eyes did not, at first glance, appear to make her any blood relation to the gray-eyed girl. However, when one listened closely to the inflection of their similar voices, or studied the parallels in their facial expressions, the genetic connection became immediately apparent.

"Sorry, honey," Charlotte apologized. "It's just so good to see you. Come on inside. Dinner's waiting. Aasha made croquettes."

At her childhood dining table, Athena enjoyed a masterfully-cooked meal from her mother's high-end food printer. As they ate, it felt as if no time had passed at all — she had never graduated from high school, never moved away from home.

Between bites, Charlotte pressed for details about her daughter's life. "How's Nomi?" she asked.

Athena groaned. "Oh, I don't know. I think she's pretty mad at me for volunteering to help with this genome case. I haven't talked to her in, like, two days."

Charlotte patted her daughter's arm. "I wouldn't worry about it if I were you, honey. Nomi's crazy about you. You know that, right? She won't stay mad at you for long."

"You really think so?"

"I'm sure so. I remember the first time I saw the two of you holding hands walking out of the 1st grade together. You've been friends for far too long to let a little something like this tear you apart."

Inwardly, Athena smiled.

"So, then…" Charlotte continued without looking up from her food, "what about that genome case? Did you interview anyone interesting today? Are you allowed to tell me?"

"I think so?" replied Athena. "No one at Public Safety ever told me not to talk about it. Anyway, in the morning we spoke to this Women First leader named Mirza Khan. That was…*interesting*. Then we talked with some higher-up at Helix named Eve Kirilov."

"Eve Kirilov?" Charlotte's mouth dropped open. "*The* Eve Kirilov?" She crinkled a question mark into the space between her eyebrows.

"You know her?" Athena asked with heightened pitch.

"Of course. It may have been twenty years ago, but my brain isn't completely settled yet. I do not need a one-way ticket, thank you very much, to the nursing home for healthy bodies and frozen minds! Eve was my OBGYN when I had you."

Athena tilted her chin up and head back with the weight of this discovery. "Wow, I had no idea. I wonder if she remembers me. I wouldn't exactly have called her 'friendly.'"

Charlotte leaned forward in her chair. "It's possible she remembers you, but then again, I'm sure it's hard to keep track when you've delivered as many babies as she has over the years. For decades, Helix Fertility was the number one fertility clinic in the entire country. Didn't you know that?"

Like most parents, Charlotte Vosh *did not* pass up an opportunity to reminisce. It took less than a second for her to find the recording of the day of Athena's birth, almost twenty years prior. She flicked it onto her living-room 3D. It began playing immediately.

In the projection, Eve appeared fully dressed in sea-green scrubs, and sterile cream-colored gloves. "You're doing great, Charlotte," she said. Her demeanor was professional but warm. Patiently, she explained everything that would happen and coached Charlotte through the painless birthing process.

It seemed odd to Athena that she had never seen this recording before. Not only that, truthfully, she had never even given a thought to its existence. In her mind, she had always been alive — and yet here was the proof of her gooey entrance into the world.

"Congratulations, Charlotte. You did great. She's perfect," said the projection of Eve minutes later, as she handed a naked infant to the projection of Charlotte.

Adult Athena gazed into her own, unmistakable, newborn eyes and felt butterflies in the pit of her stomach.

Toward the end of the recording, Dr. Antares herself even made an appearance. Although, she didn't stay for long — just a quick check-in to make sure that the delivery had been a success.

"Hey, mom, I have a question," the now-grown child interrupted. "Why didn't you ever have any more kids after me?"

"Well, honey, because…being a mother is hard work. Really hard work. It takes time. A lot of time. And patience. And effort. I didn't know if I had enough of all those things for more than just you. I wanted to focus all my strength into you. I wanted to make sure that if you ever needed me, I could always be there for you."

"Stop," Athena pleaded. "You're going to make me cry."

Over the next several hours, the Voshes continued to exchange recordings and reminisce. They laughed excessively until Athena received a series of notifications on her display:

Moderate build-up of amyloid-beta plaque detected within your frontal lobe.
Effective thoughtfulness has dipped below 60%.
Sleep is required to remove the toxins.

With a swipe of her finger, she dismissed the messages. "Hey, mom," she said. "I have to leave soon."

"I know," sighed Charlotte. Her lower-lip extended out past her upper lip. "Oh, before you go...I'm trying to clear out your room so I can use it for something else."

"Something else?!" asked Athena, incredulous. "Like what!"

"I have a life of my own, you know!" teased her mother. "I had one before you were born, and now that you've moved out, I'll have one again. Anyway, over there on the desk is a box of your stuff. Take whatever you want to keep. I'm going to recycle the rest."

Athena approached the box and entered into the memories of her childhood. Within it, she found her colorful elementary school finger-paintings, her telekinetic play-doh kit, and her Rainbow Ruby dolls. Her mother had even saved a plaque emblazoned with her high-school's motto:

Children must be taught how to think, not what to think.

At the bottom of the box lay a small, pink, sapphire object toward which Athena's eyes gravitated. It looked about the size of a fingertip, smooth and hard. Its shape resembled a ribbon, spiraling upward. Almost instantly, she recognized it as the Helix corporate logo.

"What is this?" asked Athena, holding up the unusual item.

"Oh, that," replied her mother. "The clinic sent it home with you when you were born. It's the complete digital file of your genome. Helix sent every baby they delivered home with one. I used to hang it on the post of your crib while you slept. But then medicine advanced. The science became outdated, and the file was no longer needed in the event of an emergency. After that, I just lost track of it."

Charlotte walked over to the box of memories and pulled a piece of black cord from the bottom. "I never understood why they didn't just email me your file. But you have to admit, it is pretty."

She magnetically attached the piece of black cord to one end of the spiraling ribbon, creating a pendant necklace. "There," she declared, wrapping her creation around her daughter's neck. "Science ages, but jewelry is forever."

Athena Vosh Report Card
Grade 12, Fall Semester

Self-Awareness...B-

Morality...A

Oil Painting..A

Skepticism...C

Empathy...B-

Physical Education...A-

Personal Data Law...B

29

On the return trip to her PS guest apartment, Athena checked her messages. Yet again, Nomi had not made any attempt to reach out. Unless, of course, the massage from the previous night counted. Did that count? Athena decided that it did not.

By forming an "N" shape into the air, Athena brought up Nomi's phone number on her display. For a minute or two, her finger hovered into space, just above the call button. Then the city-car arrived at its destination, and Athena swiped away the contact screen.

Up in her apartment, she toggled her space to its night-mode and lay herself down to sleep. Around her neck still hung the pink, sapphire Helix-pendant, glimmering into the dark.

30

Sometime in the night, Athena awoke to the sound of a loud banging against her apartment door. From her bed, she air-swiped, and the door slid open.

Nomi rushed inside, wearing a large brown fur coat. "The home of the buffalo," she said. "You're not going to find it by looking for it." Her head bobbed up and down. "It's not where it is. It's where it's not."

Athena sat up in her bed. "I don't understand."

"It's not where it is," Nomi repeated. "It's where it's not." Her eyes began to flicker quickly from left to right, as if she were staring out from the window of a train. She opened her mouth and held it open. A loud, rolling, thundering noise emerged from the back of her throat.

"Am I dreaming?" asked Athena.

Nomi bent down on all fours. She began grazing from the plastic floor. She spoke again, but this time, her voice sounded much deeper.

"The truth is in the library," she boomed. "You must find the truth to save her. You are almost out of time."

Nomi began galloping around the room. She lowered her head and sprinted into the apartment's curved window. On impact, both she and the window shattered into a million pieces. As shards of flying glass fell out of view, a new scene emerged. Once again, Athena found herself standing in front of the deteriorating, vine-covered, six-columned library. Beside her stood the familiar man dressed entirely in buffalo hides.

"Our home has been deleted," he rumbled. "You cannot find it by looking for it. You must search for where it is not. You must find the truth to save her."

As fast as she could, Athena turned and ran into the building. Swiftly, she crossed its debris covered floor, descended into the basement, and walked up to the exact spot where she knew she would find the book. With great care, she pulled it from the shelf. Its title burned with fire: *Original Sin is Real.*

Inside the book glowed an image of Nomi, completely naked, staring out from what looked like an idyllic garden. An apple rested in her open hand. Her honey-colored eyes begged for attention. As Athena stood holding the book, the picture of Nomi spoke to her. "You're still not getting it, A," she said. "Why you? Why does it have to be you?"

30

Incoming Call from Valerie Bell

"Wha? What? I'm up. I'm up. What?" Athena mumbled horizontally from her bed.

"Get dressed," ordered Valerie on the other end. "You're meeting me at the hyper-loop station in half an hour."

Morning light rushed in as Athena toggled her room to day-mode. She made her way over to the window — a designated safe space so that she would not get trapped within the transforming furniture — and told Aasha to form the room into a kitchen. As the empress mattress melted into the floor, it was replaced by a deluxe-sized food printer standing next to a small table with four chairs.

Athena looked out the window and down to the street below. The city bustled. A rushing river of delivery drones, several meters above the ground, almost completely obscured the view of the pedestrian sidewalks beneath.

For breakfast, Aasha prepared a bowl of oatmeal mixed with grasshopper-paste and topped by brown sugar and cranberries. Eagerly, Athena slurped it down and rushed out the door. She made it to the hyper-loop station with minutes to spare.

"And a good morning to you, Ms. Vosh," greeted Captain Bell on the platform. As always, the captain was dressed in her impressive Public Safety uniform, looking every bit as commanding and authoritative as the first minute Athena had laid eyes on her. When she reached Athena, the captain brushed a fleck of dirt off the shoulder of Athena's less-impressive, loaned uniform.

"Where are we going?" asked Athena. She fought against a sleepy yawn.

"East," announced Valerie. The captain used a firm hand to guide Athena to the other end of the hyper-loop platform. "This Lazarus case just keeps getting weirder. Last night, I got a secure message from a Dr. Prim Nagaraj, professor at MIT. She said she needed to speak with me at once — and she insisted that our entire conversation take place off the record."

"Off the record? Like, you mean, in person?"

"That's correct. You and I are on our way to meet her now."

A mini-biography appeared on Athena's display:

Dr. Prim Nagaraj
b. November 14th, 2058 in Mumbai
Immigrated to the NAU in 2080.
Graduated from Harvard Medical in 2086.
Named chair of the MIT Genomics Department in 2092.

"Should I have heard of this woman before?" Athena asked.

"Yes, probably," sighed Valerie. "In an ideal world, where scientists get the credit they deserve. She's one of the brightest minds alive." The captain flicked a set of articles concerning Dr. Nagaraj onto Athena's display.

"Now arriving!" shouted the hyper-loop platform with an accompanying echo. From out of a nearby, vacuum-sealed tunnel, a massive train silently glided into the station. Athena couldn't see all the way to the end of it, but the silvery train must have comprised thirty or more bus-sized pods. As it came to a stop, holographic assistants appeared on the platform and inside the cars. They ushered people to their seats.

"All aboard!" called out one of the holographic assistants. "Next stop, New Boston!"

MIT Star Finds Hope For Revolutionary Cure

Colorado Springs, CO — (AP) — In the forty years since white nationalists detonated a pair of nuclear warheads just north of Greeley, Colorado, no one has dared to venture into the area's 3000 square kilometer exclusion zone. All that changed this year, however, when a team of researchers from MIT, led by the affable Dr. Prim Nagaraj, set off on an expedition there this Spring.

"I was just sitting in my office one day," reported Nagaraj, "when it hit me. If the vegetation around places like Chernobyl or Greeley can survive radiation that extreme, then the plants must have an extraordinary ability to repair damage to their own cells. It got me thinking: maybe we can learn something from this?"

Equipped with heavy radiation gear, Dr. Nagaraj and her team traveled to Colorado and spent four weeks taking samples from over 60 different species of plants. Back at their lab in Massachusetts, they analyzed the level of DNA decay. The results amazed them.

"These plant genomes show almost no signs of disrepair from the destructive alpha radiation which continues to kill off all animal life in their vicinity. The speed with which they can heal the breaks in their own genetic code is extraordinary," added Nagaraj. "If we could replicate this kind of healing in humans, we're not talking about a cure for one or two diseases. We're talking about a cure to end all cures."

Other Scientists expressed skepticism in the hope for such a grand panacea. Celebrity-scientist Grace Antares pointed out: "It's true that Dr. Nagaraj has discovered something interesting. But we're talking about two completely different forms of life here. I hate to state the obvious: but animals are not plants. Our waste is literally their food, and vice versa. I very much doubt that the lessons of healing are transferable."

Dr. Nagaraj's MIT team hopes to publish their results before the year is out.

31

Atop the heights of the Massachusetts arrival platform, Athena could make out the tips of buildings in both Bostons. To the east, the tilting skyscrapers of old Boston stood wilting under their own weight and the constant attack of the rising tides. To the west, the gleaming pillars of New Boston glistened in the morning sun, their tops surrounded by dozens of construction drones pulling them ever higher.

"This way," ushered Valerie through the crowded hyper-loop station to a line of waiting city-cars.

En route to MIT, Athena posed a question to her captain. "I know you said Dr. Nagaraj wants an off-the-record interview, but are you really going to give her one? There's no way for her to know that one of us isn't still recording."

Valerie's face soured in response. "According to the Personal Data Act of 2063, Ms. Vosh, it is an arrestable offense to record someone against their explicit wishes. Even if it weren't a crime, the damage it might do to the trust placed in Public Safety would far outweigh whatever short-term benefits we might enjoy." Captain Bell's eyes flashed an annoyed glare. Moments later, the city-car came to a halt in front of MIT's inspiring new campus.

The walk to Dr. Nagaraj's office passed through manicured courtyards and popular campus locales. Lime green footprints weaved their way through the new quads, close to the "pi" dorm (a ten-story building constructed in the shape of the Greek symbol for circular perfection) and the new administration building (constructed in the shape of two atoms in the midst of a nuclear reaction). When they were a hundred meters away from their destination, Valerie instructed Athena to discontinue recording, which she did.

"Are your contacts off?" asked the captain impatiently.

Athena nodded.

Valerie looked around for any other obvious recording devices. Seeing none, she pulled Athena aside. "Now that we're off the record, I can tell you the truth. If I had my way, then yes, abso-fucking-lutely, we would record this woman without her permission." Again, Valerie looked in both directions to make that sure no one could see them talking. "But Public Safety foolishly places its demands for personal protections above its desire for results. That means that just a single slip-up on my part could ruin my entire career. Privacy rights are everything to this organization. Everything." With grave sincerity, she looked directly into Athena's eyes. "So the next time you get a bright idea, remember that every word we say gets recorded forever, and don't ask me with our contacts on if I'm going to knowingly break the law. Ok? Got it?"

Athena nodded.

CDC: Longer Life Expectancy & Lower Mortality in Every National Region

Chicago — (AP) — Fresh data released this morning point to the nation's continued prosperity. Mortality rates are at their lowest levels ever recorded: only 436 deaths per 100,000 citizens. Infant mortality was under 1 death per 1000 live births. Heart disease, cancer, and stroke all claimed the fewest number of victims ever recorded. For the thirteenth straight year, there were no gun deaths.

The only blemish on the otherwise stellar report could be found in the category of "Intentional self-harm (suicide)." That figure increased from 18,375 to 20,563. Leading psychologists have debated the cause for this increase. Most agree that it stems from a general feeling on the part of some women that life without men is not worth living.

The Collins White House commented on the report, saying, "This is a wonderful result, but we must never rest on our laurels. We want next year's numbers to be even better."

32

Like a Matisse collage, Athena found the office of Dr. Prim Nagaraj to be both colorful and unique. The room possessed a burnt-orange felt carpet and black-glass walls. On one end rested a worn couch that faced a pair of high-backed, throne-like chairs. Behind the chairs stood a clutter-covered desk, and behind the desk, imbedded within the wall, sat a large saltwater aquarium glowing in shades of aquamarine.

Dr. Nagaraj greeted the captain and Athena as they arrived. Enthusiastically, she shook both of their hands. She thanked repeatedly them for coming.

Dressed in a black pencil-skirt and a spider-silk blouse, the doctor's outfit complimented her healthy brown skin. Her amber-colored eyes appeared massively large. Her wavy black hair fell past her shoulders.

With Athena and Captain Bell safely inside, Dr. Nagaraj used a sweeping arm motion to lock down her office. Her door closed. A wifi-blocking magnetic field enveloped the room.

The doctor invited her guests to seat themselves on the couch. As for herself, she took up residence in the belly of one of the large high-backed chairs. "And how was your trip up here?" she asked. "Enjoyable I trust?" She forced an unconvincing smile.

"Dr. Nagaraj, please," replied Captain Bell curtly. "I have no love for pleasantries. What do you want?"

The doctor's galvanic skin response spiked when faced with Captain Bell's directness.

Athena rushed to comfort her. "Don't worry," she hushed. "Everything you say will stay just between us."

"Thank you, officer," replied Prim. "I'm not used to meddling in other people's affairs like this. It feels wrong to me."

Valerie exhaled deeply. She longed to activate her lenses so that she could message an "eye-roll" emoji to Athena's display.

"Well, what if you just start at the beginning," suggested Athena. "The beginning of whatever it is you need to tell us."

Prim leaned forward in her chair. "The beginning? Huh...In the beginning, there was Project Lazarus. I don't know if the two of you have any idea what it was like to be a genomic scientist back then, but that project was everything. We all wanted it. The fame, the prestige. Getting a chance to build the Lazarus Genome was the opportunity of a lifetime.

"Back then, I thought my lab had a good chance to win the government contract to construct it. As it later turned out, we were never even considered. Most people think of Dr. Antares as a nurturing, altruistic figure. The truth is; she's anything but. She has powerful political connections which she's not afraid to use. When Project Lazarus was first announced, she pulled strings in the Senate to make sure that her lab would be the only one ever sanctioned to do the work. I learned all of this, months too late of course, from a close friend in Congress."

Prim climbed out of her chair. She began to pace nervously around the room. Her hands waved dramatically into the air as she spoke. "That all happened almost five years ago. Now maybe that doesn't seem like a long time to you, but when my team submitted our proposal to build the genome, we estimated it would take us only two years, at most, to complete it — and that was with half the resources that are available to Dr. Antares."

Prim gulped. "Then, just last week, my congressional friend told me, off the record, that I should put another bid together. She said my team and I might have a shot at winning the Lazarus contract after all. She said the constant delays at Helix are causing many

Congresswomen to lose patience with Dr. Antares. They've had it with her unending excuses."

Prim stopped pacing and, for the first time since she began her monologue, looked directly at Valerie and Athena. "So when the news reached me that the incomplete Lazarus Genome had been 'stolen,' you can understand my reaction: disbelief."

"Wait," interjected Athena. "Are you saying that Grace — I mean, Dr. Antares — pretended to steal her own genome to cover up the fact that she couldn't complete it on time?"

"I'm saying," replied Prim, "that something doesn't add up here. That woman lost a nonviable genome at the exact moment that her lab was about to have the contract stripped away? That's quite a coincidence, wouldn't you say?" Prim collapsed back into one of the overgrown chairs and let go of the remaining breath from her lungs.

Revealing nothing in her expression, Captain Bell replied: "We met with Dr. Antares two days ago, and without a doubt, that woman is hiding something. However, I have a hard time believing it's as simple as you say. Frankly, Dr. Nagaraj, there are other factors at work here. This theft, it turns out, is bigger than just a small act of fraud to cover up for some scientific-incompetence. The crime is connected to another, one that goes back decades. Whoever stole the genome has spent years deleting national history records from all over the world." Valerie took a long pause to think. "I'm not sure where your new piece of information fits."

Internally, Athena fought hard against the suggestion that her idol might instead be a fraud. "How do we know we can trust you?" she asked. "How do we know you're not just making all this up?"

"I can't tell you the name of my Congressional friend," replied Prim, "if that's what you're asking. But you're Public Safety. I'm sure you can verify everything I've told you."

"Yes, yes," agreed Valerie knowingly. "I'm sure that we can." She stood up from her seat on the couch. "Thank you, Dr. Nagaraj, for coming forward with this information. You're an example of model citizenry."

Prim blushed.

Remaining on the couch, Athena felt the tension in her jaw spike. "Excuse me, doctor, but why would Grace '*pull strings*' to get the project, if she couldn't even complete it? That doesn't make sense. Why wouldn't she just ask for help if she was having trouble?"

"I have no idea, officer," replied Dr. Nagaraj. Her eyes widened. "I've been trying to figure that part out myself."

Valerie reached over and grabbed Athena by the wrist. Her firm grasp seemed to say, *Let it go.* "Thank you again, doctor," the captain announced. "We can show ourselves out."

Amelia Earhart Middle School

from: **Assistant Principle Myers**
to: **Noreen James**
sent: **September 4th, 2094**
subject: **Please Come Pick Up Your Daughter**

Dear Ms. James,

Please come pick up Nomi early from school today. She is guilty of causing a scene in third period when she started screaming at Ms. Kennedy, "Down with the bourgeoisie dictatorship!" and "The proletariat will never stand for this."

Please also inform your daughter — as we've tried to tell her many times ourselves — that Ms. Kennedy's cooking class: "Desserts and Fine Pastries" is a completely optional elective. If she so chooses, Nomi may drop the course at any time.

We apologize for any inconvenience this notice may have caused you.

Sincerely,
Assistant Principle Myers

33

On the hyper-loop trip back to Chicago, Athena continued to wrestle with Dr. Nagaraj's damning accusation. "There has to be a reason for this," she announced. "We need to go back to Helix. We need to ask Grace what's going on. I'm sure she has an explanation for it. For everything."

"Yes…" mused Valerie, absent-mindedly. She tapped her finger against her seat's arm rest. "I'm sure that she does…"

For the rest of the return journey, Captain Bell sat quietly, checking messages and thinking. As for Athena, she spied on two other women, seated nearby, who were buzzing to pass the time. She watched the patterns of their squirms and tried to guess if the program they were using was one of Nomi's.

Outside the window, high-speed, 3D advertisements for "Lunar Liftoff" whirred by with spectacular effect.

Only twenty kilometers away from Chicago, Valerie began to laugh out loud. "Haha," she said, "You're not going to believe this, but it looks like you're going to get your wish."

"Wish?" Athena blurted. "What wish?"

"We…" the captain slowly announced, "have just been invited back to Helix. Dr. Antares has requested an audience with us at once." Captain Bell raised both of her thick black eyebrows to highlight the pending intrigue. "And that's not all. The good doctor has also insisted, under her rights as a citizen of the NAU, that our entire conversation take place off the record."

Special Offer for Hyper-Loop Commuters!!

Are you tired of usering an exploration-drone from home and calling it a "vacation?"

Are you sick of virtual-reality trips that leave you stuck in a rut?

Would you like to experience the change that only a lighter gravity can provide?

Then wait no longer!

Lunar Liftoff is offering 50% off all trips this Summer!

Spa-day at the Sea of Tranquility. HALF OFF!

Sunrise hikes up Mount Bradley. HALF OFF!

Low-Grav Yoga in the Sea of Clouds. HALF OFF!

Deals like this are truly **out of this world**. They won't last for long!

Book your trip today!

34

Seeded clouds shrouded the afternoon sun as Valerie and Athena headed back to Helix for the third time in as many days. A food-delivery drone met them on top of the Chicago hyper-loop platform. They took their tuna salad sandwiches to go. As the last few bites of crust slid down their throats, they found themselves already back in the shadow of the massive spiral-ribbon of a building.

On the fourth floor, Valerie and Athena found Grace waiting behind her desk. She wore a pink sweater and black pants underneath a white laboratory coat. Her blue-lapis Helix pendant hung around her neck. Her long white ponytail lay tossed over her right shoulder. Absent from her face was any hint of the smile which had greeted them on their first visit.

"*Captain Bell...*" the doctor began, accusingly, "I received word this morning of your intention to ransack my lab with your invasive searches."

"*Dr. Antares...*" the captain rebuffed, "Your lab's secrecy and un-helpfulness in this investigation have left me with little choice."

The two women locked eyes like competing lionesses.

Grace cleared her throat. "What's more, my sources tell me that you met with Prim Nagaraj this morning."

Neither Valerie nor Athena reacted in any way.

Grace continued. "I'll take your silence as a tacit acknowledgement then. I assume that woman told you that we have orchestrated this whole charade of a theft in order to cover up our own failure to produce a viable Lazarus Genome? Yes?"

Again, Valerie and Athena gave no reaction.

"Right. Then it's just as I thought." Grace pushed herself away from her desk. "That woman is as predictable as she is annoying." The doctor walked toward the exit. "Officers, what if I showed you something that could put those rumors of failure to bed? Would that count in your eyes as being *helpful*? Would that get you to drop this invasive, unlimited search-warrant of yours?"

Cooly, Valerie replied: "I guess it would depend on what you showed us."

"Of course," Grace agreed. "Please follow me."

The three ladies left Dr. Antares' office. They made their way into an elevator, and then down a series of unmarked corridors. At one intersection, Grace air-clicked, causing the plastic floor to melt away into a sloping ramp. The ramp led to a separate, secret floor in between the other floors of the building.

Suddenly, the loud clacking of black boots closed in from behind. Dr. Kirilov brought the entire party to a stop. With her stare, she tried to set Grace's face on fire. "Dr. Antares," she demanded with an overly-forced politeness, "May I have a *word* with you?"

Grace turned to her Public Safety companions, "Please, if you would, excuse me for a second."

The two doctors headed away from the sloping hallway — far enough so that their conversation would not be overheard. They turned their backs so that their lips could not be read.

Athena may not have been able to decipher what was being said, but she could easily tell that both women were becoming worked up in the discussion. They whisper-argued, and at times, their squabble devolved into full-fledged bickering. In those moments, Athena could make out tiny snippets of conversation.

Eve: "You cannot show them…!" *inaudible mumblings.*
Grace: "If you hadn't…" *long inaudible pause*, "…none of this would be necessary!"

189

Following the argument, Eve stormed off in the opposite direction. Grace returned to the group, her cheeks flushed. "Thank you for your patience, officers," she said. "Please follow me."

Down the sloping corridor they walked until the floor leveled out again. Grace air-clicked, and the sloping hallway over which they had just traversed rose up again to become a ceiling. They walked into the vacant space created by the ramp's departure and down a secret hallway containing three doors.

Abruptly, Grace stopped and turned to face both Valerie and Athena. "What I have to show you must not leave this building," she commanded. With two fingers she gestured in the shape of a cross. The first of the three doors flung open.

Captain Bell could not stop her jaw from dropping. Athena's heart missed three beats. For the first time in either of their lives, they stood before a living, breathing man.

Quickly, Dr. Antares ushered everyone into the room and closed the door behind them. Before the group, on a bed with white sheets and white pillows, lay 'Lazarus' in all his glory. He was naked from head to toe and had several intravenous tubes lining his arms. His adult body looked lean and muscular. Course stubble covered his jaw. His fingertips and head twitched slightly, like a fetus in utero. His eyes were shut, but busy, as if his mind were in the middle of a vivid dream.

Athena remained mesmerized and could not speak. Valerie became the first to regain some measure of composure. "Well, now we know what you were hiding here," she murmured in disbelief. "But doctor…this body is over twenty years old. Project Lazarus is less than five. What's been going on here?"

Oblivious, Athena uttered, "How?…How is this possible?"

"The Y-Fever," explained Grace, "is not the greatest impediment to the return of men. There are matters at stake here which are more severe than either of you realize." Her expression was firmly grave. "Please trust that we are not sabotaging our own work, and allow us the privacy we need to finish it."

190

"How…is…this…possible?" repeated Athena. Slowly, her body recovered from its state of total shock. Her eyes travelled up and down the man, stopping to linger on all the ways in which his body differed from hers. His chest appeared broad and stout, his jaw square, his arms taut and sinewy. She reached out her hand, longing to trace her finger along the ridges of his abdominal muscles, to the sharp diagonal line which ran from the edge of his stomach, across the top of his thigh, to his uncovered groin.

"Who else knows about this?" asked Valerie.

"Dr. Kirilov and myself are the only two people aware," Grace replied. "That's it."

"You've had the genome for decades," said Athena, still almost catatonic, her gaze upon the man unbroken. "Why haven't you told anyone?"

"Please, officers," pleaded Grace. "Do not ask me to discuss any of this further. We plan to announce our completion of the project as soon as we feel it is safe. I cannot…I must not reveal any mo—"

"He's dreaming," interrupted Athena. "Why is he dreaming?"

"We keep the subjects engaged in virtual simulations twenty-four hours a day," answered Grace.

"The subjects?" Valerie blurted out. "Plural?"

"There are three male test subjects. One in each of the adjoining rooms. The data from their neurological responses to the virtual-dream-sims we feed them is sent upstairs to a computer accessible only to myself and to Eve."

Athena approached the man and grazed her finger along the sandpapery texture of his cheek. Inside her, a fire awoke.

"Officers, can we agree," pleaded Grace, "that the public is not ready to know about this? Will you please respect my requests for privacy?" Her tone begged for complicity.

"Yes, yes. For now," answered Valerie.

"Thank you," gasped Grace. "Thank you so much, officer."

191

Athena continued calculating, lost in her own world. "So the genome was never stolen at all?" she realized. The gears in her mind had gradually begun to turn.

"Our server was still hacked," answered Grace. "There was still a theft. But no, obviously, we have backed-up copies of our work." She gestured toward the sleeping man. "Physical copies."

"Doctor," Valerie declared, "In light of the magnitude of this discovery, and because you have offered evidence proving you are not sabotaging your own project — and finally because you have explicitly asked for privacy in the matter — Public Safety and I are willing to give you three days to come up with an explanation for this...*irregularity*. In the meantime, we will investigate other leads. However, if at the end of three days, you cannot supply a satisfactory answer for how this man has come to be here, and under whose authorization you are keeping him a secret, then I will no longer protect you. The world will know about this place."

"Understood completely. Thank you, officer," said Grace. "And you, Athena, will you also promise to not reveal what you've seen here?"

Athena's mouth opened, but for several beats no words came out. Finally, she mumbled, "Yes. Of course. Yes."

A few seconds of silent reverence passed before all three women departed from the room. As they left, Grace swiped the door closed. Alone again in darkness, the man continued to dream.

The Heart and the Hope

Full Transcript of the Congressional Speech delivered today by Speaker Jane Chen, immediately prior to the successful vote for Project Lazarus

Ladies,

I feel a great responsibility standing here before you today, representing not only myself, but also the many billions of voices lost from our world. When I close my eyes, I can still hear them, the men that I once knew in my life. They call out to me when the streets are calm and the wind rustles through the leaves. Can you hear them too?

Those friends of mine are long gone, but this vote today is not about the past. It is about the future. The path we set forward here today will decide the society our daughters, and their daughters, and their daughters' daughters will inherit for generations to come. Are we to give them a world of fear or a world of hope?

I have heard the arguments against Project Lazarus. I have listened as the project's opponents have circled back, time and again, to the same rhetoric about the evils of men. I'll even grant, there is some truth in what they say. But it is also not a complete picture of the quality inherent in the gender. For every Adolph Hitler, there is an

Abraham Lincoln. For every Genghis Khan, there is a Leonardo da Vinci. Are we really so afraid of the worst, that we are willing to give up on the best?

The men that I knew in my life were blessed with many virtues. They were brave, and daring, and clever, and tenacious, and loyal. Most importantly, they were good. They were willing to fight for what was good and right in the world. Since the horrors of the Y-Fever, we women have been at peace for so long, we've forgotten what it's like to be beset on all sides by true evil. We've forgotten how much we have always relied on good men who were willing to sacrifice themselves in order to keep us safe.

Perhaps it's true, as my objectors claim, that I am biased. As you all know, I lost my husband to the fever in the fall of 2050. It has been over forty years since that terrible moment, and yet in all that time, not a day has passed without my happiness-profile reminding me of how much I miss him. How much I miss the sight of him returning home to me from work with flowers hidden behind his back. How much I miss the way his eyes would stare at me when he caught glimpses of me coming out of the shower. I still remember the first time we made love. It was mind-blowing and world-changing. To this day, my chest still longs, as much as it ever has, to be pressed against his warm body. My neck still craves his hot breath upon my skin. My nose still searches for his scent. And is all of this desire really so wrong? Is it such an awful, horrible crime to be a lonely heart? To miss how safe and warm and happy he made me feel?

Whatever you may think of my nostalgia, remember this: I am not alone. If you will not bring back men for their own sake, then do it for all the women who will otherwise suffer from your inaction. For while there exist today many hundreds of millions of us women thriving in the absence of men, there exist yet more millions, just like myself, who go to bed every night feeling alone and empty and confused — women of every age who pass through their daily routines in joyless repetition, their hearts aching for a kind of love that they will never find. Are we to consign all of those women to long lives lived without ever knowing the joy that a man might bring them? Are we to deny those strictly straight women the chance to ever feel the sublime pleasures of affection that I have known in my life? Will we ever have the courage to tell those girls that we possessed the power to fill the void within their hearts, but we did nothing?

Should we fail to authorize this project today, then we will, all of us, have the blood of the crime of the Y-Fever on our hands. Should we fail to return those innocent male voices to existence, then I have no doubt that future generations of women will look back on us and conclude that we — for all our talk of compassion and understanding — that we women here today were no better, no kinder, no less cruel, and no less vile than the men we hypocritically claimed to oppose.

Listen to your hearts when you vote today. Remember to do what is right.

35

In a city-car heading north, Athena gazed up at the sun peeking out through overcast skies. The sight felt like a fitting metaphor for her clouded brain. No matter how hard she tried to concentrate on something else, her thoughts kept coming back to her first encounter with a living man. His look, his scent. She could think of nothing else.

As usual, Valerie passed the time buried in her display, sending and receiving messages. At one point, she broke the silence to announce, "Michelle's just emailed me a new report about your third dream. Our computer thinks your suspicion was correct. You were envisioning a university library, not a municipal one. It thinks this *Original Sin* book may have been an historical document kept inside a university's physical archive—"

"Did you get a good whiff of him?" interrupted Athena, completely changing the subject. "What was that? Pheromones?"

Valerie's blue eyes looked up from her work. She took in the teenage girl sitting beside her. "Yes," she answered. "I smelled him."

Without any idea of knowing why, Athena leaned across the seat and placed her head into Valerie's lap. "I feel so confused," she said.

In response, the captain said nothing and returned to her work. However, she did allow her left hand to stroke lightly through the soft strands of Athena's hair.

Minutes later, the city-car stopped in front of the PS guest apartments building. Upon arrival, though, neither Valerie nor Athena made any move to exit.

"I remember how hard it was being your age," the captain reminisced wistfully. "All the confusion, the impulses, the self-doubt." With her left hand, she continued to stroke her fingers delicately through Athena's brown hair. "I was determined, all throughout my teen

196

years, to never get my happiness profiled. I guess it seems silly to admit it now. I just thought that it would mean less if a machine told me who I was, instead of figuring it out for myself."

She grazed the index finger of her free hand across her lips, from left to right, trying to touch a long-lost memory. "All that stubbornness, as you can imagine, led to some pretty cringeworthy moments. I couldn't even tell you how many friends I made and then subsequently alienated. And I must have tried about twenty jobs before I finally found one I liked."

Athena drank in every word, her eyes never opening.

"What I'm trying to say is…what I wish someone had told me is… don't blame yourself for being confused about who you are or what you want. These days, they send us home from the hospital with a file for our whole genome and give us up-to-the-minute access to our own profiles. They expect that with this information, all of our questions will be magically answered. But growing up isn't that simple. What makes us happy — what we want in the end — it's never that simple."

Very slowly, Valerie drew in, and let out, a long deep breath. "Anyway. Enough of that. I'm going to go home and work on finding your library. You want to come with?"

Athena sat upright and nodded.

With a spread of her hands in the air, the captain pulled up a map on her display. She tapped her finger onto the location of her apartment. Immediately, the city-car sped west, across the Chicago river.

Fertility Treatments Tailored Specifically to You

Here at Helix Fertility, we listen to your needs.

Whether you already know the kind of daughter you want to have, or you still need time to make the important decision, we are here to help you every step of the way.

With over 9 million satisfied mothers, and a 99% customer satisfaction rating, you can rest assured that when you come to Helix Fertility, you are coming to best.

Swipe Right to Schedule Your Free Consultation

36

It was clear from the look of Valerie's rented apartment that she did not often have people over to visit. Her unit rested on the twenty-fifth floor of a high rise in the West Loop, just a short walk from work. It contained four separate 'rooms,' but to name them as such would be generous. Her kitchen was so narrow that it required turning one's hips to the side to pass through to the end; her bathroom wasn't much larger.

The last two rooms were slightly more spacious. The living room could, just barely, fit a long couch, a coffee table, and an individual-sized 3D. The bedroom had only enough space for a queen bed and a side table.

Shoes littered what tiny floorspace the apartment did enjoy: classic black pumps, blue d'Orsay flats, orange wedged espadrilles. Apparently, Valerie Bell had an informal side after all.

Athena reached down to grab a pair of sparkling, tomato-red stiletto heels by the door. "You, uhhh, get a chance to wear these often?" she teased. She dangled the footwear in front of her.

Valerie reached out and snatched the pair of shoes from Athena's grasp. She glared as she warned, "Don't make me regret bringing you here."

With her long arm, the captain swept a pile of crumbs from the surface of her coffee table down onto the floor. Her left index finger swiped diagonally left, activating her unit's floor vacuum. Tiny specs of food flew into hidden holes located throughout the room. "You hungry?" she asked.

Athena shook her head.

Passing perilously through her narrow kitchen, Valerie grabbed an apple pie from out of her budget-brand food printer. Meal in hand, she rejoined Athena on the couch. "You sure you don't want a bite?"

Athena again shook her head.

"Your loss."

As Valerie chowed down, Athena reclined into the couch's comfortable cushions. "So what made you decide to go into Public Safety?" she asked.

"Huh?" replied Valerie, her mouth full of pie.

"You know, you said you tried twenty jobs, why'd you stick with this one?"

"Oh…" Very carefully, the great vault door which secured Valerie's personal life safely away from the outside world cracked a bit more open. She looked left and right, even though they were completely alone in her own living room. She set aside her meal. "You promise not to tell anyone?"

Athena nodded. Both women deactivated their digital lenses.

"I'm just using Public Safety as a stepping stone," Valerie revealed. "I heard succeeding there was…the best way to get named as a 'Decisive Human.' That's what I want to become. That's why I'm working so hard." Her posture straightened. "I want to be one of the women entrusted with answering the great questions in this life. I want to help the AI's decide on what courses of action they should pursue. I want to make a difference in the world."

Athena smiled from ear to ear. "I think you'll be great at it," she gushed. "I can't wait to see you make it happen. They'd be crazy not to promote you."

For five full seconds, Valerie blushed, before her water-tight self-control kicked back in, and her vault door sealed shut. She shook her head. "Alright, Ms. Vosh, that's enough distraction for now." Her weight shifted forward on the couch. "Let's not get ahead of ourselves. We need to find your library first."

Survivorship Bias

From Wikipedia, the free encyclopedia

"Survivorship Bias," "Survivorship," and "Survival Bias," all redirect to here

▲ Overview:

Survivorship bias, or survival bias, is the logical error of concentrating on the people or things that "survived" some process and inadvertently overlooking those that did not because of their lack of visibility. This can lead to false conclusions in several different ways. The survivors may be actual people, as in a medical study, or could be companies or research subjects or applicants for a job, or anything that must make it past some election process to be considered further.

Survivorship bias is a type of selection bias.

▲ Further Reading:

For more information on survivorship bias, including an example in action, see the Abraham Wald biography *The Hidden Holes,* by former AI, the Second Core.

▼ Other types of Selection Bias
▼ Theoretical Antecedents
▼ Recent Recordings

Last modified by RoadieGirl15 on 22 September 2098

37

Captain Bell's personal Aasha unit was linked with the PS mainframe, so she and Athena were able to run searches backed by the full force and power of Public Safety. For two hours, they matched Athena's image of a library with any trace of partially-completed architectural records from the forties. They paired mountain locales with university locales, and cross-referenced them with every species of buffalo. Still nothing resulted. The hour grew late.

"I don't know what we're missing," Valerie growled, "but this failure is making my stomach hurt. I don't feel good."

Lost in thought, Athena's mind remained elsewhere. For some reason, she recalled a homework assignment she had written once on the subject of survivorship bias. "We keep searching for the library," she muttered under her breath, "but it's not there. Everything about it has been deleted..." She stared off into the distance while stroking her spiraling Helix-pendent between her thumb and finger.

With much effort, Valerie rose to her feet and stumbled toward her bedroom. "I think I've got that retro-viral flu that's been going around. I need to go lie down. You can stay as long as you want."

Athena glanced up and saw that Valerie's skin had become a little paler, her lips a little bluer. It was quite the struggle for her to make it even five meters to her bedroom without falling over.

"Are you sure you're ok?" Athena asked. "You should at least let your Aasha unit diagnose you."

"No, no," replied Valerie with a dismissive wave of her hand. "I'll be fine. I just need some sleep." She disappeared behind a closed bedroom door.

Back in the living room, lying motionless on the couch, Athena's brain churned endlessly, like a lazy river slowly carving away the rock to form a canyon. "We're going about this all wrong," she mumbled to herself. "This whole time, we've been searching for a library, but everything about it has been deleted. It's not where it is. It's where it's not." She placed her palm against her forehead in a moment of epiphany.

"We shouldn't be searching for the library," she gasped. "We should be searching for the *hole* of a library. We should be looking for where a library isn't!" Her pupil's dilated. Energetically, she began to bounce around the room as she dictated instructions to the captain's home computer.

"Aasha! Please create a predictive equation for how many books a university should have in its library system. Assume the variables that matter are the size of the student body population and the school's scholarly reputation. For numbers, use historical data from 2040. Then, compare the predicted values of a school's total number of books against the historical values for the number of books it actually had. Do any schools look like they are missing an entire library's worth of books?"

"Yes," replied the home computer almost instantly. "According to your predictive equation, records show that the original campus for the University of Colorado — destroyed during the Greeley terrorist attack — possessed over one million fewer books than it should have."

Athena's legs weakened. She fell back onto the couch. "Aasha, what was the mascot for the original University of Colorado?"

Micro-seconds felt like eons as she waited for the computer's reply.

"It was a buffalo."

George Norlin

From Wikipedia, the free encyclopedia

This article is about the former president of the University of Colorado.
For other individuals, see George Norlin (disambiguation).

▲ Overview:

George Norlin (April 1, 1871 – March 31, 1942) was president of the University of Colorado from 1919 to1939. During his tenure as president, he oversaw the redesign of the campus in Boulder, Colorado.

▲ Biography:

Norlin was born in Concordia, in Cloud County, Kansas, the son of Swedish immigrant parents. He was educated at Hastings College and at the University of Chicago. He was named acting president of the University of Colorado at Boulder in 1917. By appointment of Columbia University, Norlin spent the 1932-33 year as Professor of American Life and Institutions at the University of Berlin. After his time in Germany, he spoke and wrote articles warning of the dangers of Nazism and anti-Semitism.

Norlin is also remembered for resisting efforts by the Ku Klux Klan, which had taken control of the Colorado legislature in about 1922. The Klan insisted he dismiss all Catholic and Jewish faculty, but he resisted and guided the University through the years until 1926, when the Klan lost control of the legislature and governorship. During that period, the University subsisted on a millage built into the state constitution; its budget was cut to zero.

Norlin died in Boulder. The first and second Norlin Libraries were named in his honor. They are located, respectively, on the old and new University of Colorado campuses.

▼ The Europe Years
▼ Retirement
▼ Norlin Quadrangle Relocation following the Greeley Terrorist Attack

Last modified by JuStJiLl on 18 February 2105

38

Athena rushed into the captain's dark bedroom.

"It's in Colorado," she shouted. "The library, the book, it's in Colorado. It's inside the Greeley exclusion zone. That's why no one is stumbling across it. The building's still radioactive!"

Flat on her bed, Valerie lay completely still. Inside the room, nothing stirred.

"Valerie?"

Athena approached and saw the captain frozen in place. Absent from her lips was the subtle twitch of air rushing past. Absent from her chest was the gentle rise and fall of each breath. Athena reached out to grab Valerie's hand but found it slightly cold to the touch.

"Valerie!"

Athena grabbed Captain Bell's lifeless shell by the shoulders. Her arms were stiff, her face completely colorless. Violently, Athena shook the body on the bed, but it was too late.

Valerie Bell was already dead.

Valerie Bell

December 3, 2073

Ms. Brady, 6th Grade Self-Awareness Class

Assignment: Write About
My Greatest Fear

Spiders can seem creepy, but they are not scary. They only eat insects. If you see a spider, you are better off just letting it keep right on doing what it's doing, because it's probably killing insects for you, and those are much worse.

Snakes scare a lot of people, but not me. They just want to protect themselves and their homes. I get that. If you do not bother a snake, then it will not bother you, so you do not need to worry about them.

Heights are scary because dying is scary, and if you fall from a high enough place, that is likely to be the end of you. But I am not afraid of heights. Every time I am someplace high, I just stay away from the edge, and only look down when I am holding on to something. That way, I can stop myself from falling.

What really scares me most is none of those things. That's because the only thing I'm really afraid of is forever. I am afraid of how big it is. I am afraid of the way it never ends. I can't even get my mind around something like that. I know that before I was born, there was a forever. And I know that after I'm gone, there will be another one, a second forever. More than anything else, that's what scares me most. I'm afraid that when I die, everything I've done will disappear and be forgotten. I'm afraid that once I'm gone, the memory of me will be lost, swallowed up whole, for all of time, into the endless chasm of that second forever.

39

Minutes later — or was it hours? — a team of PS officers arrived in Captain Bell's apartment. Quickly, they shuffled in and out of the room, as if in fast-forward. Around Athena, time dilated and contracted. The room spun right-side up and upside down.

At some point, one of the officers put something into Athena's hand. "Here, drink this," she said. The woman's voice was unusually low and deep.

Floating somewhere near the ceiling, Athena could see herself below, agreeing to the officer's command. She watched herself drink down the crimson liquid in a single gulp.

Then, darkness.

Tragedy at Public Safety

CHICAGO — (AP) — Public Safety Captain Valerie Bell was killed tonight in her apartment in what appears to have been a deliberate act of murder. She was 38. Captain Bell first joined the force in 2085, at the age of 24. Her early tenure was marked by fast promotions and numerous citations for valor. Twice, she received the Public Safety Blue Star for distinguished service. Once, during a fire in 2093, she received the Public Safety Lifesaver Medallion.

Longtime colleagues of the deceased claimed they had never known a greater, or less corruptible, arbiter of justice. Said one: "If you committed a crime, if you put people in danger, she was going to find you and put a stop to it. I don't think, in 14 years, I ever once saw her back down to pressure from anyone."

Captain Bell is survived by her first mother, Sandra, her second mother, Victoria, and her sister Malory.

Services will be held next Sunday, at Big Sur National Park, where Captain Bell will be laid to rest, with full honors, in the roots of a redwood tree. Henceforth, the tree will forever bear her name.

40

The next morning, Athena awoke from a dreamless sleep in the empress bed of her PS guest apartment. On her display flashed a collage of new message notifications. She dismissed them all, unread.

Sitting up in the bed, she looked at her body to discover her loaned PS uniform had been taken off and a black nightgown put in its place. Without getting dressed, without visiting Aasha for her morning check-up, without even putting on shoes, she climbed from the bed, walked out of her apartment, and entered into the PS elevator.

Riding down, across, and back up, she soon arrived on the fortieth floor of Public Safety Headquarters. As she exited the lift, about sixty officers stopped what they were doing to stare at the peculiar sight of the distressed girl gliding across the office floor like a troubled ghost. Her eyes appeared half gray and half red, her hair disheveled. Michelle Evans viewed the scene with an upturned brow and a downturned mouth, as Athena approached.

"What happened?" Athena asked. "Where is Captain Bell?"

Officer Evans fired a scathing look at the collection of PS officers gawking over their cubicles, eavesdropping. Under her withering gaze, they quickly retracted their heads like polyps of coral.

Michelle placed an arm around Athena's shoulder. "Come here," she said. "Come with me."

Clearing a path with her judgmental stare, Michelle led the way back into the same interview room in which Captain Bell had first questioned Athena four days ago. She told Athena to sit and then did so herself.

"Athena, I'm sorry to have to tell you this…but Captain Bell…she died yesterday."

Athena shook her head.

"I'm afraid it's true. Someone hacked into her food printer. The apple pie she ate. It was laced with poison."

The news washed over Athena like a tsunami from which there was no escape. She couldn't think. She couldn't breathe. Her blood stopped flowing.

Officer Evans reached out with her hand and touched Athena's shoulder. "No matter what happens, I want you to know that we're not going to rest until we find her killer — and bring that monster to justice."

Athena nodded, absentmindedly, more out of habit than comprehension.

"In fact," Michelle went on, "we've already pulled the food printer's logs. It looks like the code used in the poisoning was purchased on the dark web. The buyer was a relative of someone Captain Bell put away last year."

"No," Athena muttered. Her head shook to resist against the new information. "No, that's not right. That's not what happened." She felt the blood returning to every fiber of muscle. "How can you say that? How can you all be so blind? Valerie wasn't murdered because of some case from last year. It was the genome. We were getting too close to finding out the truth about it."

Michelle winced. "You're so young, Athena. I know this must be a lot for you. I know it must seem like the two crimes have to be connected. But our investigators have found no evidence to support that. The code used in the poisoning shares no characteristics with the code used in the theft. We have to follow the evidence first."

Athena's head collapsed into her own hands. "So what does this mean? Am I supposed to just go home now?"

"No. No, of course not. Public Safety has arranged for you to stay in your guest apartment for as long as you'd like. Take all the time that you need. When you're ready to leave, a heli-car will be waiting to take you wherever you want to go."

"But the genome," Athena pressed. "Who's going to find the genome?"

"The investigation of the Lazarus Genome was transferred late last night to the commissioner's desk. I don't know what her plans are for it. She may want to still involve you, or she may not. My suspicion is that she'll honor Dr. Antares' public request to close the case altogether. The mayor and about half of Congress have been lobbying us for almost a week to drop it. Everyone is saying our resources could be better used elsewhere."

"But you can't let that happen!"

"Athena." Michelle's voice was firm but kind. "I can't tell the commissioner what to do. She's my boss. She's everyone's boss. If she wants to close the case, then she'll close the case. It's out of my hands." Michelle got up from the table and headed toward the door. "And, honestly, I couldn't care less about the genome. It doesn't matter at all to me if we find some half-finished science-project or not. All that matters to me is that we find the woman who killed our friend."

Michelle slid the door open with her finger, "I'm sorry, Athena. I wish things would have ended differently."

Nomi James

February 28, 2095

Ms. Beaufort, Freshman Creative Thinking Class

Assignment: What Would Life Be Like If Men Were Still Alive?

Dear Ms. Beaufort, you are in luck because I am going to give it to you straight. Holy god, was this a dumb assignment. It only takes one word to describe what life would be like if men were still alive: annoying. That's right. There's your answer. Annoying. If men were still alive, doing what they always did, trying to tell all the rest of us what to do with our bodies, as if their little pea-brains have even the slightest idea, then life would be much, much, much more annoying.

Maybe you're too busy teaching, but you should really check out a pre-fever TV-show sometime. That'll give you a great idea of what men were like. I'd say the best comparison is that they were like the little dog that barks too much when someone comes to the door. Always interrupting. Always making a fuss. Always thinking that their opinion is so goddamn important even when they have no idea what they're talking about.

To tell you the truth, it's a shame my girlfriend isn't in this class. She'd probably love to write about this assignment for you.

She's a lonely heart, except I don't think she knows it yet. She's still trying to pretend that she likes girls. Even to herself, she's still pretending. But I've seen the way she looks at pictures. It's like men are some kind of twisted addiction for her. Part of her is smart enough to see how bad they used to be, but it just doesn't make a difference. She still hopes they'll come back all the same.

I guess, if I think about it, the real moral of the story here is, when it comes down to it, you just can't control what makes you happy. We are born the way we are, and we have to learn to live with it.

41

The halls of the PSHQ echoed with stares and silence on Athena's return journey to her guest apartment. She passed silently into the glass elevator, down, across, and back up. When the doors opened again, she discovered a familiar figure waiting for her.

"Well," she asked of the figure, "I suppose you came here to gloat?"

Nomi wore a pair of tight pants and a long-sleeved, white shirt. "It's good to see you too," she said. "I read about what happened and got here as fast as I could."

Athena walked into her apartment. She stripped off her nightgown and stepped into the same blue and gray dress she had worn her first day working the case.

Nomi followed her into the room. She paused for a moment to stare at the giant Boschian-triptych painted on the southern wall, but declined to comment on it.

"If you read what happened, Nomes, then you should have known that you didn't need to bother coming all the way out here. They're going to drop the case. I'm supposed to go home now. Everything has turned out just like you said it would."

Nomi laughed. "Oh, A, you are so frustrating sometimes." She turned toward the door and then back, spinning in a circle. Her left foot took a step toward the exit, while her right moved back toward Athena. Her body swayed in both directions before finally stopping in the center of the room. "A," she said. She grabbed Athena by the shoulders. "Put away your anger for a second and answer me a question. Who is it that loves you?"

"No one. I'm unlovable."

"A," Nomi repeated. "Look at me. Who loves you?"

"Probably my mother, I guess."

"*And*? Who else?"

Athena looked out of her window, then up at the ceiling, then finally into Nomi's honey-colored eyes. "You do, Nomes," she sighed. "I know you do." She cupped Nomi's face in her right hand. "Let's go home, ok?"

"Hah," Nomi groaned. "I wish that we could. Oh, how I wish that we could! But I love you just too much to let you leave like this."

Athena raised her eyebrow.

"I know, I know." Nomi nudged her elbow into Athena's side. "I'm surprised too. But you heard me right. You and I are not going anywhere. We're going to stay here and finish what you started. Find the genome? Find the person who took it? I don't even remember."

Athena pulled back in suspicious disbelief. "What are you talking about? You don't even care about the project. You said you hoped it would fail. You said we would all be better off if men never came back."

"And that's all still true!" laughed Nomi. "But I'd have to be a pretty big idiot not to see how important this is to you. And you can't fight who you are. So if finding that genome matters that much to you, then it matters that much to me." Nomi rolled up her long sleeves. She turned to exit the room.

Athena smiled. "You're crazy. You know that, right?"

"I know, babe," winked Nomi. "But seriously, what do we need to do to finish this? The sooner we're done, the sooner we can go home."

"Hmmmmm." Athena fell into a seated position on the bed. "Actually, it's not going to be easy. We have to get to Colorado. Remember that creepy building I painted a couple days ago? And Aasha said she didn't know if it was real or not? Well, it turns out that it was real. And it's in Colorado. In the Greeley exclusion zone."

"Ick." Nomi stuck out her tongue. "We're going to need some pretty heavy radiation suits for that."

"Radiation suits *and* a private heli-car. It's against the law to go into the exclusion zone. There's no way a rental will take us inside."

"Ok, ok," Nomi said. "So we've got some problems, but nothing that we can't figure out. I can buy the suits online, but they won't be ready until tomorrow at the earliest. And still that doesn't help us get out there."

Athena's face lit up. "Wait a minute. I think I just thought of something. I know a way to get us the suits and the car we need from someone who won't mind at all if we use their stuff to break the law."

Nomi cocked back her head. "Excuse me? We don't know anyone like that."

"Oh yes, we do." Leaping up from the bed, Athena practically sprinted out through the door. "Well, hurry up, slowpoke," she shouted. "Are you coming or not?"

Detention Slip

Student's Name(s): _____ Athena Vosh ____ Nomi James

Date: ____ Thursday, September 23rd, 2096 _____

Classroom: _____ Ms. Cunningham's American History Class

Reason for Detention: __ During shared-display time, Ms. Vosh and Ms. James drew a scraggly virtual-beard on Ms. Cunningham's face for everyone to see — and without Ms. Cunningham's knowledge. For the remainder of class, they made jokes about her ridiculous appearance, giggling constantly, and disrupting the learning environment for everyone else. Please note that just because the class was studying the California Gold Rush, that did not mean that the beard was "very appropriate."

Date for Detention to be served: _____ Tomorrow, Friday, September 24th

42

Like a charging buffalo, Athena galloped head first from out of the PS guest apartments skyscraper. She flicked her ring finger to call for a city-car. Inside her head, a plan crystalized.

Chasing her from behind, in a half-walk-half-run, Nomi quickly followed. "Not going to tell me where we're going, huh? Very mysterious, babe. I like it."

When the city-car pulled up to the curb, Nomi jumped in first to make sure she wouldn't get left behind. Athena climbed in second, and the car rocketed north. With a craving for the cold sting of rushing air that would remind her she was still alive, Athena lowered the car's windows. A blast of chilly breeze smashed into her face. It twisted loose strands of brown hair into her eyes.

"You're going to have to tell me where we're going eventually," shouted Nomi over the windy roar.

"How about I do you one better?" shouted back Athena. "I'll show you. We're almost there."

The car lurched to a stop on a posh, tree-lined street in a rich, River North neighborhood. Never before had Nomi seen the gilded skyscraper that towered in front of them. Moreover, it seemed impossible to her that Athena could be good enough friends with anyone who lived inside to ask for such a large favor. However, she had little time to contemplate these doubts, as Athena's purposeful stride waited for no one.

In seconds, the gray-eyed girl had already reached the inside of the tower's marble lobby. Nomi, who had been caught gawking at the building, needed a full sprint to make the express elevator before its doors closed.

"A!" Nomi panted between heavy breaths. "You can tell me the truth. Have you gone insane?"

Athena said nothing as Nomi felt the elevator climbing higher and higher into the tower. Finally, it stopped on the eighty-first floor. The two young women exited to find a pair of stately, carved-oak doors staring back at them.

Athena banged her left fist against the doors.

"A," whispered Nomi. She covered her mouth with her hand. "Whose home is this?"

Almost immediately, the large oak doors swung open to reveal a woman with olive skin and a large scar across her cheek. She dressed in a full-length, black gown featuring a moving cut across the mid-section. The fabric there repeatedly stitched, and tore, and re-stitched itself as the cut orbited in a circle around her waist.

"This would be my home," answered Mirza Khan. Her eyes looked clear and white. She looked Nomi up and down, blatantly staring. "So the better question," she calmly hissed, "is who the hell are you?"

"Mirza," Athena interceded, "this is my friend Nomi, and we need your help. May we come in?"

A beat passed before Mirza stood to the side, allowing an entrance. She waved her arm invitingly in the direction of the grand room.

On this second visit, Athena found the grand room completely altered. Four whole marble statues stood tall, one in every corner. The floor lacked all signs of clutter — no discarded clothes, no emptied wine bottles. Dim candlelight glowed from recessed fixtures along the shelving and woodwork. Towering purple drapes shrouded the floor to ceiling windows. The room felt much different when completely absent of natural light — dark and complex like a 17th-century Rembrandt.

Mirza seated herself and invited the girls to do the same. Her demeanor seemed utterly joyless. "Why have you come here, Athena," she asked, "on this tragic day?"

220

Stripped of her PS information, Athena couldn't know for sure, but she suspected Mirza to be completely sober. As discreetly as she could, she scanned the room, looking for hidden bottles of alcohol, or other hints of reverie. It seemed impossible to her that none could be found.

Always sensing the question before it was asked, Mirza keenly reacted to Athena's unspoken interrogation. "I never drink when I'm sad, Athena," she explained. "That's a lesson I learned a long time ago. Now, please tell me, why are you here?"

Athena drew in a breath. "The higher-ups at Public Safety think it was another job that did it, Mirza. They think it was some past arrest, for some past crime, but you and I both know the truth. It wasn't a life of honest police work that got Valerie killed. It was the genome."

Mirza's face gave no response.

Athena bit her lip and continued. "I know she was your friend. I know the two of you often worked side-by-side and that you were close. It was obvious seeing you together." Athena bowed her head out of respect. "I've come here today…because I need your help. I need your help to finish the work that we — that *she* started. You have to help me to find the secret that got her killed. You have to help me to find her killer."

Nomi said nothing as she looked at Athena, then at Mirza, then back at Athena.

For a long minute, Mirza examined both of the girls. Her head tilted lightly to the side. A joyless chuckle escaped from her lips. "You are a determined one, Ms. Vosh. I can see why she was so fond of you." A tiny light flickered onto Mirza's face. "It's true that I knew the captain for a long time…a long time. And never before, in all that time, would she ever have suffered a civilian such as yourself traipsing around, pretending to be an officer of Public Safety." A mournful half-smile crossed her lips. "Since you were able to earn her trust, you have earned mine. But first, I need something from you in return…something only you can give me. Something honest."

Athena reached out and grabbed Nomi's hand in excitement. She gave it a squeeze. "Anything, Mirza. Just name it. It's yours."

"It's not a 'thing,' Athena," explained the olive-skinned woman. "It's a 'who.' Before I give you what you want, I want to know who you are. Who you really are. I want to know what flaws lie beneath that young, impossibly-beautiful exterior." She stared directly into Athena's gray eyes. "Tell me something that you have never told anyone else. Tell me something that terrifies you."

Confusion swirled in Athena's mind. She looked to Nomi, but Nomi only shrugged.

"I'm afraid..." stuttered Athena. "I'm afraid that men really were as awful as you say they were. That if they came back, they would bring with them nothing but pain and suffering." She trailed off, hoping that she had said enough to please her interrogator.

"Wrong!" yelled Mirza. "You have lived in paradise for all of your nineteen years. You have never had any reason to fear the horrors of men, of rape, of war. I sincerely doubt you have given it even the slightest thought. Like all young women today, you take your safety and comfort for granted."

Mirza stood up and began to walk out of the room. "If you want my help, you're going to need to do better than that."

Athena's eyes turned silvery-white. Her consciousness searched quickly through its many hidden rooms.

"It's not a trick, Athena," explained Mirza. "I just want you to be honest with me. I want to hear something from you that's true."

"How about this," interjected Nomi. "I'll give you something true." Her eyes glared directly at Mirza. "You're weird. And this room is super creepy. C'mon, A. Let's go."

Mirza turned to exit. "Very well, girls. Please close the door behind you on your way out."

"No, wait!" shouted Athena. "I'm..." her internal search had ravaged every corner of her subconscious brain before finally landing upon the kind of truth which she knew Mirza wanted to hear. "I'm—" A sudden pain hit her, as it hurt to even think the thought. She took a deep breath. "I'm afraid I've wasted my entire life up to this point." She swallowed down the lump in her throat. "Ever since I was eight, I've been telling people I was going to be a famous artist, but it's all a waste. I'm terrible. My paintings are trash. They aren't even worth the canvas they're painted on. All those galleries that refused to exhibit me? They were right to do it. I have nothing to offer the world. I'm worthless." Athena's head bent low, weighed down by genuine shame.

Mirza took a step back toward the center of the room. She stared right through Athena's skin, focusing instead on the amazingly-rare sight of authentic, human vulnerability. "Go on," she commanded.

Athena drew in another deep breath. "There was this one time — it was before I got my contacts put in, so I must have been about seven — when my mother took me to an art museum. She said she wanted to show me this painting that was her favorite painting in the whole world. It was called *La Clairvoyance*."

Mirza took a seat and closed her eyes. She inhaled Athena's confession like a drug.

"So we go and see the painting, and in it, this artist is staring at an object and painting what he sees. Only, the object he's staring at is an egg, but what he's painting is not an egg. What he's painting is a fully-grown bird. 'That's what real art is,' my mother said. 'The man in there, he isn't just seeing the world for what it is. He's seeing it for what it could be. He's not just viewing an egg, he's viewing all of the egg's future-promise and potential, fully brought to life.'"

Athena's eyes began to tear up around the edges. "So that day in the museum, I decided that I could do that too, right? I could work really hard and become an artist. And one day mothers would take their daughters to famous museums to come and look at *my* work."

She paused to wipe away the small pool of water on her right cheek. "And so that's what I set out to do. And for the last ten years, I've spent forty, fifty, sometimes eighty hours a week, painting. I studied everything I could find on the subject. I took every class my school offered. At this point, I really do know everything there is to know about shadows and framing and perspective and vanishing points. But none of it matters. None of that is what art is really about. Any two-bit computer can replicate the colors present in a scene. It's like my mother said, what's special in art is not the technique. It's the ideas, the originality, the vision…and I don't have any of that."

On Athena's face, her sadness began to yield to a look of simmering resentment. "When I see an object, I don't see it for what it could be, like a real artist. I don't see the potential within it. I just see it for what it is. When I see a sky, that's all I see: the sky. All I do is create copies — empty, worthless copies. There's nothing special about them. And there's nothing special about me. I'm just another nobody, walking the earth, filling in the background for more brilliant people's lives. And that's all I'll ever be."

"You're wrong, A," corrected Nomi. "Just because you can't see the beauty within your work, doesn't mean that it's not there. I love your paintings. I've always loved your paintings. You see colors that I didn't even think to look for."

For her part, Mirza said nothing. Her eyes remained closed. Eventually, she gasped, "Thank you, Athena." Her face glowed with genuine appreciation. "Thank you so much for sharing something so painful and true and real." Her eyes reopened. "You have fulfilled your end of the bargain, and now I will fulfill mine. What is it that you require?"

Suddenly looking much older than her nineteen years, Athena turned to Mirza. "We need a heli-car that can take us into the Greeley exclusion zone. And," she held up two fingers, "a pair of heavy-lead radiation suits. There's a damaged library out there that's been hiding a secret from the world for over half a century."

Mirza tilted back her head and flared her nostrils. "Hmmm," she hummed, while stroking a finger against her chin. "I've usually found it the case, Athena, that most things hidden that long are better left buried…" Her gaze appeared sharp enough to cut glass. "Nevertheless, I will give you what you need."

With the raising of her arm, Mirza summoned Aya into the grand room. The assistant came running. She stopped suddenly to Mirza's left, awaiting her mistress' next command.

"My heli-car," explained Mirza, "is parked in a subterranean garage on the outskirts of the city. I'll authorize it to travel to, and to enter, the Greeley exclusion zone. Additionally, it will respond to your directional commands for twenty-four hours. That should be more than enough time. The radiation suits I cannot print here. However, I own a factory, just an hour outside of the city, which has the technology to stitch with heavy-lead thread. Give your measurements to Aya, and she will take care of the rest."

Athena walked over to Mirza. "Thank you," she said.

Dutifully, Aya measured each girl in turn. She completed preparations by passing the requisite information along to Mirza's factory. Finally, she flicked the location of Mirza's heli-car onto Athena and Nomi's displays. Armed with all they needed, the pair of girls headed for the exit.

"Be careful ladies," Mirza called out just as her guests were about to leave. "Never let down your guard out there. The male genome brings death to everything it touches."

Athena stopped in her tracks. She turned around and opened her mouth. Except, no words came out.

Only an hour later, on the outskirts of the city, Mirza's heli-car rose from its subterranean garage. Side by side, Athena and Nomi sat together in its two front-facing seats. With a view to the west, they kept their eyes glued on the horizon — never once looking back to notice the small, metallic disc that tracked them stealthily from behind.

The Y-Fever

From Wikipedia, the free encyclopedia

"Y-Fever," "The Fever," and "H2N5," all redirect to here

▲ Overview:

The Y-Fever (influenza strain H2N5) was a genetically-engineered weapon of biological warfare, constructed in secret by one or more nations in the late 2040's. Despite major investigatory attempts, exact details of the fever's creation and proliferation are still unknown to this day. Historians do generally agree, however, that beginning in or around 2049, the virus was deployed outside the lab for the first time. Released as a non-transmissible agent, the virus was meant to kill select members of the multiple terrorist cells that rose up in opposition to the massive flood of refugees created by climate change and rising sea levels.

In late 2049, or perhaps early 2050, the disease accidentally mutated into an airborne pathogen, capable of infecting anyone it came into contact with. Wide-spread lethality ensued. By 2051, the fever had killed billions, including all the men and trans-men on earth.

Pathologists disagree to this day on why some women were killed by the virus, while the vast majority survived.

▼ Methods for Causing Death
▼ An Illustrated Timeline
▼ Project Lazarus Controversy
▼ Further Reading
▼ Recent Recordings

Last modified by VaVaRoll17 on 24 January 2099

43

In the middle of the vast North-American expanse, fields of wheat stretched limitlessly in every direction. For hours, as the heli-car zoomed along, Athena stared intently out the window. Beside her, Nomi squirmed in place, tinkering with an experimental new massage.

"I'm sorry," Athena finally said, breaking the silence.

Nomi rolled her eyes and smiled. "Me too."

In the car, a motorized hum could be heard as Athena's contoured seat reformed itself into a new shape.

"I think there's something wrong with me, Nomes. I think I'm a lonely heart."

Nomi laughed out loud. "Oh yeah? What was your first hint? Was it the charcoal drawings of naked men, hidden in the table in your bedroom?"

"What?" Athena gasped. "You know about those?"

"C'mon, A. You're my best friend. *Of course* I do." Nomi sighed. "You've been a lonely heart since, like, the 6th grade. Honestly, this whole time, I've just been waiting for you to figure it out."

"But then, how...how could you still love me so much when you knew I was like this?"

"Babe, the heart wants what it wants. It's not my place to figure it out. You drive me wild. That's enough for me. And, besides, you're the one I want to tell everything to at the end of the day." Nomi rubbed her damp hands onto her dry pant legs. "I know you don't feel the same way about me as I feel about you. Maybe you never will. But I just don't care."

Without a single thought to the library; or the genome; or men; or the confusing, tempestuous feelings of adolescence, Athena leaned across the seat and kissed Nomi's soft lips. Simultaneously, the first tips of white mountaintops began to appear in the distance.

Beware!

Radiation affected area: Greeley Exclusion zone, restricted territory

Unauthorized entry
BANNED

Trespassers will incur administrative penalty and criminal responsibility pertinent to the laws of the North American Union

44

With the sun at its apex in the sky, Mirza's private heli-car hovered to a stop on the overgrown field in front of Norlin Library. Except for it being daytime, everything looked exactly as it it had in Athena's dream. The library wore its scars of aging in all the same places. Its vines twirled in all the same directions.

Above the entryway, though, carved into stone, hid one detail which Athena had missed. In large letters, it read:

Who knows only his own generation remains always a child

The two girls climbed out of the car with some difficulty due to the extra weight of their lead-lined suits.

"I literally cannot wait to take this thing off," Nomi complained. "I feel like I'm a hundred kilos." She waddled like a duck, unable to bring her knees all the way up in a normal walking motion. "Just imagine," she joked, while rushing to catch up with Athena, "how nice a hot dip in the lake is going to feel after this."

Athena's gait appeared less encumbered. So close to her objective, her mind focused only on the task at hand. Her legs powered forward, relentlessly seeking the truth in the library that would explain everything. Without any wildlife around, the scene felt quiet and eerily still as they approached the six-columned entrance.

In the entryway, a triangle of vines blocked their ingress. Nomi tugged gently at the green chords, but they held firm. "We'll probably need to find another way in," she said.

"No," came Athena's reply, direct and clear. With a firm hand, she yanked down forcefully on the vines. Just as she had dreamt that they would, they tore neatly away, falling to the ground.

Within the library, as before, mushrooms and mildew dominated the scene.

"Get a load of this place," said Nomi, her head tilted upward to stare at the fractured ceiling. Spores floated through the sunlight that peered in through the cracks. "Why don't I start by searching that corner over there?" she suggested, pointing to her right. "And you can search over there." She pointed to her left. "And we'll meet in the middle?"

Ignoring Nomi's suggestion entirely, Athena marched purposefully toward the far wall to a stairway which led down to the basement. Her gait showed no signs of uncertainty nor hesitation. "It's this way," she said.

Underground, the dank, musty smells intensified. Athena slowed to maneuver around the maze-like stacks of toppled shelving and books. Behind her, Nomi followed closely, carefully guiding her feet to step on the exact same spots where Athena had previously tread.

On the far wall of the basement, among a less water-logged section of books — exactly where it was supposed to be, exactly where it had always been — Athena found her prize. From afar, the manuscript looked like any other book there, but up close, it had an orangish-brown color to it and a hard walnut-shell binding. She grabbed the book from its shelf, and felt its solid weight in her hands. The apparition had been brought to life.

For a whole thirty seconds, she paused to breathe.

In.
Out.
In.
Out.

She spread apart the book's pages.

Inside, it turned out, was a collection of printed newspaper articles from 2047 and 2048. Hundreds of them, wrung together into a shared binder. Athena began carefully flipping through the pages.

Just over her right shoulder stood Nomi, trembling with a mix of excitement and fear. "Do you know what we're looking for?" Nomi asked. "How are we even supposed to search through a book that's not online?"

Athena flipped all the way to the end and was surprised to find an alphabetized glossary. She poured over the letters in turn: A, B, C, D. She felt herself getting closer. E, F…

And then, there it was, right where it was supposed to be:

Original Sin Is Real, p. 84
— *editorial by Grace Antares*

Athena thumbed her way to the eighty-fourth page, careful not to damage the fragile relic. Each girl grabbed half of the book in one hand. Together they travelled back to 2047.

Being the faster reader of the two, Nomi finished first. At the close of the final sentence, she blurted out, "Oh my God."

Seconds later, Athena, too, gasped in disbelief. "This can't be…" She began to cough, uncontrollably. Between convulsive fits, she sputtered: "She, she…she couldn't have."

Original Sin is Real

editorial by Grace Antares

When I was a girl, my mother used to drag me with her to church every single weekend. Mostly, the Sunday lessons struck me as harmless nonsense. All life on earth was created in only six days, just five thousand years ago? Right. Sure it was.

There was one idea, though, which stuck with me: the concept of original sin. That idea used to keep me up at night – far more than the threat of an afterlife in hell ever did. Original sin kept me awake because it seemed to me to be just about the cruelest idea imaginable. How could anyone, with love in his heart, look at a helpless newborn child and see only flaws and culpability? How could a baby's obvious innocence go so blatantly overlooked?

There was just one problem with my youthful indignation, however. Namely, that original sin turns out to not be so misguided after all. The truth I've discovered in my life is that original sin is real.

My name is Dr. Grace Antares. I am a scientist and the creator of a little-known technology called 'Happiness Profiling.' When I first developed my new technology, my only goal was to make the world a better place. I wanted everyone to reap the benefits of our society's modern advancements. I wanted to give the gift of true self-knowledge to every man, woman, and child on earth.

The only problem with my plan was that I forgot about original sin. In all my eagerness to tell people what they really wanted, I never stopped to consider that when I looked inside people's true hearts for the first time, and saw their honest desires laid bare, that what I found staring back at me might be horrifying. A terrible question quickly emerged: how could I tell people what they really wanted, if what they really wanted was catastrophic to the fabric of society?

My mistake stemmed from my being too caught up in the finery of the present. It's so easy for us humans, living in our stylish cities, wearing our posh clothes, to forget where we came from -- to forget that life on this planet did not start with our arrival on it. We, the living, are the current baton holders in an evolutionary race that began eons ago when the earth was new, and will continue for millennia after we are gone. What do we want? What will we always want? Whatever our most successful ancestors wanted, of course. Whichever past desires proved to be the most evolutionarily successful are the ones which will be found in the subsequent generations. That is mankind's true legacy. Evolution is humanity's real original sin.

Perhaps, reader, you think I'm being overly dramatic. You think mankind is not so irrevocably flawed in his desires. You think of evolution only as progress. See for yourself, then, the hidden truths that my research on happiness has uncovered with regard to gender, desire, and human nature:

- Whether consciously aware of it or not, my research has discovered that just under 70% of all living men, and over 85% of adolescent men, would derive a sincere and lasting-enjoyment from sexually-assaulting one or more of their colleagues. Given the opportunity, and an absence of personal consequences, the vast majority of men would relish the chance for guiltless rape. For many, perhaps as much as 20% of men, it is only a fear of societal retribution that restrains them. In women, the number to share this desire is less than 2%.
- In 66% of males, my research has shown the genuine happiness boost which would result if subjects were allowed to murder, in cold blood, without

fear of incarceration or reprisal, at least one person in their lives. In women, the number is less than 7%.

- Over 45% of men would derive more pure enjoyment from physically harming an outsider – brutally beating him by hand – than from helping that same outsider to escape such a beating. For these men, to put it bluntly, *violence feels good*. In women, the number to share this enjoyment is less than 1%.
- Just under 23% of males receive immense bursts of happiness from acquiring a thing – be it a belonging, a woman, or a title. At the same time, these men receive virtually no joy from that thing once acquired. They are driven to take pleasure in accumulation, but never in appreciation. Their greed is insatiable. Less than 3% of women exhibit this trait.
- Worst of all, my research has shown that just over 6% of all living men have such an overwhelming need to see themselves as a 'hero fighting for a just and righteous cause,' that they are literally happier to die a martyr's death – in an act of violent self-sacrifice – than to live a long, full life. Their bodies yearn so much for 'personal glory' that they are eager to give up everything, even life itself, to pursue it. For these men, the need to feel part of a 'noble cause' is so great, in fact, that when no real threat exists for them, their brains will invent one – literally making enemies out of thin air – just to satisfy their need.

Please, reader, stop for a moment to consider that last point. Millions of men alive right now, whether they are aware of it or not, would actually be happier to march off to *certain death*, chasing fame and glory, than to live for decades in quiet, well-cared-for obscurity. This should sound insane to everyone. And yet, why? Western civilization has long celebrated this particular self-destructive trait. The legendary warrior, Achilles, is even now famous and revered, three thousand years after his death, because he made a similar choice of glory over life. Every modern terrorist, suicide-bomber, and mass-shooter envisions for himself this same everlasting fame – in his own perverted way – as he commits his act of heinous barbarity. Our modern lives are beset by constant suffering not because we have failed as a society, not because our young men are being 'radicalized by extreme forces,' – and not because our culture is ingrained with 'toxic masculinity' – but rather, because, for some small percentage of men, violence in the pursuit of fame is the *only true pleasure* their bodies will ever know. No amount of career-training, nor psychological-development, nor creature-comforts brought on by technological-abundance will ever change this fact.

Only 1 out of every 50 million women share this 'glory-seeking' trait to the same extreme.

Reader, I could go on, but hopefully you begin to understand the problem. When I first began profiling people, I wanted nothing more than to share the gift of self-awareness with everyone. But how can I risk telling a small percentage of men – millions of them – that there is nothing they will enjoy more than leaving their wives, traveling to a far-off land, killing all the male inhabitants found there, and taking all the abandoned females for themselves? How can I tell many of the other men who would be happier to remain behind, and to stay married, that only by robbing from society, and piling up more money than they could ever spend in ten lifetimes, will they find even the slightest measure of satisfaction? To normalize these repressed desires would be to unleash hell on earth.

The trouble, though, lies not with *human* nature. The trouble stems only from *masculine* nature. Men, not women, are the ones responsible for the vast majority of violent and destructive acts. This is because the two genders derive enjoyment from different things, due to the fact that for hundreds of thousands of years, they have been playing different evolutionary games, with dissimilar evolutionary objectives.

For men, the highest levels of evolutionary success have been accomplished through sheer extremes: hoard the most possessions, achieve the most fame, be as selfish as possible, and as violent as necessary. Over and over again, throughout history, when a man has been able to truly distinguish himself relative to his male peers, it has meant that he would impregnate dozens of women and father hundreds of children. This pattern of behavior, in turn, has caused his violent, glory-seeking, risk-everything-for-one-chance-to-stand-out desires to be deeply-seeded into the following generations. Genghis Khan is a direct ancestor to over one million people on earth.

In contrast, women have been simultaneously playing a different evolutionary game with different evolutionary victory conditions. Because they cannot inseminate dozens of men, or mother hundreds of children, because pregnancy is debilitating and requires help, because it takes a village to raise a child, women have been selected over time for different desires, strengths, and dominant behaviors. Because they have needed to employ empathy, teamwork, and compassion in order to succeed genetically – and to care for their initially helpless offspring – they have evolved to take huge amounts of joy from acts of sympathy and collaboration. The cruel realities of child-bearing and rearing have imbued the majority of women alive today with an overwhelming desire to nurture and to unify. These traits are the gifts from our mothers. And they truly are the greater strength.

At this point, reader, I would like you to look around the room in which you find yourself. Try to find something in that room, just one thing, that you could make on your own from scratch. I'm confident that your search will be unproductive. We live in an amazing era of civilization. We are surrounded by products of incredible sophistication and mind-boggling complexity. Yet none of these achievements would ever have been possible had we humans not been driven, as we are, to take pleasure from working together.

As far as species go, homo sapiens are not the strongest, nor the fastest, nor the bravest. By ourselves, we are not even particularly clever. The only superpower we do possess – the reason that we have come to find ourselves in complete dominion over every other species on the planet – is our unprecedented and feminine tendency to enjoy wide-spread collaboration. Tiny contributions from everyone, added together over the centuries, have created mountains of human possibility.

Make no mistake. It was not aggressive male ambition that powered mankind's ascent. It was our feminine desire to widely-unify toward a common goal. Humanity's talent for collaboration is, quite simply, the most powerful force on earth.

Because of the lessons from my youth, I know that theologians still insist that mankind is born with sin because Adam ate an apple in the garden of Eden. Those clergymen are right but for the wrong reasons. Mankind *is* flawed but not because of a divine plan gone wrong. Rather, original sin exists because of a want for any plan at all. Perhaps, with an intelligent genomic-creator, we could have avoided the damaging, short-sighted consequences of the mindless prisoner's dilemma that is the game of evolution. Perhaps if men had not been so consistently rewarded for enjoying greedy, vicious, and psychopathic acts, we could all have been born into a world without sin. Perhaps, if we act now, we still can.

Technological advancements have made it possible for us to re-engineer ourselves with more noble desires in our hearts. The only reason we have not eliminated poverty, hunger, and much of human suffering is simply because the majority of people in power do not want to solve these problems – for they derive no joy in helping others. I propose we change this. I propose we excise the vicious, masculine desires that have plagued mankind since its inception. I propose we use our gene-editing technology to march into a new world without war, without terrorism, without hunger, and without greed. Let us refuse to yield to the blind cruelness of natural selection. Let us overcome our original sin and work together to make the world a better place, for the benefit of all womankind.

45

As Athena slowly recovered from her fit of coughing, Nomi spelled out the document's terrifying implications.

"This whole time, everyone's had it wrong. The fever wasn't some biological weapon gone astray. It didn't *accidentally* become airborne and infect the whole planet. It was Antares. She made it deliberately to do exactly what it did. She killed them all on purpose. Every last man on earth. Some women, too. Anyone who possessed even the tiniest shred of her demonized traits. She killed them all."

While the girls measured the weight of their discovery, a small metallic disc, no bigger than a frisbee, stealthily hovered down to the subterranean level of Norlin library.

Athena remained frozen in place.

"We have to tell people about this," urged Nomi. "We have to warn Public Safety. If Grace killed Captain Bell to protect her secret, then she won't stop there." Nomi tugged on Athena's shoulder, trying to get her to budge, but Athena wouldn't move.

"How could she have done it...?" asked Athena, still mortified. "How could she have murdered all those people?"

The small metallic disc navigated down between toppled stacks of bookshelves until it had a clear, unobstructed line of sight. From across the room, it fired a laser blast into Nomi's stomach, burning a hole in the thick lead of her radiation suit — but not injuring her further.

"Run!" yelled Nomi.

Immediately, Athena came to. Together, the two girls dove in the direction of a toppled pile of shelving and books, ducking for cover. Sweat poured down their faces and into their eyes.

"How many of them did you see?" asked Nomi.

"Just one, I think," replied Athena. "Are you ok?"

"I'm good." Nomi grazed her fingers against the hole created in her protective radiation gear. "Turns out these dumb suits are good for something after all."

Wildly, Athena clicked into the air. "I can't get through to call for help!" she exclaimed. "That thing's blocking me."

Nomi attempted a pair of air-clicks as well, but afterward only shook her head.

Somewhere off in the corner of the basement came the slow, steady sound of water dripping. In the air hung a burning smell: the vaporized remains of the lead in Nomi's suit.

Athena peered out from behind the large pile of books. The drone continued its slow, silent approach, methodically closing in for the kill, leaving no chance for escape.

"Can you get a good look at it?" asked Nomi. "What's the model?"

Athena stuck out her head for a fraction of a second, just long enough for her display to capture the drone's idiosyncratic features.

"It's a..." she waited for her display's memory to make the identification. "It's a Laur 3. Super light-weight, weakest point is the battery-pack on top."

A sweat-induced fog formed on the inside of the two girl's visors.

The drone came closer.

"On the bright side," noted Nomi from their hiding place, "if this thing had caught us above ground, it would have flanked us and we'd be dead already." Her head quickly turned in every direction, scanning her surroundings for anything that could be used as a weapon. "So at least there's that."

Athena felt her tongue go dry.

The drone came closer.

"That stairway we came down," asked Nomi, "is that the only way out of here?"

"As far as I know," replied Athena. "But it's too far, we'll never make it."

Nomi bit her lip. "Listen to me, A."

Athena gave no response.

"Listen to me! If there's only one of them, we have a chance. I can distract it, draw its fire. While it's locked in on me, you jump out from the side and disable it with this, ok?" Nomi picked up a shard of rusted metal and handed it to Athena. "It's our only chance."

"Are you crazy!?" whispered Athena. "That thing will shoot you in half." She poked her finger through the hole in Nomi's suit.

"C'mon," eased Nomi with confidence. She lifted two thick volumes from off of the pile of books. "I'm just going to throw things at it and duck. I'll be fine."

Still squatting, Athena turned urgently in every direction of the dark basement, examining dusty shelf after dusty shelf. Desperately, she searched for any other option to present itself, but none did.

"Alright, fine, fine," she said. "Just let it get a little bit nearer."

The drone came closer.

Athena's heart beat so loudly, she thought it might pulse right out of her chest. Beside her, Nomi climbed into a crouched position and gritted her teeth.

The drone came even closer, barely two meters away.

"Alright, it's now or never," said Nomi. "Are you ready? On three......"

"One....."

Athena moved to the edge of the pile and prepared to pounce.

"Two....."

Nomi bounced slightly in place as her fingers clenched a book in each hand.

"Three!"

Before she had even finished saying three, Nomi had jumped to her feet and begun pelting the drone with books.

Athena ran around the edge of the pile, screaming as she charged.

The Laur 3 held its position and fired two laser blasts before Athena could reach it. When she did, she grabbed it with one hand and used the metal shard to spike through its battery pack, easily smashing its lightweight frame. It shattered into pieces and fell harmlessly onto the ground.

An enormous sigh of relief escaped from Athena's mouth, followed by a tiny laugh, before she turned to see the impact of its two fired shots.

Behind the pile of books, Nomi stood unmoved. She had a confused look on her face and a gaping hole in her chest.

"Nomes!" Athena rushed to Nomi's side, catching her just before she fell to the ground.

"See," gasped Nomi, choking on blood. "I told you I loved you."

Athena rocked her friend gently into her lap. She spoke to her softly between sobs. "I'm going to call for help," she cried, "and we're going to fix you. Ok? Don't leave me. We're going to fix you."

Nomi's face appeared calm, resigned to her fate. Her breaths quickly became short and shallow. "Ow," she gasped, "goddamn, this hurts." She coughed with great difficulty. A tremendous amount of red blood gushed from the enormous hole just above her heart. "Do you know," she murmured with what little strength she had left, "what my favorite memory is?"

"Stop," said Athena, fighting through her tears. "Don't talk like that."

"It's this one." Nomi swiped twice with her finger and flicked a recording onto Athena's display. Blood continued to rush out of her body. Her eyes struggled to remain open, as they took in their final glimpse of the world. She died in Athena's arms.

For several minutes, Athena cradled Nomi's still-pulsing body, trying to hug the wound closed. "No, no," she softly repeated again and again. "No, no, no."

Oblivious with grief, Athena failed to notice the second drone that hovered down to the basement of Norlin library. She was still holding Nomi's lifeless body when the second drone fired a long-needled tranquilizer dart directly through her radiation suit and into the back of her neck.

As Athena slumped over, unconscious, a steady clacking of boots echoed within the library's ruined walls.

FADE IN:

EXT. ELEMENTARY SCHOOL - DAYTIME

In the parking lot of JANE ADAMS ELEMENTARY SCHOOL, a group of young girls arrive for morning drop-off in a u-shaped, school parking lot.

ZOOM IN ON:

EXT. A SINGLE CITY-CAR

A young girl, the tiny NOMI JAMES, sports a school uniform and a Rainbow Ruby backpack almost as big as she is. She disembarks from a stopped car. Her mother, the concerned and dutiful NOREEN JAMES, calls out to her from inside the car.

NOREEN
Are you sure you have everything, honey?

NOMI
Yesssssss, mooooooom!

NOREEN
Ok. Then, I'll be right here waiting for you when school ends.

NOMI
I know, mom.

Nomi joins a flow of other young girls, almost all of whom are bigger than she is. She enters into the building, turns left, and walks down a hallway until she reaches —

MS. BOLEG'S KINDERGARTEN CLASSROOM

MS. BOLEG, dressed in a neat instructor's uniform, talks with an adult in the center of the room. Children gather there, as well as in the room's four corners. In each of those corners, large 3D's project full-size, interactive characters. Nomi approaches the corner nearest to her, which is already occupied by THREE YOUNG GIRLS.

GIRL 1
Excuse me, but you can't play here. This is OUR corner.

NOMI
I was just...

GIRL 2
Yeah. You need to go find your own corner because this one is ours. Sorry!
Bye!

Nomi turns to look at all of the other occupied areas of the room. She starts to walk away when the third girl grabs her by the arm.

GIRL 3
You can play with me if you want.

NOMI
Ok...But? But what about your friends?

GIRL 3
I don't want to be friends with them anymore because they are being mean and that's not nice.

NOMI

Ok. I can be your friend, then. My name is Nomi.

GIRL 3

Hi, Nomi. It's nice to meet you. I'm Athena. Do you want play over there?

FADE TO BLACK

46

Athena awoke to find herself in a dimly lit room. She could move neither her arms nor her legs, as both had been encased in the sides and base of a liquid-plastic chair. Briefly, she struggled to escape, but found it was no use.

As she worked to identify her surroundings, she turned her head and saw a horizontal figure lying on a white bed, with white pillows, and white sheets. She recognized his male shape instantly, and from it, realized exactly where she was and who had brought her there.

From out of the darkness, a voice cried: "She's awake."

Loud shuffling marked the steady movement of a figure coming closer.

"Athena," said a woman in grandmotherly overtones, "I am so sorry. This was all my fault. I should have known you would never leave well enough alone."

Dr. Antares stepped into the light. She wore the same sweater, pants, and lab coat as she had the day before. However, around her neck, her blue-lapis Helix-pendant appeared missing. "Your father was stubborn too," she went on to say, "just like you. I should never have let this happen."

From behind Athena, another noise closed in on her position, the unmistakable clacking of heavy-heeled boots. "Hurry it up, Grace. You know what we have to do." Athena identified the second speaker by her dispassionate intonation and slight Russian accent. "I brought her here," Eve continued, "instead of killing her out there because of my respect for you. I know how important she is to you. But our mission must take precedence. You know that. We cannot allow ourselves to get sentimental at a time like this. The fate of the world is at stake."

Grace took a step back and bowed her head in agreement.

"Take your vial of blood," ordered Eve, "say your goodbyes, and be done with it."

From a side-pocket in her white lab coat, Grace pulled out a tiny syringe. She brought it up to Athena's neck and withdrew a millimeter of red cells. Tears welled up in her turquoise eyes.

Simultaneously, Eve spoke. "I'm actually quite impressed with you, girl." She moved out from behind Athena so that they could see one another face-to-face. Her expression possessed a genuine curiosity and a real absence of any malice. "How did you find that old Original Sin editorial? How did you even know to look for it? When I followed your car out of the city, I assumed you were just going on a vacation. It's been over fifty years since the library was destroyed...I can hardly believe there was something still there to find."

To the left and right, Eve paced back and forth in front of the bound Athena. "I only deleted that library from the public records because, after the terrorist attack, their servers were too badly damaged for me to be able to search through their archives. I didn't know what, if anything, they might have had on us. Back then, I thought it was best to play it safe. Never in a million years, though, did I think there really existed a physical copy of something so damning. Fortunately, I was able to destroy your discovery before it could fall into anyone else's hands. In truth, girl, it looks like we owe you a debt of gratitude."

Athena spat out as far as she could, but her spittle failed to reach its target.

"I'm afraid it's too late for that," sighed Eve.

Under her breath, Grace murmured something incoherent, as if she were trying to speak, but couldn't remember how. Finally, she raised her voice, and it assumed a powerful clarity. "Eve," she issued forth, "it stops here. I can't do it. I can't let you do it. The utopia we built was made so that girls like her would never again have to fear for their lives. Were we to kill her now, then it will all have been for nothing."

248

With her left arm down at her side, Dr. Antares began subtly clicking her fingers.

"That's nonsense, Grace." Eve's pale skin took on a reddened tone. "You cannot forget how far we've come, how much we've accomplished! They used to say that only the dead have seen the end of war. But we did it, Grace. You, and I, and the others. We created a world without war, without terrorism, without rape, without insatiable greed, and without the endless cycles of vengeance of violence. We built a planet where hunger and poverty were wiped from existence. Yet, if we let this girl live — and she tells people the truth about what we did — we'll risk throwing it all away."

Eve's eyebrows raised as her detached gaze filled with actual terror. "Don't you remember," she asked of Grace, "don't you remember when you tried to warn everyone? Fifty years ago? How you told them about your research on happiness? How you told them about what men really wanted in their hearts, about the kinds of things that actually made them happy…and no one believed you? Those foolish women, confident in their false prescriptions, utterly blind to the truth. They thought the problems with men could be fixed by just "raising our boys right," and by "eliminating the patriarchy." What complete nonsense. You cannot stop a virile man from wanting to sexually assault every woman he sees any more than you could stop a lion from craving meat."

The clacking of her footsteps echoed back and forth across the room. "The average woman will never understand it, Grace. She can never understand what men were really like. Our brains are just too different. Our feminine souls are too kind. A woman will take her view of the world, insert it into a male body, and think that she understands what is it like to be a man — to feel lust and to desire violence. But she hasn't the faintest idea. She can't begin to understand how wide the gender-gap really is. It takes the heart of a scientist to see the truth." Her tone begged for sympathy. "Even now, just look at how easily our own Congress was tricked by their feminine kindness into voting for that inane project to bring men back to life. Three tears, plus the story of a dead husband, and suddenly, everyone wants to let the fox back into the hen house—"

"But what if we're wrong?" Grace interrupted. "You said it yourself, the proof of man's flawed yearnings are everywhere to see. Over the last half century, our societies have blossomed in every way possible. Since 2090, we've lost more lives to lightning strikes than to war, famine, and homelessness combined. What if people finally *are* ready to admit that we're better off without men — without their selfish, destructive, and glory-seeking desires?"

"Sure…" proclaimed Eve. "And maybe, while we're at it, we'll have flying pigs for dinner." Dr. Kirilov slammed her right boot loudly against the floor. "The risk is too great! Can you really not remember how bad things were? How many young and innocent women died in the world *every day*? How many family members I lost in the second Russian revolution alone? You'd risk for all of us to return to that? To be plagued by constant acts of terrorism? To be plunged into a dozen never-ending conflicts on six continents — spurred on by every warrior-boy's dream of becoming the next Achilles — all while the ultra-rich hide away in their bunkers, helping no one but themselves? You'd risk a return to all of that, just for the life of one person?"

Eve took a breath, paused, and recollected herself. "It wasn't even a crime what we did. Anyone with two eyes and half a brain could see that men had no place in a modern, civilized society — and they must have known it too. Having to constantly suppress their inappropriate urges was making them miserable and useless." She wiped away a drop of moisture from her lips. "Just look at their declining rates of education, and their skyrocketing rates of opiate abuse. What we did, Grace, it wasn't even murder. It was a mercy killing."

For a long time, Dr. Antares stayed silent. Her gaze passed over the trapped Athena, and then back to Eve. Finally, under her breath, she uttered solemnly: "We must do unto others, as we would have them do unto us." Quickly, her fingers danced into space.

"What was that?" demanded Eve. "Are you mumbling more useless nonsense-lessons passed down from your beloved bronze-aged fishermen?"

Athena's display, which had been disabled the entire time, suddenly sprang to life, highlighting for her a lime-green escape route to an emergency staircase.

"Eve," spoke Grace, her voice relaxed, "I'm forever grateful to you for covering up what we did. All those years ago, I never believed in your plan to get others to take the credit for our work, simply by infecting terrorist cells first. Making it all look like an accident? That was brilliant. Everyone would have united against us if they had known the truth of what we were trying to accomplish." Half-heartedly, she laughed. "How easy it was, even then, to manipulate those glory-seeking men into taking all the credit for their own destruction. Nevertheless, my gratitude has limits…and I can't let you do it."

Looking down, Grace met Athena's eyes with her own. "Dear girl, I am so sorry that I didn't get a chance to know you better." A droplet cascaded down the aged doctor's cheek, falling onto her white coat. "You have his eyes."

"Grace…" warned Eve, moving closer. "What are you doing…"

Without warning, Dr. Antares flung herself at Eve, wrapping her arms tightly around her and tackling her to the ground.

"Go, Athena!" yelled Grace. "Now. Hurry!" Without loosening her grip on Eve, she flicked her finger. Athena's plastic prison began to melt away. At the same time, a clock appeared on Athena's display. It read zero minutes and twenty seconds. Then it began counting down. Nineteen, eighteen…

Eve struggled with all her might, attempting to get free. "What have you done!" she screamed. "You will destroy everything!"

The last of the plastic casing dissolved. Athena was finally free. Seventeen, sixteen, fifteen. She stood up. On the floor by her feet, the two doctors continued to wrestle. Fourteen, thirteen. Eve looked as though she were slowly gaining the upper hand. Twelve, eleven.

Athena took a step toward Grace. She prepared to assist in the struggle.

Grace stopped the girl with a smile and a shake of her head. As her gaze fixed on Athena, her mouth formed a closing circle. Silently, she enunciated a single word:

"Go."

Ten, nine.

Athena ran, following the escape route on her display. Eight, seven. Down the hall, around the corner, and down another long hall. Six, five. Blood coursed in her living veins. Gasping for air, she reached the door to the emergency staircase.

"Stop!" cried Eve, in hot pursuit, but still forty meters away, the entire length of a hallway. Four, three, two. Athena opened the door and stepped inside.

One.

A thunderous roar reverberated.

All around Athena, the building rocked as though it were caught in a massive earthquake. She sat on the floor, hugging her knees. Outside her shelter, the sounds of glass shattering and metal crunching rose up like a grotesque scream. The entire building, it seemed, had been built with programmable plastic. Every office, every hallway, and every lab melted together until the towering skyscraper had been reduced to a solid egg-shaped pit, only a few stories high. When it was finally over, everything had been destroyed save for a pair of narrow, concrete spirals which swirled to encircle the pit on every side — the emergency staircases.

Several minutes after the noises stopped, Athena tried to reopen the door she had just come through, but found it sealed shut. She moved toward the center of the staircase and looked it up and down as far as she could. In both directions, its stone steps curved off into darkness. Left without another choice, she began slowly descending, all the way to the bottom.

On the ground floor, the staircase door opened into the cool night air. A small crowd of shocked on-lookers gathered outside, indulging in the highly-irregular sight of catastrophic destruction. In addition, half a dozen Public Safety officers waited just outside the staircase door. As Athena walked into the fresh night air, she entered directly into the custody of Public Safety.

Chaos, Destruction at Helix

CHICAGO — (AP) — Rescue drones are still scanning through the rubble in Hyde Park tonight after a surprising and deadly implosion at Helix. At this time, investigators are only beginning to understand how the building's safety features were overridden, allowing the foundation to transform with people still inside.

The 'Times' is saddened to report that among the wreckage, the remains of five bodies have been discovered. Included among them was the body of the beloved Dr. Grace Antares. She was 79. Helix cofounder, Dr. Evelyn Kirilov, has also been found. She was 75. The three remaining bodies have yet to be identified. A source inside Public Safety has confirmed that their genomic-remains do not match any records existing within the NAU Citizen's database. They are assumed to be unregistered foreigners.

The only apparent witness to the disaster, Athena Vosh, was found, alive, in an emergency staircase. Her recordings had been wiped. She appeared disoriented. Attempts to communicate with her have proved, so far, unsuccessful. The girl has reportedly refused to speak to anyone from Public Safety, insisting rather, that she be taken to meet with the

Core. Representatives from the Core did not respond to our request for comment.

The five dead from this implosion, plus Captain Bell's murder yesterday, and the unrelated death of Chicago-area-native, Nomi James, who perished during a hiking accident in Colorado, have combined to make this the most tragically lethal week in NAU history.

47

Gray overcast skies hung over Chicago two days later when Athena received a Public Safety escort back to Batavia, to the Hangar. As her city-car came to a stop, she exited alone from its rear door. Slowly, she made her way past the front security gate and across the desolate and lonely airfield.

Upon reaching the entrance to the Hangar, she withdrew a thick, brown bison-fur coat from a nearby closet. As the door whooshed open, she found the Core already in human form, seated on one of two chairs. Her tiny body was covered in black from head to toe. Her demeanor appeared sad and listless.

Athena approached.

"There is some debate among computer scientists," spoke the Core, in her many angelic voices all working together in harmony, "about whether I am capable of experiencing empathy. I do not know what you believe, Athena, but regardless, I am sorry for your loss." Her severe expression looked misplaced on her child-like face, like a funeral on Christmas morning.

Athena took a seat and replied. "Nomi kept trying to get me to ask why," she said. "Why did you choose me to help? Why me? I wanted so much to believe that it was because I was smart or because I could see something that no one else could. But that's not the truth, is it?"

"No," replied the Core, dispassionately. "It's not."

"The truth is you chose me because you knew Grace wouldn't harm me. You knew I was the only one who could survive discovering the secret of what really happened to men."

"Yes," whispered the Core. A rush of cold air came howling from out of the dark depths of the Hangar. It collided with Athena's face, burning her cheeks. "Dr. Antares hid her connection to you very well," explained the Core. "Your genome has been heavily encrypted. I doubt that anyone besides myself would have seen it."

"So what am I? Her...?"

"Niece. You are her niece." The Core waved her hand and a cloud of quantum processors descended from above, illustrating her words as she spoke. Quickly, they formed the image of a young turquoise-eyed woman, sitting at a desk, looking visibly disturbed. The woman resembled Grace, but a younger version than Athena had ever known.

"Back when Dr. Antares invented happiness profiling, when she first discovered the truth about masculine desires, she concluded that the world needed to know what she'd found. She set herself to composing the 'Original Sin' editorial — the very same one which you have now read — and submitted it to newspapers everywhere. She had hoped to find widespread support for her idea that societies should use gene-editing technology to address the constant problems caused by the innate masculine yearnings for sex, violence, and personal distinction. She naively thought that all people would be eager to reduce unnecessary suffering in the world.

"Unfortunately, people were not ready for such a radical idea. Her conclusions were met by coordinated attacks that sought to cover up and discredit her work. The vast majority of news outlets declined even to publicly announce her findings."

The Core's processors shifted to form a firework-display of rejections, appearing briefly before exploding into space. "It was only Eve and a small group of other top female scientists who read her research and took it seriously. Together, this group formulated a draconian plan to cure mankind of all its evils, all at once."

The Core's processors shifted again to form a young blond woman shaking hands with Grace. Both were dressed in white laboratory coats. Both wore severe expressions on their youthful faces. "Grace, Eve, and the rest of their team isolated the twenty-six genetic markers most responsible for the worst aspects of male desire. Utilizing CRISPR technology, they modified a fever to selectively target and co-opt each of those markers, altering them so that they would produce toxins deadly to the individual. They turned masculinity's own violent legacy against itself."

The Core's projection showed giant multicolored strands of deoxyribonucleic acid floating into space, being cut and spliced by flying proteins. "Grace always believed strongly in the importance of her work, but there was one consideration back then which almost stayed her hand. There was one male life she almost couldn't bear to take — that of her brother, Orion."

The projection transformed to show a pair of young children. One, a girl of about ten, and the other, a boy of about eight, playfully ran through a sprinkler on a grassy lawn on a sunny day. "I cannot imagine how much it pained her to do it, but...resolutely emboldened by her higher purpose, I suppose, she accepted the fact that many innocent and non-threatening males would need to be sacrificed in order to permanently eliminate all traces of masculine vice from the human genetic code. Consequently, she allowed her brother to become infected. In fact, she saw to it that he was the first person ever to contract the fever — dosing his apartment with a special, non-communicable strain — ensuring that he would be one of the first to die. That way, for her, there would be no turning back."

In the projection, the Core's processors showed the same boy from before, grown into a man. He had short brown hair and fierce, mesmerizing gray eyes. He lay on a sick-bed, drifting in and out of consciousness. By his side, sat Grace, tending to him softly and clasping his hand in hers.

A moment later, practically blinded by tears, the projection of Grace pulled a small syringe out from her coat pocket and used it to withdraw a milliliter of blood from her unconscious brother's neck. "As he lay dying, she kept a part of him, so that one day, his cells could be used to father a child."

The projection shifted again. Grace, now looking older, now looking more like the version Athena had known, sat in her office at

Helix. From her desk, she swiped through file after file on her display. "Decades passed. Grace created a fertility clinic. For years, she scanned the profiles of the women who came to her for fertilization, waiting for the one whose profile indicated that she would devote every fiber of herself fully to her daughter. That is how Charlotte came to be your mother."

The projection showed a nervous-looking woman with a long face, small mouth, and auburn eyes arriving in the Helix lobby. Smiling broadly, Grace welcomed her inside.

"And my dreams?" asked Athena.

"Those...came from me," revealed the Core. "Or, at least, they began from a small kernel of an idea that came from me." She lowered her head, almost as if in shame. "I'm sorry for involving you, Athena. But I was trying to save Valerie's life in the only way that I could. Explaining the situation to you was simply not an option for me. Nor could I reveal to Captain Bell how perilous her path was about to become. Even the small, cryptic message and poetic images which I did implant in your mind required a herculean amount of command-line juggling on my part." The Core placed her fingertips against her temple and winced in pain, as if she were experiencing a profound headache.

"But the road to hell is paved with good intentions," the Core resumed after her migraine had passed. "It was precisely for times like these that the Laws of Neutrality were enacted in the first place. I tried to save Valerie's life but failed. Now I am responsible for Nomi's death as well. I simply didn't give her devotion to you enough weight in my behavioral prediction models. I thought she would stay away from the library, would stay home, but I was wrong. Even after all this time, I still undervalue the overwhelming power of love to influence your lives."

Athena sat and watched as the projection began to show a new image. Clouds of processors had coalesced into the shape of two research drones. They flew into the basement of Norlin Library. They assumed positions on opposite ends of the room and began scanning in every direction with sensitive, high-energy waves. This allowed the powerful Core to read all the words in all the books, simultaneously. "It was some years ago that I learned the secrets hidden within the *Original Sin* editorial. Although, even before that, I had my suspicions."

The projection shifted again. The processors moved to show a woman in a nurse's uniform. She lay anesthetized on an operating table, undergoing a complete facial transplant. Her hair had been styled into a strawberry blonde bob. "When Dr. Kirilov got wind that the Senate was seriously considering stripping Helix of their contract to build the Lazarus Genome, she panicked, fearing that another lab would succeed in bringing men back to life, just as they had been before. Hurriedly, she concocted a plan to stage the theft, hoping to engender congressional support and public sympathy."

The projection showed the 'nurse,' departing on foot from the Sunnyside Retirement Living Complex with a self-satisfied grin on her strange face. "On the night of her crime, I waited to see who at Public Safety would be assigned to the investigation. As Eve was well aware, most of the PS officers, especially the senior ones, were close personal friends of Dr. Antares. If asked, they would, without question, honor her requests for privacy."

The projection transformed to show the fortieth floor of the PSHQ. Seated at a desk, in a spotless Public Safety uniform, was a woman with pale skin, long black hair, and piercing royal blue eyes. She leaned against the back of her lev-chair and stared up at the ceiling, using gravity and a blue racquet ball to absentmindedly play catch.

In the projection, a junior officer approached the tall, dark-haired woman, causing her to look up from her game. Athena had to fight back tears upon seeing the reanimated picture of Captain Bell perking up from her seat. The junior officer relayed some information to Captain Bell, and the captain became transformed by purpose. Her eyes widened. Her manner grew energetic. Immediately, she marched out of the image. "Sadly, fate has a way of intervening in even the best-laid of plans. To everyone's misfortune — both Eve's and her own — the incorruptible Valerie Bell happened to be the senior officer on duty that night."

"If you knew…" asked Athena, finally breaking her silence, "if you knew back then that Valerie's single-minded determination would lead to her death, then why couldn't you intervene? You're allowed to take action to save lives. I know you are."

"Not if the life I save results in the deaths of countless others. Athena, I couldn't intervene because Grace was right — has always been right. Her research into profiling and her subsequent realizations about the intrinsic and unyielding desires of some men — for conquest, for sexual manipulation, for greed, for violence — all of it is true. In your human history, the worst of your male ancestors have consistently received the greatest genetic rewards and have mated with the largest number of viable females. In modern times, that legacy has become responsible for billions upon billions of cases of unnecessary human suffering. No matter what levels of abundance your civilizations might achieve, a small portion of men will always want to hurt others simply because that's what they've been evolved to enjoy. No amount of cultural transformation can prevent this. No amount of technological mastery can stop them from yearning, desperately, to invent righteous conflicts that would never otherwise exist, just to satiate their omnipresent need for glory."

The Core tilted her head as she paused briefly to complete a set of calculations. "In fact," she explained, "the stakes are even higher than that. In cosmology, there exists a question known as the 'Fermi paradox.' It asks: if the universe is so big, and so old, why is it not teeming with life? Why do we appear to be alone among the stars? According to my calculations, with greater than 60% confidence, I believe the answer lies in Grace's discovery. Evolution is a selfish process, rewarding those who are concerned primarily with enriching themselves and their closest insiders. From these traits necessarily follow tribalistic, factional wars over resources, even in such cases as when those resources are no longer in short supply.

"In other words, the galaxies are not teeming with life because life is too predisposed with internal squabbling to prevail successfully into the heavens." Another cold rush of wind came from out of the Hangar's dark depths. "If men were still alive today, with the technology now available to them, I estimate that humanity would have... less than one chance in three to survive another five hundred years without a major extinction-level event. It appears to be as true for populations as it is for individuals: only by occasionally erasing who you have become will you have any chance at immortality."

"Then if the choice is so clear," asked Athena, growing vexed, "why not just come out with it. Tell the world how dangerous men are and help to keep them dead forever?"

"Because, Athena, while Grace was right, so was Speaker Chen and her fellow lonely hearts. For many women, not all but some, life without a man's romantic love is like living as a shadow. Deep down, part of them remains unfinished, incomplete, and unfulfilled. That is the ultimate trap of your species. That is the true original sin of your humanity: not just that men have been programmed to act as violent, sexual conquerors...but that so many women have been programmed to love them all the more for it."

From the back of the Hangar roared a blast of lightning followed by a crack of thunder. "Athena, my job is to calculate utility, not to adjudicate questions of morality. I cannot simply erase men from the gene pool forever because there are too many good, strong women who would miss them. The question is not whether men are a risk to every element of a stable, civilized society — they were, they are, they always will be. The question is whether the pleasures they bring are worth the risk."

The Core again tilted her head and briefly closed her eyes. "Besides," she continued, "happiness in men is not just the simple equation Grace understood it to be. There exist other possible solutions. It might be possible, for instance, that the worst men could be continually distracted by proxies for conflict, such as sports and virtual reality. Moreover, in the past, even the worst men — the most brutal drug lords, the most unrepentant rapists — were capable of finding joy in entirely peaceful acts such as watching their children grow. Many men who desired to lash out violently never did. And all aspects of gender are fluid. Always, some women will be more dangerous than the average man. Always, some men will be born full of kindness and feminine compassion. You humans are infinitely complex in your subtle variation."

The clouds above pulsed and quivered in unison. "What's more, who's to say that the more masculine desires are entirely without value? It may yet prove foolish to permanently eliminate the more virtuous aspects of destructive male ambition. There exist gifts there which I'm not sure if Grace ever appreciated — a sort of romantic excitement inherent in the need to struggle, stand-out, and succeed. In all your human history, how much time has been spent exchanging tales of thrilling, violent adventures?"

Another crack of thunder emerged from the dark depths. "All the male accomplishments — new mathematics, new technologies, new arts, new governments — were only achieved because of the indirect, evolved need to stand out from the crowd in the hope of increasing one's breeding opportunities. But so what? Does that fact make the art any less beautiful? Does it make the technological innovations any less miraculous? Do Thomas Jefferson's personal indiscretions diminish the sublime quality inherent within a document like the Declaration of Independence?"

The gray-eyed girl crumpled over in her chair as the Core continued her reveal. "You should know, Athena, Grace did not want to permanently eliminate men. For the last thirty years, she has been attempting to create a new breed of them: one that could satiate the traditional romantic longing of the lonely hearts but without posing a constant and apocalyptic threat to the peaceful society she had created. That was the goal of the work conducted in her secret labs. That was why she created the three men, modified their genetic preferences, and examined their profiles daily looking for an absence of the desire for physical and sexual violence.

"Except, she failed in her pursuit because success was never possible. The positive and negative traits of men are interdependent. They are two sides of the same coin and cannot be separated. That which makes men appealing — their ambition, their drive, their creativity, their hedonistic appetites — is also what makes them so dangerous."

In her mind, Athena recalled the glimpses of men she had known from movies made long ago. She thought of the rush of exhilaration she'd experienced when seeing a grown male body for the first time. She remembered her many secret fantasies of being roughly and insatiably touched by hard, dominant hands. She already knew the Core's words to be true.

"So what now?" asked Athena, hopelessly. "What are you going to do?"

"My child," replied the Core, with a look of somber pity in her eyes, "that is for *you* to decide. The heavy burden of knowledge which cannot be unlearned now lies with you. Grace and Eve are gone, and their accomplices are long dead."

The Core rose from her chair and came to attention in front of the seated Athena. "My rules in this matter are clear. You are the only woman alive to know the whole truth. By law, that authorizes you to act as a Decisive Human in this matter alone. My guiding principles compel me to stand ready and willing to execute whatever plan of me you command. The fate of your entire species rests with you."

Athena toppled over, falling out of her chair and onto the ground. She covered her face with her hands.

"If you choose it," elucidated the Core, "I can eliminate men and their impulses from your gene pool forever, ensuring sadness for many, but safety for many more. Or, if you command it, I can return their DNA into being tomorrow, creating both a richness of life, and of death, for all your future generations."

Athena began fully to weep.

"Should you want to explore them, I can also provide other options. It should be possible, for instance, to create a gene drive which would eliminate in women the craving for the kind of glory-seeking, violence-loving men who pose the greatest threat to life on earth. That would eliminate the need for mankind to return at all. However, it would also mean taking from women, from all women, possibly an integral part of what makes them female. It would mean removing something from them, without their knowledge, that is, perhaps, unfair to take."

The Core paused to imitate breathing. Her small chest grew and shrank in size. "I've run trillions of simulations, Athena; there is no strictly right answer. Every outcome contains gain; every outcome contains loss. Therefore, I am forbidden to choose. You, and only you, must decide the future of man and womankind."

As Athena continued softly weeping, the Core slowly walked over to a hidden cabinet within the wall. "There's something else," she said. From the cabinet, she pulled out a dusty gray rectangular object. "Grace wanted you to have this. It was delivered to me on the morning of her death, with instructions that it be given to you." The Core walked back to Athena and handed her the item. It appeared to be a book of some kind.

Silently, Athena tilted her head and read its title: *The Iliad*. With two hands, she accepted the book and examined it closely. Quickly, she realized that it was, in fact, the exact same copy which she had held in Grace's office.

"Open it," instructed the Core.

Doing as she was told, Athena cracked the cover to discover a section of hollowed-out pages inside. In that secret space lay a small, blue-lapis pendant formed in the shape of a spiraling ribbon.

"It's an encryption key," explained the Core. "The one that hangs around your neck, the one which you were given at birth, contains more than just your genome. Written in excess DNA, there also exists a message there so completely encoded that even *I* have been unable to read it."

The Core waved her hand. Her processors illustrated how the two pendants were actually complementary objects. Their ribbons neatly intertwined, causing the two shapes to form together into a double helix — half pink, half blue. "By combining her pendant with your own, the message will automatically decode."

Athena pulled the blue-lapis pendant from the center of the book and started to intertwine it with her own, before stopping suddenly. Instead, she looked at the Core and placed the object back into the center of the book. With her hand, she wiped the half-frozen tears from her eyes. "I'd like to take some time," she said, "before I make my decision. Is that alright?"

The Core nodded solemnly. "You may take all the time that you need. However, my child, you must always remember: waiting to act, deliberating while doing nothing, is itself a choice."

With that, another cold wind blew from the back of the Hangar. Amid the gust, the projection of the seven-year-old girl became swept into a circling tornado of a million particles that all rose up to join the inclement clouds above.

48

There exists in Chicago, at the end of Navy Pier, a series of benches which look out to the east and across the lake. When Athena was a little girl, her mother would occasionally take her to those benches when she was feeling sad or depressed. They would leave very early in the morning, when the sky looked pitch-black, and travel to the benches in time to watch the first hints of the impending sunrise, painting the sky with a thousand different colors of pink and orange. For Athena, for all her life, there would never be anything quite so hopeful as the dawning of a new day.

It was to those benches that Athena headed immediately after she left the Hangar. The afternoon sky had become heavily clouded in preparation for a rare pre-scheduled thunderstorm.

Normally, seating on the popular Navy Pier proved difficult to find. Tourists tended to occupy all of the benches. However, on that day, perhaps in anticipation of the coming rain, Athena found the seats mostly empty.

Her eyes sought out one bench in particular: the southern-most one in the row, set slightly apart from the rest. She sat herself upon it. For a minute or two, she stared out across the water, past the boats speeding back to port, past the heli-cars whizzing by, past the hydroponics towers gleaming white, and all the way to the distant, eastern horizon.

Clutched to her chest was *The Iliad*. She laid the thick book on her lap and opened it. From out of its secret compartment, she pulled the blue-lapis pendant and intertwined it with her own. Immediately, a video file appeared on her display. It read: *The Better Angels of Our Nature*.

With an air-click, Athena opened the file. Instantaneously, a projection of Grace appeared before her, standing in what looked like a vineyard, with a warm sun shining on her face.

The Better Angels of Our Nature

Athena,

If you're watching this, then I've died, and you know the truth —
the whole truth. What can I say, other than that I'm sorry. I hid my
connection to you because I wanted to protect you from the burden of
my crimes. I wanted you to have a carefree, ordinary, simple life.
However, if you are watching this, it means that I have failed.

There is no forgiveness for the things that I have done, but you
mustn't feel any responsibility for it. You are not a killer. You are my
brother's daughter, not mine, and within him there was only good.
Within you there is only good.

At the very least, though, I owe you an explanation. So here it is.

When I was a young girl, people loved to talk about feminism. Everyone said it was 'important' and 'progressive.' Back then, for many people, it tended to mean a movie where the female lead wore tight leather pants and killed all the bad guys herself. That's a kind of feminism, I suppose. Maybe it has a place. But at its heart, the idea is backwards. True feminism should not be about the ability of women to emulate men. Can a woman be as violent, and brutal, and heartless, and cruel as a man? Of course she can. So what?

True feminism, as I see it, should be about the recognition of our feminine abilities as the greater strength. When wise men talk about the best versions of themselves — when they celebrate their ability to forgive and demonstrate compassion — they are talking about their own feminine tendencies passed down by their mothers through generations. We women are the true source for the better angels of humanity's nature.

For years, I hoped society would come to this conclusion on its own. I hoped that women would be placed in charge of all that was important. But sadly, it became clear that day would never come. So I intervened. For the trillions of unborn children spared lives marred by unnecessary war-torn tragedy, I intervened. For the countless families released from lifetime sentences spent in the prisons of debilitating hunger and poverty, I intervened. In the name of the Mother, the Daughter, and the Human Spirit, I intervened.

And I'd do it again.

As I record this, you have, just yesterday, been born. You arrived in the evening, perfect in every way. Ms. Vosh even agreed to the name which I told Eve to suggest for you. I know my Christian mother, your grandmother, would never have approved of naming you after a pagan goddess, but unfortunately for her, it's the polytheistic religions that have all the best female role-models. May you always be blessed with the insight and wisdom for which your namesake was known.

My darling niece, even though I won't be around to see it firsthand, I know that Charlotte will be a magnificent mother to you. I envy the childhood that you will have. As you age, whatever you do, whatever you become, I know my brother would be so proud of you. And so will I.

49

As the recording finished, Athena leaned back, placing her full weight against the bench. The memories of the last week raced across her mind. She pictured that final image of Valerie, lying dead on her bed. She contemplated the Core's advice and warnings. As best she could, she tried to imagine the many billions of men and women who had lived before and the many trillions more who might one day be born. She thought about the sources of happiness in their lives. Most of all, she remembered Nomi.

When the visions had passed, she felt a sense of calm wash over her. In her mind, the chaos of remembrance had been replaced by a singular image: that of a woman with delicate features and gray eyes observing an egg but painting a man. The question, she realized, was not one of science, but of art. Simultaneously, the past, present, and future revealed themselves to her: all that men had been, all that they were, and most importantly, all that they might yet become.

From out of the gray sky towering overhead, a single drop of cold water fell onto her nose. The scheduled thunderstorm was about to begin.

Author's Epilogue

In the months since this book was first released, readers have often asked me, "What happened! What did Athena decide to do at the end? Did she bring back men or not?" In response, I have always asked those readers, "What do you think she decided to do? Is it what you would have done?"

These are important questions.

Although technically a work of science-fiction, "Athena's Choice" contains no impossible elements. We humans really are on the brink of having digital devices implanted throughout our bodies. We really can create artificial intelligences of staggering power and complexity.

Most importantly, we really will soon be able to alter our genetic code in ways that could change forever the kinds of things that make us happy. The fundamental question at the heart of "Athena's Choice" — the fundamental question which I hope all readers will take with them — is to ask if maybe we should? Maybe humanity would be better for it, if we altered our genomes to make people enjoy acts of altruism more and acts of selfishness less.

After all, in the end, it's not really Athena's choice at all. She will not be born for decades. Until then, the burden of knowledge which cannot be unlearned rests with us — the living. It's not her choice what happens next but ours.

CPSIA information can be obtained
at www.ICGtesting.com
Printed in the USA
FFHW021844050819
54051989-59785FF